"WE CAN'T SPEND ALL DAY IN BED."

Though Max was teasing Chris, his voice was full of regret.

"Sounds like a good idea to me," she suggested as she nuzzled his neck.

Reluctantly, Max pushed himself up until he was sitting on the edge of the bed. "Don't tempt me," he said, getting to his feet. "But you're welcome to join me in the shower, if you promise to behave."

"Curses," muttered Chris.

She waited until she heard the water running, then tiptoed into the bathroom, yanked the shower door open and joined him under the spray.

"Christine!" Max growled. "I told you to behave yourself."

"But I didn't promise, Max," she pointed out.

"Oh, well, that's different," he answered as he gathered her into his soapy arms. . . .

ABOUT THE AUTHOR

The idea for *Double Trouble* came to Lynn Turner when she was watching one of her favorite TV shows, *Remington Steele*. So she packed up her two sons, got in the car and drove to Daytona Beach, all the way from her home in Indiana. It was no coincidence that she arrived in time for Spring Break, which was, according to Lynn, both "terrifying and terrific." She enjoyed herself so much that she plans to go back next year.

Books by Lynn Turner

HARLEQUIN SUPERROMANCE

134–A LASTING GIFT
203–DOUBLE TROUBLE

HARLEQUIN TEMPTATION

8–FOR NOW, FOR ALWAYS
56–ANOTHER DAWN
75–UP IN ARMS

Lynn Turner

DOUBLE TROUBLE

Harlequin Books

TORONTO • NEW YORK • LONDON
AMSTERDAM • PARIS • SYDNEY • HAMBURG
STOCKHOLM • ATHENS • TOKYO • MILAN

Published March 1986

First printing January 1986

ISBN 0-373-70203-5

Printed in Canada

PROLOGUE

Evansville, Indiana, mid-March

THE LARGE ORANGE-AND-WHITE rental truck waited at the loading dock, its massive rear doors flung wide in anticipation of the cargo the vehicle was about to receive.

The narrow alley behind the large two-story brick building was dark—almost as dark as the interior of the truck's empty cargo compartment. Half a block away, a tomcat on the prowl leaped onto a garbage can, and from there up and over a boxwood hedge. The lid of the can hadn't been securely fastened, and the thrust of the cat's hind legs when he pushed off to clear the hedge sent the lid clanging onto the pavement. The noise reverberated off the walls of the buildings lining the alley, creating a startling cacophony in the otherwise quiet night.

"Did you hear that?" one of two young men inside the brick building whispered in alarm.

He nearly dropped his end of the large object they were removing from its resting place. His companion swore softly as he was forced to shift his grip to keep it from falling.

"For Pete's sake, Frank, don't go to pieces on me now," he growled. "We're almost home free."

"But that noise! There's somebody out there... maybe cops. Somebody spotted the truck and called the cops! I told you this was a lousy idea. I knew it wouldn't work."

"Get hold of yourself!" The command was an impatient hiss. "There's nobody out there. If there was, we'd have known by now. Come on, let's get this thing loaded before my arms fall off."

They slid their burden onto the waiting bier, which they then pushed onto the loading dock. From there it was simply a matter of hefting the cumbersome item off the bier and into the back of the truck. When their cargo had been safely loaded, the one named Frank sagged against the wall of the truck and wiped a sleeve of his lightweight jacket over his forehead.

"Whew. The thing's not as heavy as I thought it would be, but it sure is awkward to lug around. No wonder it usually takes six people."

His companion ran a palm over the gleaming surface of the object they'd just stolen. "But it's a real beauty, isn't it? Steel-lined, genuine mahogany exterior—this baby's built like the vault at Fort Knox."

"But... you can't *breathe* inside a vault!" Frank pointed out anxiously. "You might suffocate. There's gotta be some other way."

"There may be, but I don't have time to figure out what it is. I've got a deadline, remember? Stop worrying. I told you I had everything worked out." There was a sudden flash of white as he grinned. "And you have to admit it's the last place anybody would think to look for me."

They jumped down from the rear of the truck, closed and latched the doors, then climbed into the cab and drove away. Neither of them thought to go back and lower the large metal overhead door to the loading dock of the Diehl Funeral Home. The truck's taillights caused a faint reddish gleam to appear here and there beyond the open door, as they were reflected by the brass rails of the coffins stored in the large room at the rear of the building.

CHAPTER ONE

"GOLD'S!" Chris repeated into the receiver. You want me to go to *Gold's*? Isn't that a gym?" She imagined a large, rank-smelling room filled with overweight men straining over exercise equipment, and shuddered in distaste. "Now, listen, Elliott—"

"Calm down, Christine," the voice at the other end of the line advised patiently. "It's not a job. A buddy of mine picked up some lottery tickets for me the last time he went over to New Haven. All I want you to do is go in and get them from him, okay? I'd do it, but Darlene's home sick today and there's nobody here to answer the phone."

Chris could have pointed out that he had an answering machine, but she didn't. Elliott was too tight to entrust his business calls to a machine. She gave in with a sigh.

"Okay. Where is this place and how do I get there?"

"It's downtown, in the old Sears building."

"On Sycamore?'

"Right. When you get the tickets from Rick, bring them to me at the office. I want to talk to you about a job I've got lined up for next week."

Forty-five minutes later Chris walked into Elliott's cluttered office and slapped the lottery tickets down on his equally cluttered desk. "You owe me ten dollars.

Why didn't you pay the guy for the tickets before he bought them?''

Of course she already knew the answer. Elliott was too cheap—so tight he squeaked when he walked, to use her father's words.

''Rick knew I was good for it,'' Elliott said as he picked up the tickets and slid them into his shirt pocket. ''I always pay my debts.''

Eventually, Chris thought. *Provided whoever you owe has the perseverance to keep hounding you.* ''Ten dollars,'' she repeated flatly, and held out her hand, palm up.

When Elliott had reluctantly counted out ten crisp one-dollar bills, Chris folded the money and stuffed the wad into the bottom of her oversize shoulder bag. ''So what's this job you've got lined up for next week?'' she said.

A little over a year and a half ago, Elliott had started an odd-jobs agency to provide the kind of temporary help people couldn't usually get from Manpower or a regular employment agency. Since Chris had started working for him to supplement what she made as a substitute teacher, she'd been among other things the ''hostess'' for a new-car show, a dog-and-cat sitter, a magician's assistant and/or clown for children's birthday parties, and spent one entire weekend demonstrating video games for a computer software exhibit. That job had been one of her favorites.

''First, I need to know if you'll be free for a couple of days the beginning of next week,'' Elliott said as he leaned back in his chair.

''Sure. In fact I'll be available all week. Spring break starts Monday. The schools will all be closed.''

"That's a relief. I was a little worried about who to give the job to, if you couldn't take it. Some of my regulars might have balked at this one."

Chris eyed him suspiciously. "I'm almost afraid to ask why. It's not another job for that guy who cleans out septic tanks, is it?"

Elliott looked as sheepish as he was capable of looking. "No, it's nothing like that. First thing this morning I got a call from a woman down in Florida. She'd just been notified that her only son died of an apparent drug overdose last night, here in Evansville."

"Oh, how awful," Chris replied. "They just called her on the phone and told her?"

"Evidently. She sounded pretty upset. Anyway, she's elderly and a semi-invalid. She can't come up here herself to take the body back to Florida for burial, and she doesn't have any relatives who could do it for her, so..."

"So she was forced to contact a perfect stranger about making arrangements to get her son home. The poor woman. Can you imagine how she must feel? How tragic."

Elliott shifted restlessly. Chris had noticed before that any display of emotion seemed to make him uncomfortable. "Yes, tragic," he agreed gruffly. "He was found by some other students, apparently. They tried to revive him, but it was too late. He was pronounced D.O.A. at the Welborn emergency room."

"He was a student at UE?" Chris asked.

"Yeah, a sophomore. I've got his name here somewhere." Ruffling through the papers littering his desk, Elliott produced a sheet from his memo pad. "Here it is. Gollum. Cy Gollum." He handed her the paper, then cleared his throat and shifted around in his chair some more. "The authorities insisted on an autopsy, and they won't be ready to release the body until Monday morning. I've already made the arrangements. You'll accompany the coffin to Daytona Beach, where you'll turn it over to the director of a local funeral home. Mrs. Gollum's already contacted him, so there'll be a hearse at the airport to meet you. You can fly back home the next day."

Chris glanced up from the paper with a frown. "Daytona Beach? Elliott, next week's spring break. Do you have any idea how many high school and college kids are going to be descending on that town next week? There's no way I'll be able to get a room for the night on such short notice. I might as well fly back the same day."

"No problem," he assured her. "Mrs. Gollum has a friend who owns a motel. She's already reserved a room in your name for Monday night. The only hitch is that you'll have to be out by noon Tuesday. So is there any reason you can't take the job?"

Chris gazed down at the piece of paper in her hand and thought about a nineteen- or twenty-year-old boy named Cy Gollum and his elderly invalid mother, and how each of them had been the only family the other had. She blinked the sudden moisture from her eyes.

"Of course I'll take it," she told Elliott huskily. "Just give me the details and tell me what time to be at the airport on Monday."

RATHER THAN PAY the exorbitant rates for airport parking, Chris begged a ride from a neighbor who worked at the Whirlpool plant near the airport Monday morning. She checked in, then decided to make sure the item she was escorting to Florida had arrived and been loaded onto the plane.

"Could you tell me if the...uh, cargo from Diehl's was delivered all right?" she asked the clerk behind the ticket counter. "It's supposed to be on the same flight."

The young man began leafing through the pages on his clipboard, muttering, "Diehl's, Diehl's" in a ponderous tone. "Ah, here it is! Yes, the man from Diehl's delivered the casket a little while ago. The paperwork was all in order, so it's probably been loaded by now." Bestowing a look of commiseration on her, he added somberly, "I'm so sorry about your loss. Please don't hesitate to let us know if there's anything we can do to make the trip easier for you."

Chris decided to forego an explanation and smiled wanly instead. She arrived at the departure gate just as the plane was loading passengers.

There was a three and a half hour layover in Atlanta, which made it a little after twelve-thirty when they finally arrived at Daytona Regional Airport. Chris saw the coffin placed in a baggage handling area, then went in search of the hearse that was supposed to be waiting. As she'd expected, the small terminal building was swarming with vacationers, and it took a few minutes to collect her overnight case and make her way to the exit marked Taxi and Bus Service.

There were taxis and buses, all right, but no sign of a hearse. *Great,* Chris thought as she craned her neck in a futile attempt to locate the vehicle. There must have been some kind of mix-up. Maybe the funeral home had got the flight number wrong or something. She went back inside and found a bank of pay phones, then dug the name of the establishment—Holloway's Eternal Rest—out of her purse and looked up the number in the directory.

The man who answered didn't know anything about a delivery at the airport that day, and there was a delay while he went to find the funeral director. Chris shifted her coat, which she'd needed in Evansville but removed on the plane, to her other arm and tapped her foot impatiently. These people seemed extremely unprofessional. What if she'd been a relative of the deceased, for heaven's sake?

The man who'd answered the phone said, "It wasn't supposed to be here till the end of the week, was it?" and for a moment Chris thought he was talking to her. Then another male voice made an indistinct response, and she realized he'd been addressing someone there at the funeral home. There was another brief exchange that she couldn't quite make out, and her irritation increased as she was forced to wait. By the time Mr. Holloway himself came on the line, she was ready to give him a piece of her mind; only he sounded so sincerely apologetic that she didn't have the heart to chew him out. After repeatedly assuring her that this kind of slip up was extremely rare, he promised to send a hearse at once.

As she turned away from the phone, Chris glanced at her watch. She'd spent almost an hour straightening things out. *You're going to owe me extra for this one, Elliott,* she vowed as she slung her coat over a shoulder. She supposed she'd better go back to the baggage area and explain the delay. Who'd have believed a dead person could cause so much aggravation?

At first she thought they must have moved the coffin to make room for passenger luggage or something. But after she'd spent half an hour questioning everyone in sight and practically turning the entire area upside down and inside out, it had become horrifyingly obvious that Cy Gollum's coffin was gone. Vanished. And Cy Gollum with it.

IT WAS A NIGHTMARE. That must be it. She was having an incredibly realistic nightmare, Chris thought several times during the next hour. Things like this simply didn't happen, at least not to her. She doubted they happened to anybody, except in movies or on TV shows. Coffins didn't just up and disappear without a trace, for heaven's sake!

Just about the time she despaired of getting any cooperation from the baggage people, the hearse arrived and she had to deal with the driver. She could tell from the way he glowered at her that he didn't believe a word she said. She couldn't really blame him—even *she* had trouble believing what was happening.

Eventually it became clear that she wasn't going to get any help from either the airline employees or the guy from the funeral home, so she took the next logical step—she got into a cab and went to the police station.

The place was an even bigger madhouse than the airport had been. The receiving area was packed with people of all shapes, sizes, ages and colors. Chris had no idea why the rest of these people were here, but she figured their business couldn't possibly be any more serious or urgent than hers. Pushing and shoving, she made her way to the front of the crowd and tried to get the attention of a harassed-looking uniformed officer who was gripping a clipboard as if he thought he might soon be called upon to defend himself with it.

"Excuse me, but I'd like to report a disappearance."

"Sorry, lady, you'll have to wait your turn," he said without even glancing at her.

"But this is an emergency!" she told him as she ruthlessly shouldered an obese woman in a flowered muumuu out of the way.

The officer heaved a long-suffering sigh while he scrawled a brief notation. He still didn't look at her. "Lady, everybody here has some kind of emergency that requires my immediate attention. Unfortunately, you've got me outnumbered. Like I said, you'll just have to wait your turn."

Meekness had never been a virtue Chris prized highly. Neither had blind obedience. Her patience had already been exhausted by the nitwits at the airport who'd somehow managed to lose a coffin and its contents, then deny any responsibility for the loss. She wasn't about to face Cy Gollum's poor mother without knowing she had done everything humanly posible to retrieve his remains.

"All right, officer, I won't bother you anymore," she said in a deceptively humble voice. "If you'll just tell me who I should talk to about this... disappearance, I'll let you take care of the others. I'm sure the simple theft of a corpse can't begin to compare with their problems."

It took a few seconds for the policeman to react to what she'd said. However several of the people around her weren't quite so preoccupied, and Chris's mouth curved in a satisfied smile as pandemonium broke loose.

"A corpse!" someone echoed in a horrified voice. "Did she say somebody stole a corpse, as in dead body?"

"Where? Where did this corpse get stolen?"

"Right here, I think."

"It got stolen out of the police station! Land sakes, a person's not safe anywhere nowadays."

"What was the danged horse doing in the police station in the first place? There ain't hardly room for all the people in here, let alone a horse."

"Will somebody tell that old fool it was a dead body that got stolen."

"Eh? The horse was dead, you say? Now that's *really* stupid. I'm goin' home."

There was a chorus of "Good!" from the others as the crowd parted to let the old man through. By the time they closed ranks again, the officer had belatedly decided to seize control of the situation.

"Where was this alleged corpse, miss?" he asked brusquely as he made a few furious scribbles.

"It wasn't an *alleged* corpse, officer," Chris answered testily. "It was real enough, and so was the coffin it was in. They were both taken from the baggage area out at the airport, between one and two hours ago, while I was arranging for a hearse to be sent out from Holloway's Eternal Rest funeral home. After I got off the phone I went back to check on the coffin, only it was gone."

"And you're sure it's missing? You couldn't have just overlooked it?"

The look Chris gave him contained equal amounts of exasperation and disbelief. "A seven-foot coffin is sort of hard to overlook, officer. And anyway, I searched the place thoroughly before I decided to come to the police. It's not there, believe me. Now what are you going to do about the theft? Aren't there some forms I should fill out or something?"

What the officer decided to do was get her off his hands as fast as possible. He pointed her down a hall behind him and told her to talk to Sergeant Vincent. Chris gave him another hard stare before she turned on her heel and walked away in a huff, but he didn't notice; he was already listening to somebody else's story and adding more scribbles to the copious notes on his clipboard.

MAX DECKER was shooting the breeze with Quinn Vincent in Quinn's office when the young woman burst in without bothering to knock. Both men glanced up, but neither rose to his feet—at least not right away. Then they both got a good look at her and simultaneously vacated their chairs.

No more than five one or two, she was perfectly proportioned with slender, almost dainty hands and feet, delicately formed features in a small oval face and a flawless ivory complexion. She looked like an almost-life-size Barbie doll, but with dark hair. It was a rich, glossy brown, cut medium short so that it sort of fluffed around her face and set off her high cheekbones and enormous blue eyes. Max decided on the spot that she was the best-looking woman he'd ever seen. Everything about her spelled "Class" with a capital C. He was uncomfortably conscious of his faded and patched jeans and the red T-shirt that smelled of fish and beer and had a peeling picture of Farrah Fawcett on the front.

She spared him a brief but comprehensive glance and then turned her attention to Quinn. "You must be Sergeant Vincent. I've come to report a stolen corpse."

She sounded as if she held him personally responsible for the crime. Max saw Quinn's blond brows rise half an inch, and his own mouth twitched in amusement before he got it under control.

"Well? Aren't you going to take down my statement, or whatever it is you do when somebody reports a theft? I'd like to have the matter resolved today, if possible."

The men exchanged a fleeting glance, and then Quinn motioned for her to take the vacant chair beside Max. Since Max hadn't been asked to leave, he settled back to listen, his hands linked across his stomach and one foot propped on the opposite knee.

He knew what Quinn was thinking: he'd immediately assumed she was just another prank-playing college student, out to have some fun at the expense of the local police department. At first Max shared the assumption, but the longer he listened to her, the more he tended to believe she just might be for real. Quinn's calm, tolerant attitude seemed to irritate her as he wrote down the pertinent facts in neat block letters. After ten minutes of answering his succinct questions, she was clearly on the verge of blowing her top. Her cheeks were flushed, and there was a tight look to her mouth and an angry glitter in her eyes.

"I *told* you, for pity's sake, I didn't even know the guy!" she snapped, as Quinn sought to establish exactly what her role in the alleged theft had been. "I was hired to escort his coffin down here and then turn it over to a local funeral home. How many times do I have to say it? And what does it matter whether or not I knew him, anyway? You should be concentrating on the fact that somewhere in your lovely city there's a pervert running around with a dead body, for crying out loud. Find him and start asking *him* questions, why don't you."

Quinn fixed her with a calm, steady gaze and assured her that someone would be assigned to look into the supposed theft as soon as possible. Then he added that it might take some time, though, since at the moment they had their hands full just dealing with the yearly migration of college students and their idiotic practical jokes. If the barb hit its intended mark, she didn't show it. She just gave him a disgusted look and curtly told him the name of the motel where she'd be spending the night, then stood up and left the office as abruptly as she'd entered it.

"Do you believe it?" Quinn muttered after she'd gone. "These kids get more inventive every year. A stolen coffin, yet."

"I'm not convinced she wasn't on the level," Max said quietly. He was still slouched in his chair, but Quinn knew him too well to be fooled by the indolent pose.

"Come on, Max," he scoffed. "Don't tell me you swallowed that story. You could drive a tank through some of the holes in it. She's just another college kid from up north, getting her kicks by pulling a fast one on the local cops."

"You could be right," Max conceded lazily. He stretched both legs out in front of him, flexing the right one a little before he got to his feet. "Then again, it could be that you called this one wrong. Personally, I think she was telling the truth."

As he turned to leave Quinn jumped out of his chair. "Hey, hold it. You can't drop something like that on me and then just walk out. What makes you think her story's legit?"

Max paused at the door, his hand on the knob. "Call it intuition."

"More likely infatuation," the other man suggested dryly. "You were so busy taking inventory of Miss Hudson's obvious assets, I doubt you even heard her missing-coffin story."

"You could be right about that, too," Max agreed mildly as he opened the door. "Then again—" his sudden grin was full of mischief "—it just might be I heard something you missed, Sergeant Vincent. See you later."

"Hey, come back here!" Quinn yelled as he hurried after his departing friend. "What did I miss? Max, you dirty rotten— What the hell am I supposed to have missed?"

Max didn't stop or even slow down as he threw the answer back over his shoulder. "Something you probably haven't heard in a while—the sound of sincerity."

There was a derisive snort from behind him. "Sincerity, my big toe! You're going after her, aren't you?" He didn't wait for an answer, which was just as well, because he didn't get one. "Okay, it's your time to waste. But if you come up with anything, you damn well better bring it to me!"

Max paused just long enough to glance back and flash another grin. "Don't I always?" he said just before he followed Christine Hudson out of the building.

CHAPTER TWO

WHEN CHRIS STEPPED OUT into the bright sunlight, she was so agitated that for a minute or two she just stood on the sidewalk and steamed. Her coat was still slung over her left arm, and her right hand had the handle of her overnight case in a death grip. *Idiots!* she thought furiously. *Imbeciles! Incompetents!* Well, if she couldn't count on the police to find Cy Gollum's coffin, she supposed she'd just have to do it herself. She followed the sidewalk around to Nova Road, the heavily traveled street behind the police department building, and started scanning the oncoming traffic for a taxi.

When Max exited the building, she was rounding the corner, heading west on Orange. He had to really stretch his legs to catch up with her.

"Miss Hudson." Chris turned her head impatiently when the quiet voice spoke her name, then frowned when she saw that it belonged to the man from Sergeant Vincent's office.

"What is it—did your boss think of some more asinine questions to ask me?"

Before he could answer, she spotted a taxi heading their way. It was in the outside lane, and unless she caught his attention quickly the driver would probably go right past. She sucked in an enormous breath and stuck the index finger and pinkie of her left hand into her mouth, then cut loose with a whistle guaranteed to get the attention of anybody within a radius of half a mile who wasn't already stone deaf. At the same time, she held up her overnight case and waved it over the curb like a semaphore flag.

"Holy Moses," the man beside her said as the cab swerved across two lanes of traffic and made a beeline for them. It screeched to a halt with the rear door handle within reach of Chris's fingers.

"Nice driving," she told the cabbie as she opened the door and tossed her case inside. Her coat was thrown on top of it before she ducked to slide onto the seat.

The driver shrugged modestly. "Where to, lady?" Chris gave him the name of the motel as she closed the door. He nodded and started to swivel toward the steering wheel, then noticed the slightly scruffy-looking man loitering beside her door. "Ain't your friend coming?"

"What?" Glancing out the window, Chris saw that the man who'd followed her out of the police station was still standing on the sidewalk with his hands thrust into the back pockets of his jeans.

Turning from him with a haughty expression, she told the driver, "He's no friend of mine. He's just a cop."

The cabbie's eyes widened comically as he jerked around and rammed the gearshift into first. "Jeez, lady, you tryin' to lose me my license?" he complained.

Max leaned forward to speak to her through the half-open window. "I'm not..." he began, but the cab pulled away from the curb—at a conspicuously safe speed—and he didn't get to finish the statement.

He watched until it turned east onto Volusia, his lips pursed and a quizzical expression in his hazel eyes. This was the woman he'd taken one look at and labeled Classy with a capital C? He grinned as he turned to walk back around the building to the enclosed parking lot, where he'd left his battered old Dodge pickup.

Chris had just hung her coat in the closet and was rummaging in her purse when there was a sudden burst of insistent rapping on the door of her room. *What now?* she thought as she went to open it.

"You!"

Before she could slam the door in his face, Max pushed it open and stepped past her into the motel room that was no bigger than a postage stamp.

"You should always use the peephole," he told her sternly. "Or at least leave the chain on until you know who's at the door. This place is really a dump."

Chris couldn't argue with the assessment. "I was lucky to get a room at all. Mrs. Gollum arranged it for me. Why are you following me? Why aren't you out looking for the person who stole her son's coffin—that's your job, isn't it?"

There was only one chair—an uncomfortable-looking straight-backed wooden one—and Max was leery of helping himself to a seat on the bed, so he took a chance and perched on a corner of the rickety dresser, careful to keep one foot flat on the floor in case the thing collapsed under him.

"No," he replied with a slight smile. "That's not my job." He watched her perfectly arched brows draw together in confusion, and thought that she was even lovely when she frowned. ''I'm not a cop,'' he explained. ''At least, not anymore. I am a private investigator, though—got a license and everything.''

Which was true enough. He did have a license...somewhere. The last time he'd checked, it was in his wallet, sandwiched between his driver's license—which had expired—and his Social Security card. He didn't see any point in telling her that, or that he couldn't remember the last investigative job he'd taken on. He casually folded his arms over his chest and waited, giving her time to decide whether to bite. A successful fisherman often had to exercise patience, and Max rarely returned from a fishing trip empty-handed.

''Honest?'' Chris said. She looked skeptical. In fact, she was still standing by the open door, as if she thought it might be wise to stay close to the nearest escape route.

''You're really a private detective?''

''Investigator. Honest, I really am. Maybe you'd like to see some identification.'' Max slowly reached for his right hip pocket, hoping she'd say it wasn't necessary. He couldn't be a hundred percent sure that license was still in his wallet.

''No, I'll take your word for it.'' Chris stopped frowning and gave him a tentative smile as she pushed the door closed. ''I've never met a private investigator before. Is it as exciting as they make it look on TV?''

''Not quite,'' Max answered dryly. ''In fact, most of the time it's pretty boring.'' Which was one reason he so seldom made use of his license that he couldn't even vouch for its present whereabouts.

"Well, look, Mr... uh, I don't believe you told me your name."

"Sorry," he said with a crooked grin. "It's Decker. Max Decker." He held out his hand, and when she took it her grip was firm and strong. He liked that.

"Well, Mr. Decker, I suppose you followed me because you thought I might be in the market for a private investigator. Right?"

Max refolded his arms and leaned back against the wall. "The thought had crossed my mind. I don't think you should bank on the police finding this coffin for you. At least, not anytime soon."

"I'd already figured that out for myself," Chris muttered as she crossed to the bed and plopped down on the sagging mattress. "Are they always so...thick, or did Sergeant Vincent just take a dislike to me personally?"

Max ordered himself not to smile. He could imagine how Quinn Vincent, who possessed two master's degrees and a Ph.D. and was attending night school to obtain his law degree, would react to hearing himself described as "thick."

"Vincent's really a pretty decent guy," he told her, and inferred from the way she rolled her eyes that she had her doubts about that. "It's just that he took you for a college student playing a practical joke. Now don't blow your stack—it happens a lot more often than you might think. Every year the department gets dozens of phony calls and reports during spring break."

Chris stared at him in angry astonishment. "And he automatically assumed this was just another stupid practical joke? Without even bothering to check my story? Of all the nerve! Do I look like some silly, bubble-headed college student to you? Well, do I?"

"No, of course not," Max assured her hastily. "If I hadn't believed your story, I wouldn't be here, would I?"

"I guess not," Chris conceded after a moment. She was still miffed that Sergeant Vincent hadn't taken her seriously. Her youthful appearance had always been a sore point, anyway.

For the first time, she looked beyond his shabby clothes. She estimated his age at somewhere around forty-five. He was neither too tall nor too short—right about an even six feet, she'd guess—with slightly wavy medium brown hair that was starting to go gray at the temples and needed trimming, and intelligent hazel eyes that were marked by crow's feet at the corners. He was neither lean nor fleshy, but as he silently endured her appraisal she noted that with his arms folded like that, his biceps bulged impressively. He looked... competent, as if he could and would handle whatever task he took on.

"Tell me, Mr. Decker," she said impulsively, "why did you believe my story, when Sergeant Vincent didn't?"

The question didn't seem to surprise him. He hitched his left shoulder in a careless shrug. His expression remained impassive. "Your suitcase, for one thing. Either you'd really just come straight from the airport, or you were going to an awful lot of trouble for a practical joke."

"You said 'for one thing,'" Chris prompted curiously.

Now his expression did alter. A couple of extra creases appeared in the weathered skin of his forehead and his lips pursed slightly, as if he were considering his answer before he spoke out loud.

"There wasn't one specific thing you said or did that convinced me. I guess you'd just have to call it a gut reaction. All my instincts told me you were telling the truth, and I usually go with my instincts."

Chris liked the answer. It was simple and straightforward. She had a feeling Max Decker was the kind of man who would keep silent rather than lie. And before you asked him a question, you'd better be darned sure you wanted to hear the unvarnished truth, because that was exactly what you'd get. She admired that kind of uncompromising honesty, maybe because her father had always possessed it in such abundance.

"Elliott would never go along with hiring a private investigator," she murmured, more to herself than to Max Decker.

His response was a quiet, unconcerned "Who's Elliott?"

"My boss. He's a little . . . oh, why not tell it like it is—he's a cheapskate."

"Something of a penny-pincher, huh?" Max's tone was dry as his gaze took in the peeling wallpaper, water stains on the ceiling and dilapidated furnishings.

"You could say that. In fact, he's so tight he—"

"Squeaks when he walks," he finished with a grin.

Chris was momentarily startled into silence. "Well, yes, that's one way to put it. He'd never let me hire you to find Cy Gollum or his coffin, the old tight-wad."

"So don't tell him."

Chris blinked, not sure she'd heard him right. "What?"

"Don't tell him. If I locate the coffin, I'll send him a bill for services rendered. If I don't—" he shrugged "—I'll waive my usual retainer. Fair enough?"

In truth, it hadn't even occurred to him to charge her anything, but to admit as much would sound unprofessional as hell and would probably put her off the whole idea. She had no way of knowing that he lived very simply and didn't need to supplement his modest income by working as a private investigator, and he didn't particularly feel like going into the reasons why. And if he just came out and told her he'd been feeling edgy and restless lately and that her case presented an interesting challenge, she'd no doubt think he was some kind of a crackpot. He waited for her reaction to his offer, and was surprised to realize how much he was hoping she wouldn't turn it down.

"Fair?" Chris echoed in amazement. "Why, of course it's fair. It's more than fair! But are you sure you want to do this? If it turns out you can't find the coffin, you might end up wasting a lot of time and effort when you could have been working on some other case."

Max dismissed her concern with a wave of his hand. "No problem." Forcing himself to meet her eyes, he added with a straight face, "I'm between cases right now, anyway."

"Well, if you're sure . . ."

"Positive." Sliding off his precarious perch, he hesitated for a moment when he felt a warning twinge in his right knee, then slowly took the three steps necessary to get him to the foot of the bed. He covered his cautious movements by gesturing toward her shoulder bag, which lay behind her with its contents partially spilling onto the worn spread. "Have you got anything in there that might be of help?"

Chris swiveled to dump out the rest of the things in her purse, and missed seeing him bend over slightly to knead the knee in a brief, almost punishing gesture.

"I don't know. I was just going through everything when you got here," she murmured absently. "Let's see . . . here's the name and phone number of the funeral home." She laid the scrap of paper to one side, and Max picked it up as she continued sorting through the rest of the junk that had accumulated in the bottom of the capacious bag. "And the receipt for this room. And...omigosh, I'd forgotten all about this!"

"What?"

She held a bunch of folded papers out to him, and he risked leaning forward to take them. Thankfully, his bum leg didn't pick that moment to give way and send him sprawling facedown on the mattress.

"It's the papers for the coffin—the forms the airline had to have filled out before it could be shipped. That was all I managed to get out of those bozos at the airport. Maybe there's something on one of them."

Max scanned the first sheet of paper, which was basically nothing but a description of the cargo. Beneath it was the burial transit permit required by law to ship human remains from one state to another. Not much help there. He progressed to the third form. "Bingo," he said softly.

"What? What is it?" Chris scrambled to the foot of the bed and rose up on her knees to peer over his arm. A light, flowery fragrance rose from her body. Max did his best to ignore it.

"The address of the dear departed's next of kin, a Mrs. Leona Gollum, by name. We can at least go see her and explain what's happened."

Chris tipped her head back to look up at him. Her expression was decidedly unenthusiastic. "I guess we have to, huh? We couldn't wait until we've found the coffin?" The look Max gave her brought a faint flush to her cheeks. She ducked her head and muttered, "Forget I said that, okay?"

He smiled down at the crown of her shining head. "It's possible she might know something that could help us out," he said as he folded the papers and stuck them into his hip pocket. "For instance, whether her son had any enemies who hated him enough to have stolen his body."

THE HOUSE was in the twenty-eight hundred block of South Atlantic, which appeared to be a fairly posh neighborhood. Somehow the well-maintained two-story structure, with its curving drive and private strip of beach, wasn't the kind of place where Chris had imagined the elderly, semi-invalid Mrs. Gollum would live. It just didn't fit. But then neither did Max's ancient pickup, she thought as she gingerly stepped down from the cab. She was tempted to suggest one of them stay with the truck. If they left it unattended for any length of time, one of Mrs. Gollum's neighbors was liable to have it towed off to the junkyard.

"Let me do the talking, all right?" Max said as they walked around to the front of the house, which, like its neighbors, faced the ocean. Though he had phrased it as a suggestion, the authority in his quiet voice didn't allow Chris the option of disagreeing. She nodded somewhat reluctantly.

She had tried to brace herself for the ordeal of facing Cy Gollum's mother and confessing that she'd managed to lose the body of the old woman's only child. Still, she was a bundle of nerves when the door started to slowly swing inward. She tried to summon a reserved but polite smile.

Instead of smiling, her mouth almost fell open. She instantly recognized the man in jeans and an unbuttoned work shirt who'd opened the door. Who wouldn't? He and his partner were welcome guests in millions of living rooms every week, including Chris's. Tall and broad-shouldered, with that thick head of glossy black hair and the blinding smile that caused feminine hearts to flutter on two continents, he was even more impressive in person than on a television screen.

"You're Julio deCosta," she blurted in a dazed voice.

The actor inclined his head graciously. Max Decker stared down at her as if he might be questioning her mental health.

"So I am, lovely lady. And who might you be?"

While Chris struggled to remember her name, Max took it upon himself to answer for them both. "I'm

Max Decker, and this is Christine Hudson. We'd like to see Mrs. Gollum, if she's in."

DeCosta's bushy black brows pushed together over his nose. "Mrs. Who?" He sounded as if he, too, suspected he might be the victim of some kind of joke.

Max repeated the name and then spelled it for him. "We're here about the recent death of her son. Is she in?"

"It's really important that we talk to her," Chris interjected. "But if she's not up to having visitors right now, we could come back."

DeCosta's gaze swung from one of them to the other, his expression an attractive mix of confusion and curiosity. "You'd better come inside so we can straighten this out," he suggested. "Somebody's leg is being pulled here. There's no Mrs. Gollum at this address, and as far as I know there never has been."

As they followed him down a hall toward the rear of the house, Max bent his head to mutter, "You know this guy?"

Chris glanced up at him in surprise. "Didn't you recognize him?" she whispered. "Julio deCosta's the hottest thing on TV. His series has been number one in the ratings for almost a year." Max's expression remained blank, and she released an exasperated breath. "You must have seen it. It's about two Federal undercover agents who—"

"Let me guess. Who devote their days to keeping the world safe for democracy and their nights to the pursuit of big-busted blondes. Sounds really original. Can't imagine how I've missed it."

Chris gave him a dirty look and a sharp jab in the ribs with her elbow before she marched off ahead of him. He squashed the grin that tried to lift the corners of his mouth. She might resemble a china doll, but the lady was nowhere near as delicate as she looked.

Julio deCosta seemed to be enjoying his role as host, though Max suspected the silver tea service and expensive china he'd trundled out were produced for the express purpose of impressing Chris. The suspicion was reinforced when the actor placed himself beside her on the sofa and immediately started trying to seduce her with his rehearsed accent and million-dollar smile.

Max had heard a lot of accents in his time, and deCosta's was as phony as a three-dollar bill. He'd be willing to bet those choppers were just as phony—caps, probably—and the only place he could ever remember seeing hair like that was on a department store dummy. He shifted a little in the uncomfortably soft chair he occupied, and his gaze suddenly collided with Chris's. She was staring at him with a hard light in her eyes. He had the crazy feeling she'd been reading his mind. He gave her a tight smile and sipped the brown sugar water deCosta had served them, and somehow managed not to grimace.

"You're sure that Mrs. Gollum has never lived at this address?" he asked the actor, whose attention didn't waver from Chris as he answered.

"As I told you, the house belongs to a friend of mine. He's a producer," he added as he smiled into Chris's eyes. Max could have sworn he was a couple of inches closer to her than he'd started out. "Freddie rarely uses the place, and when I wanted to get away from L.A. for a while he generously offered to let me stay here. I know for a fact that there's been no Mrs. Gollum in this house for the past two weeks."

"But how about before you got here?" Chris asked. "Couldn't he have loaned the house to someone else . . . maybe a friend or a relative?"

DeCosta seemed a little put out that she insisted on sticking to the subject of Mrs. Gollum and her whereabouts, when he was obviously trying to direct her attention elsewhere. Releasing a resigned sigh, he apparently decided to abandon both the accent and his unsuccessful attempts to impress and/or seduce her.

"I seriously doubt dear Freddie would have offered his hospitality to any female and especially not one who was old and infirm," he told her bluntly. "Freddie's personal taste runs more to strapping young football players, if you get my meaning. And before you ask, this Mrs. Gollum you're looking for couldn't possibly be his mother, because she died about ten years ago."

"Oh," Chris responded in disappointment. She turned to Max. "Well, I guess we've reached a dead end."

"Maybe," Max said as he rose to his feet. "Thanks for the information, Mr. deCosta. We've taken enough of your time."

Chris could take a hint as well as the next person. She added her thanks to Max's as deCosta walked them to the door and waited until they were back in his truck before she asked what he thought about their meeting with the actor.

"What do you think?" Max inquired as he pulled out of the drive. "Setting aside your obvious hero worship of the guy, that is."

"Oh, come on," Chris protested. "Okay, I admit I was a little... startled, when he opened the door, but—"

"Your eyes nearly fell out of your head and you forgot your own name."

"Well, who expected the nation's newest sex symbol to answer the door?" she retorted defensively. "Anyway, we're not talking about me. We're talking about him. Did you believe him or not?"

He shot her a look that was too brief for her to interpret. "Any reason I shouldn't have?"

Chris twisted around so that she was sitting sideways on the seat with one knee drawn under her. Once again, she was frowning. "What is this, twenty questions? How should I know whether you should believe him or not? You're supposed to be the private detective here, remember?"

"Investigator," Max corrected mildly. "Humor me for a minute, okay? What kind of guy did deCosta strike you as being?"

"A professional charmer," Chris said with an impatient shrug. "The kind who has to make a conquest of every woman he meets. Shallow, vain... a phony. Do you think he might be a closet homosexual?"

A pleased smile had settled on Max's face at her perceptiveness, but the question she casually tacked on at the end nearly made him choke. He risked taking his eyes from the road long enough to slide an amused glance at her.

"Do you assume every shallow, vain guy you meet is gay?"

"Of course not—don't be ridiculous. I just wondered if there might be more to his relationship with 'dear Freddie' than he was letting on, that's all. I didn't assume you were gay," she added soberly.

Did that mean he'd struck her as shallow and vain? Max decided not to ask. "Thanks, I think."

"Are you?"

Chris saw the corner of his mouth twitch as he realized she was teasing him. Funny, she hadn't noticed until now what an attractive mouth he had—firm, yet mobile, with a fullness to his lower lip that was positively sensual.

"Not so I've noticed," he said in answer to her question. "*My* personal taste runs more to—"

"Big-busted blondes," Chris interrupted with a grin. "Right?"

"Actually, I was going to say petite brunettes." *What's sauce for the goose*... Max thought as he steered the truck into the parking lot of the motel where she was staying. When he switched off the ignition, he turned to find her staring at him with a speculative gleam in her eye that made him just a little uneasy. She didn't comment on his provocative remark, though, which was a relief until he started to wonder why.

"So what's the next step in this investigation?"

"I'll need an hour or two to check out deCosta's story. Meanwhile, I think you ought to call that boss of yours. See if you can pry any more information out of him about the old lady. I'll get back to you in a couple of hours."

"Okay," Chris agreed as she reached for the handle of her door. She started to hop down from the truck, then hesitated. "Max, do you think this whole thing could be some kind of hoax, that maybe Mrs. Gollum doesn't even exist?"

"I wouldn't rule out the possibility. On the other hand, the coffin *did* exist, and it doesn't make sense that whoever shipped it would have gone to this much trouble setting up a phony story if it was empty."

Chris's eyes grew even larger as she absorbed the implications of that. "No," she agreed softly. "It doesn't, does it?" She jumped down from the cab and slammed the door in her excitement. "I'll go call Elliott right now. Be sure to let me know the minute you find out anything, okay?"

She practically ran to the door of her room, then had to postpone making her call until she located the key in the bottom of her bag. Max could hear her muttering to herself as she dug for it. On impulse, he stuck his head out the window to yell at her.

"Hey, Chris!" She glanced up in question, but her hand continued to search for the key. "Be sure to reverse the charges when you call the old skinflint," he said with a grin.

She laughed. "I will!" Triumphantly holding up the key, she turned to unlock the door and let herself inside. Just before she closed it again, she waved and called, "Talk to you later, Max!"

He sat staring at the tarnished number eight on the door and tried to convince himself that her laugh hadn't really sounded as wonderful as he knew it had, and that hearing it wasn't what had brought on this peculiar tingling sensation in his chest.

It was just one of the old scars making itself felt again, he told himself as he shifted the truck into reverse. Every now and then one of them would start to ache for no apparent reason... unless it was to remind him of his own mortality, he thought with a grim smile. And if the occasional twinges and aches weren't reminders enough, he could always rely on the nightmares to bring everything back in vivid detail.

Irritated at the direction his thoughts were taking, he swore softly and pressed the accelerator to the floorboard as he pulled out of the motel parking lot. The truck backfired in protest, then belched a cloud of oily black smoke into the air.

The thin young man who'd spent the better part of the afternoon watching room number eight turned his head away from the noxious fumes with a muttered oath. He coughed a couple of times, stuck his fingers under his glasses to wipe at his eyes, and then headed for the manager's office.

CHAPTER THREE

AS CHRIS HAD EXPECTED, Elliott wasn't overjoyed to receive a collect call from Florida. Once she started relating what had happened since she left Evansville, however, his complaining came to an abrupt halt. In fact he stopped talking altogether, which wasn't at all like Elliott.

She told him everything that had happened so far—up to and including the visit with Julio deCosta—but deliberately omitted any mentioned of Max Decker. Elliott had been upset enough about the collect phone call; the suggestion that he pay a private investigator to find a dead body would probably have sent him into cardiac arrest.

"Elliott?" she prompted when there was nothing but silence from the other end of the line. "Are you still there?"

"What? Oh...yes! Sure I'm here." He sounded odd, slightly nervous.

"Well? Can you tell me anything else about the woman who called you and claimed to be Mrs. Gollum? It might help me find out what's going on down here."

There was a lengthy pause before Elliott answered. "Listen, Chris, I don't see any point in getting ourselves involved in this situation any more than we already are. You've been to the police. Why don't we let them handle it?''

Chris's exasperation got the better of her. ''Elliott, I told you, the police didn't even take me seriously. They think I made up the whole story. I doubt if they'll even look into it.''

''Maybe it would be better if they didn't,'' Elliott said.

Chris bit back the sharp retort that formed on her tongue. She shouldn't be surprised by his attitude, she told herself; she'd always known he was self-centered and utterly lacking in any sense of responsibility.

''In other words, you're telling me I should just drop the whole thing, is that it?''

''I think that's exactly what you should do. If there really isn't any Mrs. Gollum, it stands to reason that her dead son never existed, either. The police could be right, you know. This whole thing might be nothing more than an elaborate practical joke.'' Pausing a moment, he added on a less optimistic note, ''On the other hand, we could be mixed up in something a lot more serious. As I said, I'd rather not get ourselves any more involved than we already are. I really think you ought to stay out of it from here on. You did your job, you got the coffin down there, for Pete's sake. Hey, tell you what—why don't you stay on a couple of extra days and soak up some of that famous Florida sunshine. I'll even pick up the tab. Just bring me the receipt for your motel bill when you get back.''

For a moment Chris was too stunned by the offer to reply, and by the time she'd recovered, Elliott had apparently taken her silence for assent and hung up. She slowly replaced the receiver in its cradle, then stared at the phone as if she expected it to suddenly sprout legs and crawl up the wall.

Of all the weird things that had happened in the past several hours, this had to rate a place near the top of the list. The day Elliott voluntarily offered to "pick up the tab" for someone else's Florida vacation was the day they'd carry him off in a straitjacket. What's more, she had the uneasy feeling that he'd been holding something back, that he knew more than he'd been willing to tell her. What on earth was going on?

WHILE CHRIS SAT puzzling over Elliott's uncharacteristic behavior, a conference was being held in one of two adjoining rooms at one of the nicer beachfront motels several blocks away. Present were five young men. They were all approximately the same age, all were dressed in either cutoffs or track shorts and T-shirts, and at the moment they all wore identical expressions of acute boredom. They had arrived in Daytona Beach early that morning and spent the rest of the day in the adjoining rooms.

Outside, the city that billed itself as "the world's most famous beach" had begun to fill with young people making the most of their few days in the sun. Cars packed with students cruised up and down the major thoroughfares and the wide white beach, and by midmorning it was difficult to see the sand in places for the beach towels and oiled bodies covering it. Radios blared. Bruce Springsteen and Bryan Adams had made the trek south. So had David Lee Roth, Madonna and the Pointer Sisters, but Prince and the Jackson clan were noticeably absent this year.

The sky was a clear, bright blue, the incoming swells were exactly the right size for body surfing, and the sun and sand were warm but not scorching—altogether it was a perfect day for vacationing students to shed their warm-up suits and their inhibitions and forget about everything but what a wonderful time they were having.

Yet of the five young men who'd driven down together from Evansville, Indiana, not one had left the motel to so much as take a walk on the beach or dip his toes in the ocean.

"This stinks," one of them muttered from the double bed where he lay sprawled. "I might as well have stayed home and helped my dad paint the garage this week. At least I'd be getting some fresh air, maybe even a tan."

"Hell, Kev, you don't have any room to complain," one of the others said from the floor. "If you hadn't come, you'd just have spent the whole week scraping paint. *I* could have been in New York with my uncle."

"The one who works for the modeling agency? Damn, Mel, why didn't you go?"

Mel Braverman rolled to his side to face the skinny boy in the wire-rimmed glasses who'd spoken. "Because, Stanley, like the rest of you idiots I let David talk me into coming to Florida, instead. It's a decision I'm already regretting, believe me," he added morosely as he flopped onto his back to stare up at the ceiling. "When I think of all those gorgeous cover girls I could be fondling..."

"You guys are all talk, no action," the fourth young man in the group said as he raised his arms in a bone-cracking stretch. "I didn't come all the way down here to stay cooped up in a lousy motel room the entire week. There must be a couple of thousand nubile, half-naked females between the ages of sixteen and twenty-five out there, and first thing tomorrow morning I intend to start introducing myself to as many of 'em as possible."

"Awright!" Mel approved with an exuberant grin. "I second Roger's motion. All in favor—"

"Just a minute." The fifth and until now silent member of the group spoke as he pushed himself off the second bed. "We're all in this together, and we all agreed that the way to do it was to stay at the motel in case he shows up."

His speech drew a quartet of groans. "He's not *gonna* show up, for Pete's sake," Mel said irritably. "There's no way. There's just no way, I tell you. He hasn't got a snowball's chance."

"I agree," Roger said. "He couldn't possibly get out of Evansville without being spotted, much less sneak into Daytona Beach . . . not with all the people we've got watching for him. If we sit around waiting for him to show up, we'll just be wasting our time."

"Kevin? Stan?" The young man who was arguing in favor of staying in the motel rooms turned to the other two for support. "How about it—are you ready to call it quits, too?"

"He'd love that, wouldn't he?" Kevin grumbled. "It would prove what he's always saying about us."

"Kevin's right." Stan turned his solemn gaze on Roger and Mel. "If we don't see this thing through, we're exactly the kind of jerks he claims we are. I think we should stick to David's original plan."

"Oh, hell," Roger swore under his breath. Then a good-natured grin spread over his face. "Guess all those nubile, half-naked females will just have to do without me for another year."

"Maybe not." Four heads turned at the quiet statement, and David, who'd brought them all together in the first place, gave them a benevolent smile. "There's no reason for all of us to stay here every minute of every day. Why don't we work out a schedule? One of us should stay in each of the rooms at all times, but when it's not your turn to be here, you can do whatever you want. Does that meet with everybody's approval?"

Judging by the excited babble of voices as they started bickering about what "shift" each would take, it did.

MAX FELT LIKE A GRADE-A JERK. He thought he probably looked like one, too. The last time he'd worn anything but jeans, Carter had been in the White House. He worked in jeans—when he worked—played in jeans, and as often as not even slept in jeans. He *belonged* in a pair of soft, faded, comfortably snug blue denim jeans. Anything else was totally out of character. So why in heaven's name had he spent fifteen minutes hunting down a pair of chinos in the bottom of his closet and another fifteen ironing them?

He was a jerk, that was why. And maybe a little bit crazy, on top of it.

He parked his truck and pocketed the keys as he walked to the door of number eight. His knee seemed fine tonight. In fact everything seemed fine; he couldn't remember the last time he'd felt this good. He glanced down at himself to make sure there wasn't a grease stain on his shirt or that he hadn't left his fly unzipped, then gave the door a couple of brisk raps.

When Chris opened it, her smile hit him like a jab to the midsection. She'd changed out of the neat skirt and sweater she'd been wearing earlier. Max didn't know whether to laugh or groan as he took in her frayed cutoffs and bright yellow T-shirt. Talk about crossed wires. When his gaze lingered on the front of the shirt to read the printed message—Sexism Is a Social Disease—he discovered that she wasn't wearing a bra. Fortunately she backed up to let him inside; otherwise he might have spent the rest of the night standing in the doorway gaping at her chest.

"I told you to always use the peephole," he said gruffly as she closed the door behind him.

"I heard your truck and looked out the window, so I knew you weren't some pervert who'd come to molest me." She grinned, and a dimple appeared in her left cheek. "You're not, are you?" she asked as she tucked her hands into the back pockets of the cutoffs.

Max hesitated a second to make sure his voice wouldn't crack, then lied. Convincingly, he hoped. "No."

"Darn. My luck's been lousy all day. Oh, well, if you're not going to molest me we might as well talk business."

She brushed against him in passing, and Max suspected the contact had been deliberate. The room was small, but not that small. He watched as she gracefully sank onto the bed, and when she swung her legs up to stretch out full length, his brows scrunched down over his eyes in a wary frown.

Chris smiled up at him. She was aware that her provocative behavior had him puzzled and for some reason made him uneasy. She hoped it was because he was responding as she wanted him to, and not because he found her attempts at enticement irritating or immature. A pair of butterflies played a game of tag in her stomach. She'd never come on to a man like this before. But then no man had ever affected her the way Max Decker did.

She'd thought about him a lot after he'd dropped her off at the motel—probably much more than she should have, considering that she knew virtually nothing about him except his name.

She'd still been thinking about him when she heard the distinctive rattle of his truck's engine and looked out the grimy window. She'd watched him get out and start walking toward her, and it was as if a lightning bolt had suddenly come down out of the clear blue sky and knocked her flat. She wanted him. Just like that, with no prior warning; she'd looked at him as he crossed the pavement toward her and wanted to make love with him. Badly. Then and there.

The revelation surprised her and even left her a bit shaken, but it didn't shock her in the least. Chris considered herself liberated, socially and sexually. She knew perfectly well that a woman's sex drive was every bit as strong as a man's. She'd read most of the feminist literature on the subject and had listened to all the talk show hosts discuss female sexuality with the experts. So of course she wasn't shocked by her sudden, alarmingly powerful desire for Max Decker. Or so she told herself as she went to answer the door.

When she opened it and looked up at him, she was totally helpless to prevent her gut reaction. Up close, he was even more desirable than when viewed through the dirty window. For one thing, the short-sleeved knit shirt and khaki slacks seemed to emphasize his compactly muscled build. For another, he smelled like Old Spice now, instead of dead fish. Chris had always had a weakness for Old Spice, and on Max Decker the cologne seemed to have magically assumed the properties of an aphrodisiac.

Oh, yes, she definitely wanted to go to bed with this man. *The sooner, the better,* she thought.

The problem was, she'd never known a man like him before, and didn't have any idea what kind of woman appealed to him. She'd impulsively gambled that he would want maturity, a casual, "we're both consenting adults" attitude toward sex. But the frown on his face as he stared at her reclining form had her reconsidering the assumption. Had she misjudged him? Or—God forbid—was it that he'd got the message, but just wasn't interested?

Max felt backed into a corner. He had to make a spur-of-the-moment decision. Should he follow up on her flirtation, take what she seemed to be offering and he definitely wanted—even though it would be against his better judgment and he suspected they'd both regret it later? Or should he do the decent, gentlemanly thing, and pretend he either hadn't seen the bait dangling in front of him or was so stupid he hadn't recognized it for what it was?

Some choice, he thought resentfully. He was damned if he did, and damned if he didn't. In the end he came up with a compromise that he suspected would only be a delaying tactic at best, and knew good and well was motivated more by cowardice than ingenuity.

"I didn't say I wouldn't molest you, only that I'm not a pervert," he told her dryly. "If you've got your heart set on being molested, we'll see what we can work out later. But right now I'm hungry. Put on some shoes, and we'll go get something to eat."

Chris struggled against the urge to roll off the bed and then slither under it. So much for her obviously meager talents as a siren. Flashing a grin that was half bravado and half embarrassment, she quipped, "You're on," as she leaped to her feet.

She ended up changing back into the pale peach skirt and sweater she'd flown down in, since she didn't know where he intended to eat. When she emerged from the tiny bathroom, Max gave her a lopsided, slightly uncertain smile.

"Ready to go?"

"All set," she said as she collected her bag and hefted it over her shoulder.

"Why don't you leave that thing here," Max suggested. "It makes you tilt to port," he explained when she glanced at him in question.

She laughed softly. After removing the room key and handing it over to him, she willingly dropped the heavy bag onto the bed. Max suggested they leave the truck and walk, since there were several restaurants and fast-food joints within a few blocks of the motel. They didn't make it to any of them, though. Less than a block away they came across a hot tamale stand. Max bought them each two tamales and a canned Coke.

"Let's grab one of those benches before somebody else does," Chris suggested as they left the stand. "I'm starving."

But Max had other plans. "Hang on for just a few more minutes. There's a nice little park about a block away. It looks right out over the ocean, and we can talk in peace and quiet."

"Peace and quiet, huh?" Chris teased him when they'd finally managed to find an unoccupied bench in the park.

Max grimaced as he looked around at the hordes of young people who'd apparently had the same idea and were devouring pizzas, hamburgers and heaven knew what else all around them. "Your motel's so far from the main drag, I figured this place would be empty. Look, we can go someplace else, if—"

"Forget it," Chris interrupted. "My stomach won't wait another second." She took a huge bite of her first tamale, and as soon as she'd swallowed it, a long drink of Coke. When she looked at him, her eyes were watering. "Now that's what I call a hot tamale!"

Max laughed and reached over to dab at the corner of her mouth with a paper napkin. It was a casual enough gesture on his part, but Chris's reaction to it was anything but casual. Their eyes met, and she knew he'd seen what that brief, innocent contact had done to her. His hand was abruptly withdrawn.

"Max," she said tentatively.

"You want to tell me what kind of game you're playing?" Though his voice was soft and controlled, his anger still came through. "What was all that nonsense back at the motel about?"

"Nonsense!" Chris echoed sharply. If Max hadn't been so busy trying to control his own agitation, he might have noticed the indignation in her voice.

"You ought to be locked up, you know that? For your own protection. Your mother never should have let you loose on your own!"

"My *mother*!"

His narrowed eyes scrutinized her flushed face as she glared at him. "How many men have you been to bed with?"

Chris's jaw dropped in disbelief. "That's none of your business!"

"How many?" he repeated in a low, warning tone.

"Four! Five, if you count Denny Merton. But believe me, he wasn't worth counting. Anything else you'd like to know?"

The shock on Max's face was almost comical. "Five men!" It emerged as an astonished croak. "A kid your age—"

"Kid! Who are you calling a kid?" Chris challenged belligerently.

"Five!" he repeated in a stunned mutter. He looked a little like a basset hound as he hung his head and stared down at the half-eaten tamale in his hand. An involuntary smile suddenly curved Chris's lips.

"How old do you think I am, Max?"

His shoulders moved in a restless shrug. "Twenty, maybe a fast twenty-one."

"Try twenty-seven."

His head jerked up and around. "No." He made it a repudiation, a flat refusal to accept her word for it.

"Almost twenty-eight," Chris said straight into his doubting eyes.

"You can't be."

She released a slightly impatient breath. "I'd show you my birth certificate, only it didn't occur to me to pack it. I guess we could find a phone and call my mother, if you insist on some kind of verification."

"You don't look twenty-seven. You don't even look old enough to vote!" He didn't sound quite so skeptical now.

"I know," she said with a grimace. "But I am, cross my heart." She hesitated, then asked, "Was that why you got so uptight about the way I was flirting with you—because you thought I was younger than I really am?"

For a second or two she thought he wasn't going to answer. He frowned down at his feet, his expression withdrawn, almost brooding. Finally he murmured, "That was one reason," so quietly that she barely heard him.

"Max?" she prodded gently.

"Eat your food before it gets cold."

Chris opened her mouth to press him for a more satisfactory answer, then decided not to push her luck and bit into her tamale instead.

Max started talking before she could interrogate him. He told her he'd checked the property tax records and found that Julio deCosta had been telling the truth about the house where he was staying—it was owned by Frederick Marchand, whose permanent address was listed as Reseda, California. Marchand had owned the place since '73, and the previous owner's name had been Rosencranz, not Gollum. He added almost as an afterthought that he also had a friend checking deCosta's personal background.

"Why?" Chris asked curiously.

Max shrugged. "Old habits die hard, I guess. I like to cover all the bases."

She wadded up the wrappings from her tamales and the paper napkin she'd used to clean her fingers, then tossed the ball smack into the center of a nearby trash bin.

"I'd forgotten, but you said that you used to be a cop, didn't you?" she said lightly.

"Did I?" Chris could tell from the terse reply that the subject was off limits, but this time she decided not to back down.

"Was it here in Florida?"

"No." Max tried to sink his own wad of paper into the bin the way she'd done, but his shot went a foot wide. He heaved a resigned sigh. "It was on another planet—commonly known as New York."

"New York *City*?" She was obviously impressed.

"That's right. Did you call your boss?"

"Yes." Chris wasn't about to let him distract her. "I'll tell you about it in a minute. How on earth did a New York City cop end up as a private detective in Daytona Beach, Florida?"

"Private *investigator*," Max corrected patiently. "You're a persistent little thing, aren't you? I'll bet you drove your parents nuts when you were a kid."

"Max!"

The obstinate look on her face made him smile. "Impatient, too. Oh, all right, don't blow a fuse. There's not much to tell. When I retired from the force, a buddy who'd relocated in Miami talked me into moving down there. I stuck it out for a couple of months, but Miami was too much like Central Park in the summer. About the time I decided I'd had enough of the place, Quinn Vincent left New York's finest to take a job with the Daytona force. As soon as he was settled, he invited me up for a visit. Somehow I never got around to leaving. Okay, miss nosy britches? Satisfied?''

''You're not old enough to be retired,'' Chris said flatly.

He stared at her a moment, then turned his head away. She thought he was irritated, maybe even angry, until he faced her again and she saw that he was grinning.

''You're something else.'' He made it sound like a compliment. ''Now tell me about the call you made to your boss.''

''But I want to know—''

''Later. Maybe. It's a long, very boring story. The call, Christine—what did the old miser have to say?''

Realizing he wasn't going to satisfy her curiosity, at least for the moment, Chris repeated her conversation with Elliott almost word for word. When she'd finished Max looked as perplexed as she'd felt when Elliott hung up on her.

''This is the same guy you told me about, right—the cheapskate?''

''One and the same. When he told me to stay on a couple of extra days at his expense, I nearly swallowed my tongue. But the thing that really bothers me is his attitude about this whole situation. As far as he's concerned, the agency—meaning yours truly—is out of it. And unfortunately, he's the boss. I guess that's it,'' she said with a dejected sigh. ''Looks like I'll never know what was really in that coffin, who sent it or who was supposed to receive it."

A surprised frown flickered across Max's face. "I didn't take you for a quitter."

"I'm not a quitter!" Chris retorted. "But what choice have I got? I'm no longer involved. At least, not officially. And considering Elliott's attitude, I certainly can't ask you to go on with your investigation. He'd just claim I was acting without his approval when I hired you and refuse to pay you a cent."

"Are you trying to get rid of me? I haven't provided the results you were hoping for, is that it? You have to realize these things take time, Chris."

"No! Of course that's not it." She stared at him in exasperation. "Max, haven't you been listening? It has nothing to do with you, for heaven's sake. It's Elliott!"

"Oh, him," he said, as if Elliott was of no consequence whatsoever. "Well, as long as you're not dissatisfied with my work, I think I'll go see the owner of the funeral home in the morning." He rose and smiled down at her. "Ready to head back?"

Chris's mouth opened and closed several times before she finally settled on what she wanted to say. In the meantime, he'd taken her empty Coke can, tossed it into the bin and started guiding her around the outside of the park. "Listen, Max, I appreciate what you're doing, really I do, but I'm telling you Elliott absolutely will not—"

"I'm not working for Elliott," he said mildly.

That brought her up short. "Well, I hope you don't think you're working for *me*! I can't *afford* to pay what you must charge!"

Max's lips twitched as he took her arm and started her moving again. "I'm working for myself, okay? Call it a bad case of professional curiosity. Watch your step—the ground's a little uneven through here."

"Through here" was a narrow footpath that wound down to a sliver of beach that apparently hadn't been discovered by the vacationing students yet. The narrow strip of sand was deserted except for an elderly couple collecting shells some distance away.

"Why are we going this way?" Chris asked as she struggled along beside him on her two-inch heels. "Is it a shortcut or something?"

Max stopped, knelt to remove her shoes, and she discovered what an erotic experience it was to have a man's fingers caress her insteps. When he stood beside her again she was a little short of breath. He grinned as he turned the shoes over in his hands.

"You know, when you opened the door at the motel, for a second I thought you'd shrunk." Chris's soft laughter ended abruptly when his teasing gaze lifted and their eyes met. And then she saw the shoes fall out of his hands, and he was reaching for her.

"No, it's not a shortcut," he said as his arms closed around her.

Considering the urgency she'd felt before, Chris was a little surprised that she wasn't responding with more passion now that she was actually in his arms. But as he snuggled her up against his chest and stared solemnly into her eyes, all she could think of was how *good* he felt—how strong and warm and comfortable. How right.

Her arms slid around his neck as his head slowly descended, and they both kept their eyes open until their lips actually made contact. The kiss was a gentle testing, an experimental tasting and exploring. It wasn't hard, or impatient, or even particularly passionate, but it moved Chris more than any kiss ever had. When Max pulled back just enough to look into her eyes again, a dozen questions had been asked and answered, for both of them.

"I want you," he said huskily as his hands moved on her back in slow, delicious circles.

Chris smiled softly, dreamily. "I want you, too."

She stepped out of his embrace to bend and collect her shoes, but when she straightened he tucked her under his arm to keep her close as they turned to walk back through the park. They didn't kiss again, or even speak. It was as if they were saving all the kisses and caresses and low, intimate words until they were behind a locked door.

By the time they reached the motel, Chris was burning with anticipation. She knew by the way Max's hand trembled when he inserted the key in the lock that he was just as impatient to get inside as she was, and the knowledge made her shiver with longing. Just before he pushed the door open he lifted a hand to lightly caress her cheek. The gesture was so gentle, so tender that her eyes misted over and her breath caught painfully.

She was still carrying her shoes as she ducked under his arm and entered the room ahead of him. Max pushed the door closed, then leaned back against it and circled her waist with one arm to pull her to him as he reached for the light switch. He was bending his head to kiss the side of her neck when the lamp beside the bed came on. He stiffened as his gaze fell on

Chris's purse. She felt the sudden unnatural tension in him, and lifted her head from his shoulder.

"Max?" she said softly. She sounded confused and a little apprehensive.

His arm tightened around her in an instinctively protective reaction as anger surged through him. "Somebody's been here," he said with a deadly calm. "While we were out, somebody came in and searched the room."

CHAPTER FOUR

"WHAT! How do you know? Are you sure?"

Chris turned as she spoke, so that her back pressed against Max's chest. His arm contracted at her waist for a moment before it fell away.

"Positive," he said as he stepped around her and crossed to the bed. "Take a good look at your purse."

Chris went to join him. She stared down at her shoulder bag for a moment before she saw what he wanted her to see: its contents were spilled helter-skelter onto the spread, and two items that should have been at the bottom of her bag—her wallet and the bottle of sunscreen she'd brought along—were poking out the top.

"It looks like everything's been dumped out and then just shoved back any old way," she said as she picked up the wallet. "I may not be the most organized person in the world, but I'm not this sloppy, either. That's funny—my money's all here. There's not even a dime missing."

"How about your credit cards?"

"I only have Visa, and it's here. So are my check cashing card for the supermarket back home and my driver's license. I don't get it. Why would somebody break into the room and go through my purse, then leave without taking anything?"

"Whoever was here didn't break in. The door was locked, remember? I used your key to open it. Check your suitcase."

While Chris lifted her overnight case onto the bed to examine its contents, Max went to the room's one window, pulling the cheap drapes aside to check the latch.

"Now this makes me mad!" Chris declared hotly, causing him to turn from the window. She was glaring down into the opened overnight case. "That creep went through my suitcase, too, including my underwear!"

Max almost smiled. "He was probably looking for something, and whatever it was, when he didn't find it in your purse he tried your suitcase."

"Well, he must not have found it here, either. There's nothing missing," Chris said as she closed and zipped the overnight case. "What I don't understand is why anybody would search my room in the first place. There's nothing here worth stealing."

"That we're aware of," Max reminded her as he entered the tiny bathroom. He emerged a second later carrying her yellow T-shirt in one hand and her cutoffs in the other. The pockets of the cutoffs were turned inside out. "Did you leave these this way?" he asked as he held them out to her.

Chris took them with a frown. "No. And there wasn't anything in the pockets, not even spare change. I just threw these things over the shower rod when I changed."

"They weren't hanging on the shower rod. They were lying on the floor," Max told her. He abruptly bent to grasp the handle of her overnight case, swinging it back up and onto the bed. "Is there anything else you need to pack—makeup, toothbrush, anything like that?" he asked as he opened the case and dropped her T-shirt into it.

Chris stared at him in surprise. "What are you doing?" His response was to pluck the cutoffs out of her hand and toss them on top of the T-shirt. "Max! Answer me!"

Before the exasperated words even cleared her lips he had crossed to the closet and was slipping her lightweight all-weather coat off its hanger.

"You're not staying here tonight," he said as he carelessly folded the coat in half and laid it on top of the other things in her overnight case.

"Don't do that! It'll get all wrinkled," Chris complained, lifting the coat back out. "What do you mean, I'm not staying here? I most certainly am staying here. My reservation's good through noon tomorrow. Will you stand still and talk to me, darn you!"

The last sentence was directed at his back as he disappeared into the bathroom again. He came out carrying her toothbrush, tube of toothpaste, hairbrush and comb.

"Is this it? Have we got it all now?"

Chris watched in mounting irritation as he stuffed the articles into the inside pocket of her overnight case. "Who gave you permission to order me around?" she demanded. "Take those things back out of here right now! I told you, I'm stay—"

Max heaved an impatient sigh. "No," he said quietly. "You're not staying here. The door wasn't forced open to gain entry, and that window's sealed with about eight coats of old paint. Whoever searched the room either had a key or is damned good at picking locks. And he didn't even bother to cover the evidence of his search. That means he probably wasn't a professional, just somebody who was either desperate or in an awfully big hurry. Now are you ready to go?"

She shook her head decisively. "There's no reason for me to move out. Whoever was here either found what he was looking for, or he didn't. Either way, he isn't likely to come back. Besides, it would probably take the rest of the night to find another motel with a vacancy, *if* I could. I'm staying, and that's that."

Max's level gaze held a combination of irritation and mild disgust. She had to be one of the two most stubborn women he'd ever known. At this rate, they could spend the better part of the night arguing.

He suddenly put both arms around her and tugged her against him, catching her by surprise. His mouth closed over hers as it opened on a startled gasp, his arms contracting in case she tried to push him away.

She didn't. At first she was too surprised to resist either the embrace or the kiss; and then his tongue entered her mouth, and resistance became unthinkable. Chris slumped against him as her arms instinctively found their way around his waist. This kiss was nothing like the one on the beach. He held her tightly, pressing her body to his with a determined, purposeful strength, and his lips and tongue were no longer gently exploring but hard and aggressive.

When Max felt his control start to slip, he forced himself to lift his head. He looked down into Chris's wide, dazed eyes and had to master the urge to fall onto the bed with her still wrapped in his arms. Kissing her had been a mistake, he realized belatedly.

"I've got a neighbor you can stay with tonight." He was aware that his voice was a little unsteady, but there was nothing he could do about it. Not giving Chris a chance to argue, he released her to collect her suitcase and purse and then started her toward the door with a light shove between the shoulder blades.

HIS NEIGHBOR turned out to be a slender woman with snowy hair that Chris decided must be prematurely white. Max introduced her as Jess—nothing more.

While Max explained that she needed a place to stay and asked Jess to put her up for the night, Chris studied the other woman with a critical eye. She was undeniably attractive, probably mid-forties. Though her tan was deep and dark, her skin didn't seem to have been dried out or toughened by the intense Florida sun. She had the posture of a physically active woman, and the curious, intelligent eyes of one who was mentally agile, as well. Max had described her as "a neighbor," but Chris found herself wondering if there might be more to their relationship than he'd implied.

As for Jess, she was at first stunned, and then elated by Max's request. Her deep-set brown eyes sparkled as she gave Chris a brief but thorough once-over. Chris had the ridiculous feeling the older woman was mentally rubbing her palms together as their eyes met.

"Of course she can stay," Jess said with a sunny smile. "I'll just make up the sofa. Won't take minute."

While she busied herself gathering sheets and pillowcases, Max drew Chris to the front door of the compact but comfortable three-room apartment.

"You'll be okay here." He gave her a reassuring smile, which widened into a grin as he added, "If anybody tried to break in, Jess would probably clobber him with one of her cast-iron frying pans."

Chris returned his grin with a wry smile. Somehow she didn't doubt that the other woman might do exactly that. "That was a sneaky trick you pulled back at the motel," she accused under her breath. "Kissing me just to stop me from arguing with you."

Max instantly sobered. "My methods might have been a little underhanded, but I did what I did for your own good. Hasn't it occurred to you that if the guy who searched your room didn't find what he was after, he might assume you have it and come after you next?"

Chris blinked in surprise. "No," she replied. "It hadn't occurred to me. Do you really think that could happen?"

"If I didn't believe it was a possibility, I wouldn't have brought you here. And as for that kiss..." He inhaled an impatient breath and consigned his hands to his pockets to keep them from impulsively reaching for her. "It might have started out as a way to shut you up, but after about two seconds it turned into something else entirely, and you damn well know it."

A mischievous smile curved Chris's lips. "Yes, but it's nice to hear you admit it. Listen, I have a suggestion." A tentative note entered her voice. "Instead of leaving me in Jess's protective custody, why don't you invite me to come home with you?"

Amusement at her directness flickered in Max's eyes. "Sounds like a terrific idea." He spoke softly so that Jess wouldn't overhear, but there was still a distinct hoarseness to his voice. "But I'm not going home. After I report what's happened to the police, I'm going back to the motel. I plan to spend the rest of the night in your room, in case whoever was there decides to come back for another look around."

Chris's forehead creased in anxiety. "Is that really necessary? If he does come back, what will you do?"

"I'll decide that if and when the time comes." He glanced past her, to where Jess was spreading a light blanket on the opened sleep sofa. When his gaze returned to Chris's wide, blue, candid eyes, he felt as if he'd stepped out of a cave into blinding sunlight. "Walk me to the truck," he asked in a suddenly strained voice.

Chris had heard that strained note and read the message in his eyes, so she thought she knew what to expect when they reached his truck. She was wrong. There was a barely controlled urgency in the way he swept her against him, an almost desperate hunger in his mouth as it claimed hers, that took her completely by surprise. Yet, even while she wondered at the reason for it, her arms were lifting to close around his neck, her body leaning into his with eager abandon.

When Max felt her yield, he almost lost control. Any other woman would have taken violent exception to being grabbed and kissed as roughly as he was kissing her. But not Chris. If anything, she was encouraging him, egging him on. Her mouth moved strongly beneath his, and her fingers were clenched in his hair as she tried to pull him even closer.

He forced himself to tear his mouth away. This was madness, total insanity. He hardly knew her, for Pete's sake. She'd be going back to Indiana tomorrow, and in all probability they'd never set eyes on each other again. He *knew* that, dammit. And yet he had this crazy, nearly overwhelming desire to lock her up somewhere so she couldn't leave—or, better yet, chain her to his side. He decided his trolley must have gone off its track as he convinced his arms to let her go.

Chris rested her head on his shoulder and tried without much success to regain her equilibrium. She felt as if she'd just been given a glimpse of an alien world, one in which none of the physical rules that govern this one exist. She was stunned and bewildered, but at the same time exhilarated and undeniably aroused.

"I'm sorry," she heard Max say. He sounded a little dazed—as if he, too, had been shaken by that devastating kiss. "I didn't mean to . . . Are you okay?"

Chris nodded as she took a reluctant step backward. "Of course," she lied gamely. Her head bobbed again in reiteration. "Fine."

Her voice sounded weak, slightly raspy. She cleared her throat in a sudden attack of embarrassment, and then had to stifle a nervous giggle as it occurred to her how ridiculously they were both behaving. He'd apologized for kissing her and now she was mumbling and avoiding his eyes like a tongue-tied vestal virgin.

"Well . . ." Max's voice trailed off uncertainly before he gave himself a good kick in the pants. "I'd better go make that report to the police. Stay inside the apartment, just in case anybody followed us over here. If nothing happens at the motel tonight, I'll come back first thing tomorrow morning."

Without another word he climbed into the cab of his pickup and closed the door. Chris continued to stand on the pavement until she realized he didn't intend to leave before she was safely back inside. She gave him a limp wave and then turned and walked quickly to the door.

The instant she reentered the apartment, Jess descended on her like some kind of fairy godmother. She insisted that Chris must be half-starved and about to perish of thirst. In no time at all Chris found herself sitting barefoot at the dinette table, munching granola-and-molasses cookies and sipping some potent but delicious herbal tea Jess had brewed. As fairy godmothers go, she thought, Jess would probably have to be considered just a bit unorthodox.

But she was also warm and friendly and delightfully extroverted, so much so that after half an hour in her company, Chris felt as if they'd known each other for years. Jess had a knack for drawing a person out without appearing to pry, and as Chris started on her second cup of tea she found herself willingly answering all sorts of questions—about herself, her family, even her religious beliefs and political opinions. By the time Jess got around to casually slipping Max's name into the conversation, she was too comfortably relaxed to feel shy or ill at ease.

"You haven't known each other long, have you?" Jess asked as she filled Chris's cup for the third time.

"We met this afternoon, at the police station. I was there to report a stolen coffin," Chris explained between sips.

Jess's brows—which, unlike her hair, were still dark—rose half an inch and her bright eyes glittered with interest. "Really?" she murmured as she rested her chin in her hand. "Well, that's certainly an original way to go about meeting men. I'll have to try it sometime."

Chris laughed and nearly choked on her tea. "Good grief, Jess, I didn't arrange to have it stolen so I could meet men."

"Still, if it hadn't been stolen, you wouldn't have met Max," Jess pointed out with a smile. "And please forgive the presumptuousness of this remark, but I have to tell you how enormously pleased I am that you did."

Chris glanced at her in surprise. "You are?"

"Oh, my, yes. You're exactly the kind of woman I'd have picked for him myself. He usually tends to gravitate toward blondes whose bust measurement exceeds their IQ," she added dryly. "After a couple of weeks he's naturally bored out of his mind."

"He usually goes for big-busted blondes, huh?" Chris muttered darkly. Then a mischievous grin suddenly claimed her mouth. "Well, at least I won't have to worry about competition from you," she teased with a pointed look at the front of Jess's faded green sweatshirt.

Jess laughed delightedly. "Gracious, no!"

They sat up talking until well after midnight. Long before they went to bed, Chris had told Jess more about her brief association with Max than she'd have confided to her own mother.

THE NEXT MORNING Chris awoke with a nagging headache, which wasn't helped by the fact that at nine o'clock Max still hadn't returned or even called to tell them what—if anything—had happened during his all-night vigil.

Jess was equally impatient for information, and at nine-thirty they both climbed into her fire engine red Honda Civic and headed for the motel. Max's truck was parked around the corner, on a side street, but when they knocked at the door of number eight, there was no response.

"He probably fell asleep," Jess said as she pounded on the door again. "Max! If you're in there, open the door."

They waited, but the door remained closed and locked, and there wasn't so much as a snore from inside.

"Keep trying," Jess suggested. "I'll go see if I can get somebody to bring the master key."

While she was gone Chris kept knocking, with no better results than Jess had had. By the time Jess returned with the motel's Cuban manager, her knuckles were sore.

"Maybe he went out for breakfast," she said as she stepped aside to make way for the manager. Jess pursed her lips and shook her head.

"I doubt it. When he eats breakfast, which isn't all that often, it's usually not before noon."

The manager, who looked as if he hadn't been up long himself, frowned at Chris as he inserted the key in the lock. "I understood that you would be using this room, Miss Hudson."

"I did. That is, I was, until last night. The man who's supposed to be in there took me out to get something to eat, and while we were gone somebody came in and went through my luggage and my purse. Max insisted on moving me out, but then he came back to spend the night in the room, in case whoever searched it returned to the scene of the crime, so to speak."

Judging by the scowl on his swarthy face, she concluded that the manager didn't appreciate being informed that a room in his motel had been illegally searched. He was probably afraid she'd insist that the police be notified, or worse, that her room deposit be refunded. Chris considered reassuring him on both counts, then decided to let him stew. Max had said that whoever searched the room might have had a key, which meant it could conceivably have been the manager himself.

The door finally swung open, and Chris was the first one through it, with Jess right behind her and the still-scowling manager bringing up the rear. "Max?" Chris called as she stepped inside. "Are you here?"

He was there...sprawled facedown and unconscious on the floor at the foot of the bed.

CHRIS CRIED OUT IN ALARM and threw herself to her knees beside him. Jess yanked open the drapes to let in some light and then joined her, frowning in concern as she reached for his wrist. The manager stood just inside the door as if his shoes had been nailed to the floor and started babbling in rapid, panic-stricken Spanish.

"Omigod," Chris whispered. "Is he...? He's not—"

"No, just out cold," Jess said in relief. Releasing Max's wrist, she slid her fingers into the hair at the back of his head an probed gently. "And no wonder. He's got a knot the size of a billiard ball behind his right ear. Probably from that," she added grimly. She indicated the telephone, which lay on the floor about a foot beyond Max. "See if it still works. He'll need an ambulance."

Chris pulled the phone across the floor by its cord and lifted the receiver to her ear. "There's no dial tone."

"I'm not surprised. Whoever clobbered Max with it probably knocked the stuffing out of the thing. He's lucky he's got such a hard head. I've never seen a lump this big in all my life." Turning to the manager, Jess ordered briskly, "You go back to the office and call for an ambulance."

The man didn't move. He just kept staring in fascinated horror at Max's prone form, wringing his hands while he mumbled to himself in Spanish.

"Hey, senor!" This time Jess's voice was a sharp bark, and he jumped as if she'd thrown a bucket of water on him. You deaf or something? We need an ambulance. Pronto!"

Bobbing his head frantically, he muttered, "Yes, of course, an ambulance," pried his feet loose and darted out the door.

Less than three minutes later an emergency ambulance sped into the parking lot, siren screaming and lights flashing. The EMTs were still scrambling out when a car pulled into the space beside the ambulance. Quinn Vincent jumped out of it. "What's going on?" he demanded of one of the paramedics.

"Don't know yet," the young man replied as he hurried toward room number eight. Vincent stayed with him, matching him stride for stride. "We got a call that somebody had been attacked."

It crossed Chris's mind that the room really wasn't big enough to hold all these people, as two EMTs and a frowning Quinn Vincent surged through the door to join her, Jess, Max and the motel's manager, who'd returned as soon as he'd finished making the call.

Vincent spoke first, his voice stern as he edged to one side of the crowded room, trying to stay out of the way and still see what was going on. "This guy tells me somebody was atta—Good Lord . . . is that Max?"

"Good morning, Quinn," Jess said from her place on the floor. Turning her attention to the paramedics, she told them in the same calm tone, "He was apparently hit with the telephone, just behind the right ear. His pulse is a little erratic, but strong, and his respiration seems normal. I'd say he'll be lucky to get off with nothing worse than a mild concussion and a lulu of a headache."

"You a nurse, ma'am?" one of them asked her as he strapped a blood pressure cuff on Max's arm.

"No," Jess replied with a smile. "Just a mother."

The young man grinned at her before turning his attention to his patient. Max started to come around when the cold end of the stethoscope was shoved inside the neck of his shirt and clamped firmly on his chest. He mumbled an incoherent protest, instinctively rolling away. When the back of his head made contact with the floor, a pained grunt escaped him. It was immediately followed by a torrent of furious swear words as his eyes flew open. They quickly snapped shut again when the sunlight streaming through the window hit them.

"Hush, Max," Jess scolded. "Such language. No, don't sit up yet," she ordered as his shoulders tried to lift off the floor. "How does your head feel?"

"Like it just lost a knock-down drag-out fight with a sledgehammer," he growled in response. "Son of a bitch, what hit me?"

"I'll tell you what's *going* to hit you, if you don't stop swearing," Jess warned crisply.

His heavy groan sounded more exasperated than pained. "Give me a break. You'd swear, too, if some-body'd just used your head for batting practice.

Chris leaned over to lay a sympathetic hand on his shoulder. "Actually, it was only the telephone," she told him gently.

Max pried one eye open and tried to focus it on her face. "Thanks," he muttered. "That makes me feel a hell of a lot better."

The paramedics started stowing their equipment back in the bag one of them had carried in, and the older one said to the younger, "We'd better use the stretcher, Eddie."

"Right. I'll get it."

"Hold it," Max snarled as he struggled to sit up. "I don't need any damned stretcher."

"Of course you do," Jess contradicted brusquely. She and Chris each hurried to slip a supporting arm around him. "Don't be a horse's behind, Max."

"Yes, Max," Chris put in helpfully. "Don't be a horse's behind."

Max scowled at them both and scooted back to prop himself against the dresser.

"I'd listen to them, if I were you," Quinn Vincent advised, stepping away from the wall where he'd been lounging. He added that a concussion was nothing to sneeze at as he helped himself to a seat on the bed.

Max spared a glare for him, too. "What the hell are you doing here?" Wincing, he gingerly pressed one hand against the back of his head to keep it from falling off. "Never mind," he moaned. "I don't think I want to know."

Eddie returned with the stretcher, and Max decided enough was enough. But when he started to stand, agonizing pain exploded simultaneously in his right knee and his head. He fell back against the dresser with an involuntary gasp.

"Hell," he swore faintly. His knee felt as if someone had driven a red hot spike into it, and his skull wasn't in any better shape. He heard Chris's frightened voice cry out, but what she said didn't quite penetrate the red haze fogging his brain.

He must have passed out, because the next thing he knew he was lying flat on his back, strapped to a stretcher in the rear of a moving ambulance. Damn, they were taking him to a hospital! His hands clenched at his sides in frustrated anger, which he welcomed, even encouraged to grow. *Yes, dammit, get mad!* he told himself fiercely. He could use the anger to hold off the panic that was trying to creep in, keep it at bay for a while, hopefully until he'd regained enough strength to meet it head-on and beat it down.

Before the emergency room attendant even got the door open, Jess and Chris were hurrying across the parking lot. Quinn Vincent was hot on their heels. All three of them could hear Max swearing angrily and volubly as he was taken to a small treatment room down the corridor.

"He's terrified of hospitals," Jess confided to Chris as they entered the room.

"I *hate* hospitals!" Max corrected with furious precision. Turning a baleful stare on the young intern who'd slipped in behind Quinn Vincent, he added in a vicious snarl, "Almost as much as I hate doctors."

"Stop that!" Chris said. She crossed the room to frown down at him sternly. "You're behaving like a five-year-old."

Suddenly she bent over him, bracing a hand on each side of his head as she brought her face close to his. "Listen, you big lunk," she said softly. "We're all worried about you, okay? Is that some kind of crime in your book? Now settle down and behave yourself, or Jess and I will take you back to her place and start practicing our Florence Nightingale impersonations."

"That's extortion." Though his voice was a resentful mutter, there was a gleam in Max's hazel eyes as they met hers. Chris smiled, and he felt something flutter in the pit of his stomach. Trying to hold on to his anger became an exercise in futility; but it was all right, because as long as she kept gazing into his eyes like that, the panic didn't have a chance in hell.

"I really do hate hospitals," he told her gruffly.

"So do I. You can ever get anything but 'easy listening' music on the radios, and the nurses all have cold hands. Still, sometimes they're a necessary evil." She paused, then added in a low, husky voice, "For instance when somebody you care about's been hurt, and you want to make sure he's going to be all right."

Max couldn't have responded to that if his life had depended on it. *Heaven help me,* he thought dazedly. *What is she doing to me? What has she already done to me?*

Chris saw the confusion in his eyes, mingled with the pain and exhaustion, and wanted very much to do or say something to ease his distress. The trouble was, she was experiencing the same unsettling mix of emotions she sensed in Max, and so far she hadn't had a great deal of success in understanding them herself, much less coming to terms with them.

She was dimly aware that a nurse had entered the room to gather whatever information the hospital needed before Max could receive treatment. She impulsively lifted one hand to lightly stroke his temple, thinking she'd have to move away so the nurse could question him. But then she heard Jess speak up, saying she could tell them whatever they needed to know about the ungrateful son of a gun with the rotten temper and worse manners that the ambulance had just brought in.

A grin tugged at Chris's lips. No doubt about it, Jess was not your typical fairy godmother. Then she heard something that caused her to stiffen in reaction. Max heard it, too. His hand came up to curl around hers and a rueful smile quirked his mouth to one side.

In response to the nurse's brisk "Next of kin?" Jess had replied, "Jessamyn Decker, mother. That's me, dear."

CHAPTER FIVE

AN HOUR LATER Max had been admitted to the hospital against his will and despite his adamant insistence that except for a lousy headache, he was fine.

It was obvious that he was far from fine. Though the skull X ray had ruled out the possibility of a fracture, he was definitely concussed, and the doctor who examined him was equally insistent that he should be admitted and kept under observation for the next twenty-four hours.

He was assigned a cheery, sun-washed private room, which should have improved his disposition, but didn't. His growling and grumbling continued unabated, until Chris finally decided she'd heard enough.

"Excuse me, please," she said to the student nurse who was trying in vain to convince Max to don a hospital gown. So far, his only concession to pain had been to stretch out, fully dressed, on the bed. Stepping between the girl and her patient, Chris glared down at him, both hands planted firmly on her hips. Max glared right back at her.

"Are you trying to win some kind of award for obnoxious behavior?" she asked tersely. "Okay, so you don't like hospitals. Who does? But you're here for the night whether you like it or not, so why don't you just stop snarling at everybody in sight and make the best of it."

"Save your breath, Christine. I'm not wearing that thing, and that's all there is to it," Max retorted, eyeing the gown in disgust.

The student nurse looked at her with a hopeful, almost pleading expression, and Chris released an exasperated gust of breath. "Max, for pity's sake—"

Jess decided to intervene before Chris built up a really good head of steam. "Do you still have those pajamas I gave you last Christmas, Max?"

He frowned, then answered with obvious reluctance. "Yeah, I think so. But—"

"Good. I'll go get them. Let's see, you'll want your shaving kit, too, and some clean clothes to wear home tomorrow. No need for you to come, Chris. It won't take long—I know where everything is."

Of course you would, Chris thought. She still hadn't recovered from the astonishing discovery that Jess was Max's mother. She wasn't even sure that her brain had fully assimilated the fact yet, but she was still flustered enough to feel a little awkward in Jess's presence. It was a relief when she said she'd be back in two shakes of a lamb's tail and bustled out of the room.

"She's your mother!" Chris blurted the second Jess was out of earshot. She made it sound like an accusation. "Your *mother*, for crying out loud! Why didn't you tell me?"

Max threw an arm over his eyes and emitted a faint moan. "Would you mind closing the drapes." There was a feeble quaver to his voice that didn't fool Chris for a second. "The light . . . my head . . ."

She marched to the window and yanked the drapes together, them immediately spun back around. Max watched her through one slitted eye. A smile hovered at the corners of his mouth, and he knew she'd seen it when her chin jutted forward and a tiny frown line appeared between her brows. "Max Decker, you rotten low-down skunk, if you didn't already have a lump on your head, I'd put one there!"

They'd both completely forgotten Quinn Vincent, who had stayed behind when Jess left. Before a full-blown argument could erupt, he rose from the chair he'd been occupying and casually perched on the edge of Max's bed.

"Speaking of your lump," he said as he withdrew a notebook and pen from the inside pocket of his sport coat, "I guess you didn't get a look at whoever brained you."

Max grimaced. "No, dammit."

"Probably because he was sound asleep," Chris sniped from the position she'd taken at the foot of the bed.

Max shot her an indignant frown. "I was not asleep! For your information, I was using the bathroom." Turning back to Vincent, he added, "That must have been when he came in. I guess I surprised him. He sure as hell surprised me."

Vincent bent his head and made a brief notation. "You're not giving me much to work with, Max. Didn't you see anything at all?"

"Just a pair of shoes as I went down. White leather high tops. They looked expensive, and new...no scuff marks. About a size twelve. And he was wearing a really strong cologne. I can't name the brand, but I'd know it if I ever caught a whiff of it again. He smelled like a French—''

Glancing at Chris, he caught himself just in time.

''Anything else?'' Vincent asked as his neat block letters filled two more lines on the notebook page.

Max thought for a moment. ''I don't think so,'' he said, grimacing in pain and frustration.

Vincent nodded absently as he made another brief note. ''According to the report you made last night, whoever searched the room earlier didn't force his way in.''

''That's right,'' Max confirmed. ''When I went back I double-checked the lock, just to be sure. It wasn't jimmied. This guy was either a professional or he had a key.''

''And professional burglars usually don't go around bashing their victims in the head with the telephone,'' Vincent remarked wryly. ''Think it could have been the manager?''

Chris impulsively answered before Max could. ''No way. He almost went to pieces this morning when he let us into the room and we found Max. He was every bit as shook up as Jess and I were. And he wasn't faking, I could tell.''

''He did seem pretty rattled,'' Vincent murmured as he closed the notebook and slipped it and the pen back into his pocket. ''Probably afraid he'll lose his job.''

''Which reminds me,'' Max said with a puzzled frown, ''what were you doing at the motel? Did you pick up the emergency call on your car radio?''

Vincent shook his head. ''I didn't know a call had gone out for an ambulance until I pulled into the parking lot right behind it. I was there to talk to Miss Hudson."

Chris stared at him in surprise. "You were coming to see me? What about?"

Vincent swiveled around to face her. "About the coffin you reported as missing and supposedly stolen yesterday."

Chris felt a sudden, disquieting flicker of anxiety as he focused his attention on her. While he'd been concentrating on Max, his voice and manner were low-key—professional, yet comfortably relaxed. But that Quinn Vincent had vanished the instant he turned toward her. He'd shed his casual, easygoing attitude the way a snake sheds its skin. Now he was all business: somber, keenly observant, and—Chris had to admit—more than a little intimidating.

"Have you found it?" she asked hopefully.

There was a speculative, measuring look in Vincent's eyes that puzzled her and at the same time made her feel nervous, uneasy. She had the distinct impression that he was sizing her up.

"No, but we will," he said. Abruptly rising from the bed, he shoved his coat aside to thrust his right hand into his trouser pocket. His direct, intense blue gaze remained fixed on her face.

"When I arrived at my office this morning, there was a wire report from the Indiana State Police waiting on my desk. Care to guess what it was about, Miss Hudson?"

Frowning, Chris obliged. "The coffin?"

She thought she detected a trace of cynicism in Vincent's fleeting half smile, and also—for just an instant—in his piercing blue eyes. "Come on, you can do better than that." She *knew* she hadn't imagined the sarcasm in his voice. Her frown intensified in reaction.

"What are you getting at, Quinn?" Max asked. He sounded a tiny bit irritated, Chris noted with satisfaction. Of course it could just be that his head hurt and he needed to rest.

Vincent apparently decided to stop baiting her. He strolled over to the window and leaned back against the narrow ledge, casually crossing one ankle over the other. Chris suspected his sudden switch from sarcastic cynicism to lazy nonchalance was an act, and her frown remained in place.

"You wouldn't happen to know a man named Brian Peters, would you, Miss Hudson?"

Chris didn't even try to sound polite or respectful. "No, I wouldn't. Why do you ask?"

Her abruptness didn't seem to bother Vincent. In fact he actually smiled a little, though the smile couldn't by any stretch of the imagination have been considered friendly.

"I asked because you and Brian Peters both happen to reside in Evansville, Indiana, and both also decided to leave town at approximately the same time yesterday morning."

"So what?" Chris's frown had settled in for the duration, and her eyes were flashing storm warning signals that Vincent couldn't have failed to notice. "So did a couple of hundred other people."

"Get to the point, Quinn," Max suggested from the bed. "What's the connection between Chris and this Peters guy?"

"There isn't any connection!" Chris snapped before Vincent could answer. "I just told him, I don't *know* anybody named Brian Peters."

Max gingerly clasped his hands behind his abused head. "Calm down, Chris," he murmured. "He's obviously leading up to something. Okay, Quinn, let's stop with the cat-and-mouse games and get down to it. Who is Brian Peters and what law or laws has he broken?"

"What!" Chris exclaimed, her voice cracking in astonishment.

Quinn Vincent's gaze slid to Max.

"This doesn't concern you, Max. You're not involved."

"Wrong. Chris is my client."

Vincent just stared at him for a moment. "Your what?"

Chris finally recovered the power of speech. "His client. I hired him...well, sort of. By proxy, you might say. To find Cy Gollum's coffin. What did Max mean about Brian Peters breaking some kind of law? Who *is* Brian Peters, anyway, and what makes you think I have anything to do with him? I've never even heard the man's name before, and I certainly don't go around associating with criminals!"

Vincent opened his mouth to speak once or twice during her tirade, then decided he might as well wait until she was finished. Meanwhile, he lifted a hand to restlessly comb long, slender fingers through his hair.

"Let me get this straight. You hired Max to find the coffin you claim was stolen from the airport?" From the tone of his voice, he either didn't believe her or thought she was missing a few marbles.

"That's right," Chris replied brusquely. "After my interview with you, it was obvious I couldn't rely on the police to find it. And he is a private detective, after all."

"Investigator," Max corrected mildly. The expression on Quinn Vincent's face almost made him grin; the sergeant looked as if he couldn't make up his mind which of them was the more seriously deranged. "Got a license and everything."

"Great," Vincent mumbled. "Wonderful. So now you're both involved. That really makes my day."

"I'd offer my sympathies, Quinn," Max said dryly, "but so far I don't have a clue what it is we're supposed to be involved *in*. What say you put an end to this unbearable suspense and lay your cards on the table."

Vincent gave him a hard stare, raked his hand through his hair again, and apparently decided he had little choice but to do as Max suggested.

"A couple of months ago Brian Peters, a.k.a. Bruce Patowski and Brian Malone, was indicted by a Federal grand jury for operating an interstate credit card theft ring. His trial was scheduled to begin in Evansville next week. The U.S. Marshal's office and the FBI both had people assigned to watch him, in case he tried to jump bail, but early yesterday morning he managed to give them the slip.

"Peters is known to have contacts in Florida," Vincent added with a sharp glance at Chris. "And it's suspected he may try to use them to leave the country. The state police and all the local departments have been alerted to locate and apprehend him for extradition to Indiana."

Chris wasn't a total idiot. Long before Vincent finished speaking, it had dawned on her that he suspected her of smuggling this credit card thief out of Evansville and into Daytona Beach...inside a coffin! Her open-mouthed stare was a result of astonished disbelief, rather than confusion or a failure to comprehend his ridiculous implications.

"You don't honestly think—" she began, but Max's curt voice cut her off.

"Are you saying that Chris is under suspicion for abetting and harboring a Federal fugitive?" he demanded in a tone she'd never heard him use before. Her gaze darted to his face. It had become a hard, unyielding mask.

Vincent released a weary sigh. "Officially, no, she's not under suspicion. But you have to admit it looks pretty damn strange, Max. Yesterday morning she left Evansville with a coffin—which, by the way, was reported stolen last Saturday morning from the Diehl funeral home there—at *exactly* the same time Peters pulled his vanishing act. Later the same day both she and the coffin just happen to turn up in Florida, where Peters is known to have contacts. Let's say that at this point I have a lot of questions and not nearly enough answers."

"Let's say you're out of your mind!" Chris retorted indignantly. "Or does it make sense to you that I'd have reported the coffin missing if I'd been trying to smuggle somebody out of the country in it, for pity's sake!"

Her outburst caused a dark flush to spread over Vincent's cheeks. "Reporting the coffin as stolen might have been a shrewd move on your part, Miss

Hudson,'' he answered tautly. ''It could have been a ploy to divert suspicion from yourself, just in case anything went wrong with the plan.''

''Oh, for God's sake,'' Chris said in disgust.

''It's a wonder you don't lock her up and throw away the key,'' Max remarked. When Chris frowned at him in question, he explained, ''His theory is so full of holes you could use it as a strainer.''

''You're speaking as a completely objective observer, right?'' Vincent shot back.

Surprisingly, Max grinned. ''Not on your life. Through no fault of my own, it looks like I'm in this case up to my eyebrows.''

Vincent made a disgruntled sound in the back of his throat. ''Much as I hate to admit it, it looks like you are. Okay, Mr. Private Investigator, what have you come up with?''

While Chris looked on in angry astonishment, Max filled Vincent in on their own investigation, providing details of their visit with deCosta and the information he'd subsequently obtained that Frederick Marchand was the owner of record of the house where the actor was staying. Vincent pulled out his notebook and pen again and wrote everything down, then turned to Chris and asked her for the name and phone number of the employer who'd ''allegedly'' assigned her to escort the coffin to Daytona Beach. He didn't give any indication that he noticed the resentment in her voice when she supplied the information.

''I guess that's it for now,'' Vincent murmured as he replaced the notebook and pen in his pocket and turned for the door. On the point of leaving, he stopped to glance back at Chris. ''Oh, and Miss Hudson . . . it wouldn't be wise for you to take any sudden trips without notifying me first, unless of course it's to go back to Indiana."

"That's what he wants me to do, isn't it?" she demanded of Max as soon as Vincent had gone. "That's what he was telling me—that I should remove myself from his fair city as soon as possible and go back home? Well, he can forget it! I'm not going anywhere until my good name's been cleared and I know what the hell's been going on the past few days."

Max tried to squelch the unexpected and probably foolish pleasure her heated declaration gave him. "It might be better if you did go home, Chris," he said quietly. "There's no telling what that boss of yours has gotten you mixed up in."

"Elliott!" She pronounced the name as if it left a bad taste in her mouth. "I hope Vincent really puts the old tightwad through the wringer," she added maliciously. "What I wouldn't give to see his face when he gets that call."

"Remind me never to make an enemy of you," Max said dryly.

Chris grinned as she carefully perched on the edge of the bed. "You want to stay on my good side, do you?"

Thinking that she didn't have a *bad* side, he answered, "Damn right. You're scary when you're mad."

Chris smiled into his eyes. "How do you feel? Can I get you anything?"

"A new head?" Max suggested hopefully. He didn't mention his knee, which he'd decided he must have banged into the bed or the dresser when he fell. He hadn't tested it since they brought him in, but as long as he didn't try to put any weight on it, it didn't seem inclined to flare up again.

Her expression instantly softened with contrition. "I'm sorry. I apologize for yelling at Sergeant Vincent, too. Not that he didn't deserve to be yelled at, but the noise couldn't have done your head any good."

Max's lips twitched briefly. "It was worth it to see the look on his face when you told him he was out of his mind. I'd swear he almost swallowed his tongue."

"Yes, well, I admit I have a tendency to fly off the handle," Chris confessed sheepishly. "I've always had a pretty short fuse—just one of my many faults. I don't think I can get you a new head, but I know something that might make it feel better."

She got up and went into the adjoining bathroom, returning a minute later with a washcloth that she'd wrung out in cold water.

"This ought to help," she said as she sank back onto the mattress. Her hip pressed against his as she folded the cloth into a strip and leaned forward to place it on his forehead. Max resisted the desire to shift just an inch or two closer. "Close your eyes and try to relax." Her voice was soft and gentle, as soothing as the cool cloth.

He let his eyelids droop with an inaudible sigh. Normally he detested having anyone fuss over him, but it wasn't as if she was making a big production out of it. And it *was* nice to lie there and smell her light, flowery perfume, and feel the brush of her fingers at his throbbing temple and the warm pressure of her hip as it rested against his.

"You'd make a terrific nurse," he mumbled drowsily.

"Shh. You're supposed to be resting." Her voice was a whisper, her breath warm on his face, telling him that she was very, very close.

"I am resting. In fact, I'm almost out of it."

Chris watched his eyelids flutter and found herself fascinated by even this simple movement. "Max?" The sudden huskiness in her voice surprised her.

"Mmm."

"Why didn't you tell me last night that Jess is your mother?"

He stirred slightly, shrugging his shoulders. "Couldn't." His voice was slurred, causing the word to emerge as an indistinct mutter.

"You couldn't tell me?" Chris asked with a frown.

"No. Have to protect her... keep the bad guys from... Dad said... protect and defend..."

He was rambling, Chris realized, possibly delirious from the concussion. Sighing, she removed the washcloth and went back into the bathroom to wring it out again. When she returned and gently replaced it on his brow, Max's eyes suddenly flew open. She almost recoiled at the wild, uncontrolled panic in them. He looked positively terrified.

"Max!" she breathed in alarm.

One of his hands shot out, his fingers locking around her wrist in a bruising grip. *"No!"* he shouted hoarsely as he lurched upright on the mattress. "God, no! Don't— You sorry sonuvabitch..." His voice splintered on the last tormented word, and his fingers gripped Chris's wrist so tightly that they cut off her circulation.

"Max! Max, please, don't," she pleaded frantically as she tried to urge him back down. The thought never entered her head that he might hurt her. Her fear was all for him—what if he was having a cerebral hemorrhage or something? The call box was on the other side of the bed, and though she flung herself across his lap and stretched her free arm to its limit, she was unable to reach it.

In desperation, not knowing what else to do, she abruptly hauled herself upright again and started trying to pacify him, thinking that if she could just calm him enough to free her wrist, she could run to the door and yell her head off for a nurse.

"Max, Max, shh, it's all right," she soothed in as calm a voice as she could manage. "It's all right."

She lifted the hand he wasn't holding and began to gently stroke his hair, as if he were a child who'd just woken from a nightmare and needed comforting. Max's eyes remained glazed and unfocused, but she felt the tension gradually begin to drain from his body. When she thought he would let her, she slowly pulled her wrist from his grip and eased him onto his back. He didn't resist, but as she started to slide off the bed he suddenly reached out again, groping for her hand. Chris immediately gave it to him, instinctively linking her fingers with his.

"Chris?" He sounded confused, and there was a trace of fear in his voice that tugged at her heart. She smiled into his eyes, wanting to reassure him but doubting that he was fully conscious. He wasn't, she realized as he sighed and his eyes drifted closed.

Acting purely on impulse, she leaned down to place a soft kiss on his mouth. When she straightened, the sound of someone's throat being cleared behind her made her swivel around to see who had entered the room. Expecting it to be a nurse, she felt her cheeks burn as Jess's twinkling eyes dropped from her face to where her hand and Max's lay clasped together on the bed.

"Is he asleep?" Jess asked in a stage whisper.

"I think so. Either that or unconscious." Glancing back at Max, mainly to avoid Jess's all-seeing eyes, Chris added, "He was delirious for a little while. I think it would be a good idea if somebody stayed with him."

"One of the student nurses is going to, as soon as they finish dispensing the noon medication. One will be assigned to this room for the night, too. He'll be all right, Chris," she added gently. "He's survived far worse than a knock on the head."

Chris nodded, then carefully slipped her hand from Max's slack clasp and rose from the bed. Never one to beat around the bush, she turned to Jess and said bluntly, "I think we need to have an old-fashioned heart-to-heart."

Jess smiled her beaming, fairy godmother smile. "I agree."

Chris faltered for a moment, then nodded briskly. "Good." She took a deep breath, preparing to politely ask for the explanation she felt the other woman owed her, but just then the student nurse who'd been there earlier returned and deposited herself in the armchair beside Max's bed.

Chris looked at Jess. Jess smiled again. "He'll probably be out of it for quite a while yet. We might as well go back to my apartment and have our talk there.''

Chris was frowning as she followed Jess out of the hospital. She didn't know why exactly, but she had the feeling she was being manipulated again. Not by Max this time, but by his mother. She tried to tell herself she was being silly, but she couldn't manage to shake the feeling. It didn't help that Jess just kept smiling that serene ''I know something you don't know'' smile all the way back to her place.

Without so much as an inkling that she was going to do it, Chris heard herself abruptly ask, ''How would you feel about having a houseguest for a few days?''

Jess parked the car, removed her key from the ignition, pivoted to face her and said without a trace of surprise, ''Why I'd be tickled pink, dear.''

CHAPTER SIX

"YOU'RE FEELING A LITTLE EMBARRASSED, aren't you?"

Chris hastily set the mug of tea she'd been about to sip from back on the table, reflecting that Jess had a real flair for understatement.

"Embarrassed?" she repeated, her tone dry. "Well, yes, you could say I feel just a tiny bit embarrassed. Not to mention stunned, confused and more than a little—"

"Annoyed," Jess interrupted with an understanding smile. "I don't blame you. It was wicked of me not to tell you I was Max's mother last night. I realized right away that he hadn't, and I knew from past experience that he probably wouldn't."

Chris frowned as she picked up her mug again. "Why not?"

Jess calmly folded her hands on top of the table. Her smile was still in place, but now it looked a bit strained. "To understand that, you'd have to know something about Max's past. Unfortunately, that's a subject he never discusses."

"He told me he used to be a policeman in New York," Chris murmured over the rim of her mug.

"He did?" Jess both looked and sounded astonished.

"Mm-hmm. He said he'd moved down here after he retired, and I told him he wasn't old enough to be retired."

"You're right, of course," Jess said with a brisk nod. "He looks older, but Max is only thirty-eight. I'm sixty, in case you were wondering. He is officially retired, though," Jess assured her. "Six years ago he was wounded in the line of duty, and as a result of his injuries he was given an early retirement with full disability pension."

Chris paled. "Wounded?" Her voice wobbled over the word. "You mean . . . shot?"

"It happens sometimes," Jess said with a fatalism Chris found difficult to accept. "Though thankfully not nearly as often as the police shows on television would have you believe. He tried to stop a liquor store robbery, without any backup. He was hospitalized for almost six months."

Chris replaced her mug on the table before it fell out of her hands. "No wonder he hates hospitals."

"Yes," Jess said. "I almost lost him. His heart stopped twice during emergency surgery, and then there were...complications. But that's all in the past, thank God. I try not to even think about it, and Max . . . Well, Max chooses to pretend it never happened. I'm amazed that he told you as much as he did. Except for Quinn Vincent, I don't think anybody in Daytona Beach even knows he was a police officer before he came here. I think it's an encouraging sign, don't you?"

Chris blinked in confusion. "I'm afraid you've lost me, Jess. What's an encouraging sign?"

"Why, that he opened up to you, even a little bit. He wouldn't have, if he didn't think of you as someone special."

Chris arched her brows in question. "The kind of woman he'd bring home to meet his mother, you mean?"

Jess chuckled appreciatively. "I knew it!" she declared. "I knew the second I set eyes on you that you were exactly what he's been needing to shake him up, light a fire under him. And I was right! He's probably already wondering what hit him."

"Jess!" Chris didn't know whether she was more amused or exasperated. "For heaven's sake, you make me sound like a one-woman demolition squad."

"Oh, no, dear," Jess said earnestly. "That implies that I think of you as a destructive force. On the contrary, I fully expect you to have a very positive effect on that hardheaded son of mine. You already have, as a matter of fact. Yesterday he actually put on something besides blue jeans for the first time in I can't remember when. And if that isn't proof enough, I could swear he was wearing after-shave last night."

"Old Spice," Chris supplied. "Listen, speaking of last night . . ."

"Yes, of course. You want to know why neither Max nor I saw fit to inform you that I was his mother. Well—" spreading both hands palms up, Jess flashed one of her charming, impossible-to-resist smiles "—I'll freely confess that my motive for keeping silent was a case of plain old-fashioned curiosity. Max has never—not *ever*, in the four years I've lived here—brought a woman around to meet me. When he showed up with you in tow, I nearly expired of shock.

I was afraid that if you realized I was his mother, you might start to feel nervous or uncomfortable, and we wouldn't have the chance to really get to know each other."

"So you conveniently forgot to tell me," Chris responded dryly. She tried to resurrect at least some healthy indignation, but it was next to impossible. "Okay, that explains your part in last night's little deceit. But what about Max? It was really rotten of him to not tell me that you were his mother. He could at least have given me some warning!"

Jess's smile was sympathetic, but her eyes danced with unholy glee. "Oh, but if he'd done that, you wouldn't have been so relaxed and *open* with me!"

Chris's cheeks felt ready to burst into flame. She lifted a hand to hide behind as she muttered in mortification, "I don't remember half of what I said to you last night, but I have an awful feeling most of it was excruciatingly personal."

"You told me that you and Max had the hots for each other," Jess informed her cheerfully.

"Oh, God."

"And that if your motel room hadn't been ransacked while you were out, you'd probably have spent the night together there. Forgive me for offering an unsolicited opinion, dear, but I think it's just as well the evening didn't turn out the way you two had planned."

Chris just shook her head, at a complete loss for words.

"I took a good look at that place this morning," Jess continued chattily. "It's hardly the ideal site for a romantic interlude. Can you imagine how awful it would have been, for both of you, to have had to face each other in that tacky room this morning? It would have been a terrible way to start your relationship, don't you agree?''

Chris made a strangled sound behind her hand, then spread her fingers to peek out from between them. ''You're something else,'' she said to Jess.

Jess beamed in response. ''Why, thank you, Chris,'' she replied sincerely. ''What a nice thing to say.''

Chris's hand fell away from her face. She stared at Jess for a moment, and then they both burst out laughing. ''All right,'' Chris said as she helped herself to more tea from the earthenware pot on the table. ''You've distracted me long enough. I want to know why Max deliberately kept me in the dark about your identity last night.'' Before Jess could answer, she added pensively, ''Does he feel he has to look after you—protect and defend you?''

''Protect and defend,'' Jess repeated in an oddly subdued voice. ''Where did you hear that expression?''

''It was something Max said when he was delirious. Does that phrase have some special meaning?''

Jess nodded solemnly. ''Yes, it has a special meaning. She gazed across the table at Chris for a moment, then seemed to reach some kind of decision. Chris waited in silence, somehow sensing that what Jess said next was going to be important to both of them.

''Max's father was a police officer, too,'' Jess told her without preamble. ''He was killed in the line of duty when Max was sixteen. Max worshiped the ground he walked on. He never wanted to be anything else but a policeman, just like his dad, from the day he was old enough to understand what the word meant.'' She paused briefly, her mouth curving in a reminiscent smile.

''Joe—that was my husband—took the responsibilities of his job very seriously, and he passed that attitude along to Max. They were both detectives, and they both specialized in undercover work. I spent a lot of sleepless nights just sitting and waiting . . . watching the clock and wondering if one or the other of them would make it home.''

''I can imagine,'' Chris said.

''Yes.'' Jess's soft sigh sounded resigned. ''As I said, they were both deadly serious about the responsibility that went with the job, but unfortunately they both also carried that sense of responsibility a little too far at times. Joe, and later Max, was always afraid that sooner or later someone who had a grudge against him might take it into his head to come after me. They were both almost obsessive about keeping their professional and personal lives strictly separate. It's a fairly common syndrome, but in Max's case I often worried that he was carrying it to an unhealthy extreme. I suppose it would be asking too much to expect him to change an attitude he's held most of his life.''

''Old habits die hard,'' Chris responded, and knew from Jess's expression that that was something else she'd heard often over the years. ''Did you move down here with Max?'' she asked, thinking that he might have insisted Jess come with him so he could keep a protective eye on her.

''Oh, no. Max has been in Daytona Beach a little more than five years. I stayed in New York for almost a year after he left. But with both my husband and son gone, and no other family there, I saw myself starting to slip into a rut—an hour or two of gossip over coffee in the mornings, and either volunteer work or a matinee in the afternoons . . . Lord, what a depressing way to live," she said with an exaggerated shudder. "Anyway, Max had settled here, and I was ready for a change, so one day I packed up the things I wanted to keep, called the Salvation Army and told them to come and get the rest, and bought a ticket on the first plane to Daytona Beach."

Chris was impressed by Jess's courage and spirit of adventure. At fifty-six, she must have needed quite a bit of both to make such a drastic change in her lifestyle. Still, Chris sensed that there was more to the story than Jess was telling.

"And how do you like it here?" she asked casually. "Are you ever sorry you came?"

"Never!" Jess said with conviction. "I have a small but wonderful circle of friends and a very active social life. I come and go as I please, dress as I please, and I haven't had a cold since I moved down here."

"And, of course, you're close to Max," Chris said, still casual.

Jess's eyes twinkled and she chuckled softly. "Not much gets by you, does it?" Sobering, she answered Chris's unspoken question. "He'd been through a lot in the year before he moved to Florida. Part of the reason he relocated here was to try and put the past behind him. I'm his mother—of course I was worried about him. His scars aren't all physical, Chris. And please don't ask, because I can't say any more than that. I hope he'll tell you himself, but it has to be his decision."

Chris nodded. "All right. I can accept that." A frown line appeared between her brows as she hesitated. "But please don't set your hopes on any happily-ever-after endings where Max and I are concerned, Jess. We only met less than twenty-four hours ago, and I *will* be going home, as soon as we have answers to the questions that keep piling up about that dumb coffin and what was or wasn't in it."

Jess didn't dispute what she'd said, but there was something about the older woman's expression that made Chris distinctly uneasy as Jess encouraged her to "Fill me in" on the events of the past two days.

Since it appeared that Max would be off the active duty list for a couple of days, the two women decided they might as well do a little investigative work on their own. The idea was originally Chris's, but Jess didn't need much encouragement to go along with it. They agreed to start with a visit to the owner-proprietor of the Holloway Eternal Rest funeral home. They reasoned that Max *had* said he intended to speak with the man before he was sidelined with a concussion. They also assured themselves and each other that they were only standing in for him, acting in his place until he could, as Jess put it, "Get back out in the field."

"But I don't think we should tell him," Chris said as they rummaged in Jess's closet. Except for a couple of inches' difference in height, they were approximately the same size, and Jess had generously offered her the loan of whatever clothing she might need for the rest of her stay. "He'd just worry about us if he knew.'' Holding up a hot pink jumpsuit, she swiveled toward the full-length mirror on the back of Jess's bedroom door. ''Oh, I love this! What do you think?''

''Take it. It's perfect for you. And you're absolutely right about Max. He might work himself into some kind of seizure fretting about us . . . needlessly, of course, but why put him through that? Besides,'' Jess added as she withdrew a pair of sunny yellow slacks and flowered blouse from the closet for herself, ''he might decide to play at being a dictatorial male and order us not to go, and then we'd just have to do it behind his back. Do you think this it too frivolous to wear to a funeral home?''

Chris flashed a fiendishly wicked grin and assured her that the outfit looked terrific.

WHEN THEY STROLLED INTO HIS ROOM together, Max was scowling at the television screen and using the remote control tuner to zip through the available channels.

''Do people actually watch this stuff?'' he said in disgust. ''I can't get anything but game shows or soap operas.''

Chris walked around the bed and plucked the tuner out of his hand. ''At this time of day, that's about all you can expect to find.'' She smiled and pressed the Off button with her thumb. ''Aren't you lucky we're here to entertain you?''

''Oh, yeah,'' Max muttered glumly. ''I'm the luckiest son of a gun I know. Where did you two take off to, anyway?''

Jess and Chris exchanged an indulgent glance. ''I do believe he missed us,'' Jess said as she sank onto the armchair beside the bed. "That's sweet, Max. Where's your nurse? Have you frightened her away already?"

"No, I haven't frightened her away," he said indignantly. "She was making noises about giving me a sponge bath, and I told her she'd better be damned sure I was either unconscious or dead before she came near me with a bar of soap. She got all huffy and pranced out with her nose in the air."

"Max," Jess chided gently.

"Give me a break," he mumbled, closing his eyes. "I'm not the first one to refuse a sponge bath and I sure as hell won't be the last."

His voice was unnaturally flat and even more low-pitched than usual. Chris suspected it was because even talking caused the pain in his head to intensify. She went into the bathroom to fetch another damp washcloth, and when she gently laid it across his brow Max released a soft sigh.

"Thanks."

"You're welcome."

Chris couldn't resist the urge to let her fingers administer a light, stroking caress to his cheek, and wasn't really surprised when Max turned his head just enough to allow him to brush his lips across her palm.

"Where did you go?" he murmured against her skin. Chris felt a twinge of guilt, because she also heard the other question, the one he couldn't or wouldn't ask aloud: *Why* did you go, when you knew I needed you?

"I thought you'd be out of it for a while, so Jess and I went back to her place for a couple of hours. I'm sorry one of us wasn't here when you woke up," she added softly.

Max didn't respond. He didn't know how to react to her gentle and obviously sincere compassion. He'd heard about soft, nurturing women, read about them, seen them portrayed in movies, but he'd never actually known one before. Jess had always been...well, Jess. Pragmatic, levelheaded, both feet planted firmly on the ground—her brand of loving and caring had always been perfectly suited to the personalities of her men. Neither he nor his father would have been comfortable with embarrassing displays of emotion, something Jess had realized long ago.

But Chris wasn't Jess, and he couldn't deny that it gave him pleasure to know that she cared—and what's more, that she wasn't at all hesitant to show it. The brush of her cool fingers against his unshaven cheek was soothing, easing an ache inside him that had nothing to do with his concussion. He wanted the soft caress to go on and on, right through this lifetime and into the next; yet at the same time he also knew he wanted more. Sex, yes; he definitely wanted to go to bed with her. But there was more to it than that. It was stupid and irrational, but he felt very strongly that Chris could somehow give him something he'd been searching for all his life, if only he would let her.

The women stayed the rest of the afternoon, looking after Max without seeming to fuss over him when he was awake, and talking to each other in excited, conspiratorial murmurs whenever he dozed off for a while.

As the day progressed, his periods of drowsiness became fewer and further between as the effects of the concussion started to subside. More and more of the time he was wide awake and alert as he lay with his eyes closed and tried to make out what they were saying to each other.

He was surprised that the two of them seemed to have hit it off so well, considering the difference in their ages and the fact that he'd deliberately misled Chris about Jess's identity the night before. He'd seen the shock in her eyes this morning, when she'd found out Jess was his mother, and had fully expected her to be furious with him. But maybe Jess had soothed her ruffled feathers. She was good at that.

As the afternoon wore on, he began to realize that there was definitely something in the air; and, furthermore, he was deliberately being excluded from it—whatever "it" was. They were just a little *too* buddy-buddy, and their whispered exchanges sounded more like strategy-planning sessions than idle chitchat. He wondered briefly what they were up to, but then Chris came over to check on him, her cool fingers gentle as she stroked a few strands of hair from his forehead, and he forgot what it was that had been puzzling him.

When visiting hours were over for the day, both Chris and Jess started bustling around the room, gathering their purses and hastily making sure Max had everything he needed. Jess smiled and patted his shoulder, Chris bent down to give him a quick kiss, and then they sailed out of the room together as if they were late for Bloomingdale's semiannual white sale.

After they left, Max lay staring at the door, a brooding expression in his eyes. What the devil were they up to?

"Do you think he suspects anything?" Chris said as they climbed into Jess's Civic.

"Probably," Jess replied dryly. "He's got a naturally suspicious mind—a result of all those years he spent hobnobbing with the criminal element, I suppose."

"Doesn't it worry you that he might have guessed what we were planning?"

Jess shrugged. "What could he do about it, even if he did guess? He's safely tucked away in the hospital for the rest of the night, with one of the student nurses standing guard over him. Anyway, it's not as if we were doing anything *wrong*. We're only going to have a pleasant little chat with this Mr. Holloway, not tie him up and interrogate him with a rubber hose. When you called the funeral home, what time did they say visitation would be over tonight?"

"Nine," Chris answered. "We're cutting it kind of close. It's almost a quarter after eight already."

"Oh, forty-five minutes should be more than enough time to find out what we need to know," Jess assured her with a confident smile.

From the hospital, she zigged and zagged a couple of times to get onto Nova Road, then raced the light at Orange to make a left turn and head east. The light turned yellow well before they reached it, but Jess didn't even slow down.

Chris had the address of the funeral home, but she wasn't familiar enough with the streets to help with directions. Jess didn't appear to require help, anyway. When she reached Palmetto Avenue she made a sharp left turn, then a sharp right at Magnolia and another right onto Beach Street. As they made each hair-raising turn, Chris was positive that two of the Civic's tires had parted company with the pavement and half the tread on the others had been left behind to mark their passing. When Jess abruptly braked to a halt, she realized she was clutching the sides of her seat in a white-knuckled grip.

"Well, here we are," Jess announced as she switched off the engine. "Holloway's Eternal Rest."

Chris released a pent-up breath and flexed her cramped fingers. "That was some ride."

Jess seemed to take the remark as a compliment. She smiled happily as she replied, "Would you believe that until I moved down here, I'd never driven a car in my life."

"Yes," Chris murmured as she extricated herself from the fire-engine-red death trap. "I'd believe it."

They entered the funeral home, and while Chris glanced around for someone who looked as if he might work in the place, Jess wandered over to an alcove where the registration book for visitors lay open on an ornate white stand. Chris didn't see anyone who even remotely fitted her image of a mortician, but she did spot a door marked Office down the hall. Turning to summon Jess, she spotted the older woman stooping to pick up something she'd apparently dropped.

She hurried over to the alcove, urging, "Come on, I've found the office." As Jess came to meet her, she absently shoved the object she'd just retrieved from the floor into her purse. It looked like an address book. "Now let's just hope Mr. Holloway is in," Chris murmured as they started down the hall.

He was, but the "pleasant little chat" Jess had predicted turned out to be more of a hostile confrontation. Mr. Holloway looked *exactly* the way Chris thought a mortician should—thin and ghastly pale. His dark suit and white shirt added the finishing touch.

His voice was low-pitched and soft, but there was a slight whine to it that set Chris's teeth on edge. As soon as she identified herself, his thin lips compressed in displeasure, though he didn't speak until she'd finished telling her story and explained her reasons for coming to see him.

"So," she said with an encouraging smile as she ended her recital, "if it wouldn't be too much trouble, could you check your records to see if you might recently have had a . . ." She faltered momentarily; what did morticians call the people they worked on, anyway? "Uh, a client named Cy Gollum?"

"That won't be necessary," Mr. Holloway told her coldly. "I would certainly remember such an unusual name as that. I can state without hesitation that no one named Gollum had passed through Holloway's since I assumed management, and that was five years ago."

"Oh," Chris said in disappointment. "Well, not that I'm questioning your memory, you understand." She paused and inserted another smile, making a conscious effort to remain pleasant. "But it wouldn't hurt to just take a peek at the books, would it?"

The mortician's beady little eyes shot daggers of ice at her. "As I've already said, that won't be necessary. You've caused quite enough trouble for this establishment, young lady, without creating more. In case you've forgotten, I refer to the unnecessary trip my hearse made to the airport yesterday, as a result of your ridiculous prank."

"Prank!" Chris echoed sharply. "Now, just a doggone min—"

"While you're here, allow me to personally present you with our bill for that trip," Holloway went on smoothly. He riffled through some papers on his desk, and after a moment produced some kind of statement. "Ah, here we are. The total charges come to one hundred and forty-five dollars. Will you be paying in cash, by check or would you prefer to use a credit card?"

Chris was fuming as she and Jess stepped out the front door of the funeral home five minutes later. Stuffing the Visa receipt in the bottom of her purse, she complained angrily, "That man has got to be the most mercenary—not to mention the rudest—person I've ever met. A hundred and forty-dollars, can you believe it! It's getting so a person can't even afford to *die* anymore."

"It does seem like a lot for one trip, and his manners could certainly stand improving," Jess sympathized. "And on top of everything else, it would seem our visit was wasted."

"No, it wasn't," Chris contradicted. "Not entirely. Mr. Holloway is hiding something—I'd stake my last dollar on it. If his files really wouldn't show any record of the name Gollum, why didn't he bring them out and prove it? And there's something about him . . . I don't know how to explain it, but I wouldn't trust him any further than I could throw him."

"He reminded me of President Nixon," Jess remarked as they rounded the corner and headed for her car. "Well, what now? Back to my place?"

Chris came to an abrupt halt in the middle of the sidewalk, her chin jutting obstinately. "No. I want a look at those records, darn it."

"You're going back? Oh, dear, I don't think that would be wise."

"I'm going back, all right," Chris confirmed. "But not right away. Let's drive around for a while." Then, remembering the wild ride from the hospital to the funeral home, she hastily retracted the suggestion. "On second thought, let's take a stroll. You can show me some of Daytona Beach while we wait for this place to close for the night."

JESS DIDN'T LIKE THE IDEA one bit, but Chris wouldn't be deterred. The more Jess argued against her plan, the more determined she became to carry it out. Finally Jess resigned herself to the fact that with or without her help, Chris was going to reenter the funeral home after it had closed to have a look at the records. She reluctantly agreed to stand guard outside.

Chris was a little disappointed when the first door she tried at the rear of the building was unlocked. It didn't seem as exciting, somehow, to just open the door and walk right in. Now if she'd been able to try her hand at picking a lock . . .

It was a big building, and she realized it might take a minute or two to get her bearings. At the moment, she seemed to be in some kind of large storage area. As her eyes adjusted to the lack of light, she recognized the outlines of a couple of vehicles—hearses, probably—and decided this must be the garage. Treading carefully, she crossed the cavernous room to a partially closed door, using the narrow strip of yellow light at the door's edge as a focal point.

On the other side of the door was a hall, which she recognized as the one leading to Holloway's office. It was dimly lit by a couple of wall sconces that had been left on. And it was empty.

She eased around the door, careful not to move it in case the hinges squeaked, and started tiptoeing down the hall. She actually had her hand on the knob of the office door when the muted but distinct sound of a man's voice alerted her that there was at least one person inside. She froze. *Terrific,* she thought as she snatched her hand back, and then *Damn! Why was he still here, and how long did he intend to stay?* Thinking she might get some indication from the conversation being conducted inside the office, she cautiously pressed her ear to the wooden panel.

"The next shipment's due when?"

Chris frowned. That deep, melodious voice definitely didn't belong to Mr. Holloway.

"Tomorrow or the next day, if everything goes according to schedule." Now *that* was Mr. Holloway.

There was a brief pause, and then the first man spoke again, his voice conveying impatience. "I don't like this setup. Shipping the merchandise across the country by common carrier is too risky. You never know when some gung-ho cargo chief will decide to make a random inspection. I need the money, but not badly enough to risk ending up in prison."

Mr. Holloway muttered something that was apparently intended to placate the other man, but Chris wasn't really listening. She was stunned and shaken by what she'd already heard, and equally upset by the certain knowledge that the second man's voice wasn't totally unfamiliar to her. She couldn't immediately place where or when, but she was positive she had heard that deep, velvety baritone before . . . and fairly recently, at that.

It suddenly occurred to her that this was definitely not a good place to be caught eavesdropping. Whatever the two men were involved in, it sounded unquestionably shady, probably illegal and possibly dangerous. Deciding that sneaking a look at the funeral home's files would just have to wait, she quickly but silently retraced her steps down the hall and slipped back around the partially closed door to the garage.

When she was within ten or twelve feet of the door by which she'd entered, she finally released the breath she'd held in her lungs all the way down the hall and lengthened her stride to hasten her departure from Holloway's Eternal Rest.

She was less than five feet from the door when a hard arm suddenly snaked out of the darkness and hooked her around the waist, hauling her back against an equally hard chest. Her instinctive scream was muffled by the callused palm that clamped over her open mouth a second later.

CHAPTER SEVEN

CHRIS REACTED WITH INSTINCTIVE FEROCITY, kicking and scratching to set herself free. A gruff voice swore softly in her ear, and her struggles ceased as she went rigid with surprise. A second later the hand on her mouth was removed and she was forcibly spun around.

"Max!" she said in a breathless, astonished whisper as her breasts collided with his chest. "What are you doing here?" she hissed. "You're supposed to be in the hospital, recovering from a concussion."

"I knew the two of you were up to something, and after you left I finally figured out what," Max answered in a subdued growl. "Dammit, Christine, I ought to turn you over my knee. Of all the crazy, irresponsible things to do! If you'd been caught breaking into this place, both you and Jess would have ended up spending the night in jail, you little idiot."

"I didn't break in," Chris said defensively. "I was going to, but the door wasn't locked. So even if I had been caught, I couldn't have been charged with breaking and entering."

"No, just malicious trespass," Max snarled. He was obviously furious, and Chris judiciously decided not to argue with him.

"Where's Jess? Did you see her outside?"

"Oh, yes, I found my mother crouched behind a trash can in the alley, playing lookout." Chris winced at the sarcasm in his voice. "She was having the time of her life. I gave her a good dressing down and told her to wait in her car. You're going to join her, and then we're all going back to her apartment, where I'm sure I'll think of a few more things to say to you both."

His arm remained around her waist as he turned her toward the door; but when he started forward he seemed to stagger a little, and his free hand came up to clutch the side of his head. Chris hurried to brace her shoulder under his arm.

"Oh, Max! You're out on your feet, aren't you?" She lifted a hand to gently stroke his cheek. "I'm so sorry. You should be resting in bed, not chasing all over town after Jess and me. Come on. Let's get you home, and I'll fix you an ice pack or a hot water bottle or something."

Her honest concern and remorse were very nearly Max's undoing. He *was* out on his feet. The desire to turn to her and let her wrap her arms around him and lavish him with her tender compassion almost overwhelmed him. But he was afraid that if he didn't keep pushing himself, he'd end up facedown on the garage floor of Holloway's Eternal Rest funeral home.

"If you'll throw in a couple of aspirin, you've got a deal," he said with a lopsided grin. "Come on, before Jess decides we've been captured and embalmed or something, and calls the police."

They started for the alley again, but before they reached it they both heard the distinct sound of a door closing inside the funeral home, and then approaching footsteps.

"Oh, great," Max muttered. "Just great."

"Shh!" Chris hissed. "Listen."

He scowled down at her and tried to pull her toward the door to the alley, but she stubbornly resisted. She was certain the two voices in the hall were the same ones she'd overheard inside Holloway's office. Thinking this might be her only chance to get a look at the second man, she impulsively steered Max behind what seemed to be some kind of partition jutting out from the rear wall. Fortunately he was either too exhausted or too weak—or both—to put up a fight as she pushed at him to get them both concealed before the men entered the garage.

"What the hell do you think you're doing?" he whispered furiously next to her ear.

"I'll explain later," Chris whispered back. "Just trust me, okay?"

Max said something unintelligible under his breath, and then uttered a soft but distinct oath. "Terrific hiding place you picked here."

"What?" Turning to see what he was talking about, Chris discovered that rather than being concealed behind a solid wall, they were standing behind a set of floor-to-ceiling open shelves, about half of which held large rectangular boxlike objects. The remainder of the shelves were empty. There was more than enough open space for them to observe the door leading to the funeral home, which meant that whoever came through it would no doubt also be able to observe them.

"Coffins?" Chris whispered curiously.

"Give the little lady a cigar. What did you expect to find in a funeral home—microwave ovens?"

The anger in Max's voice had reached an ominous level, and Chris could almost feel his eyes boring holes in her back. She had just about decided that it might be best to slip outside while they still could, when the door to the funeral home abruptly swung open and two figures stepped through it.

Chris hastily dropped into a crouch, grabbing Max by the elbow to drag him down with her. She heard him inhale sharply as he half fell against her, almost knocking her over before he managed to right himself. She didn't dare ask if he was all right; the two men were standing just inside the garage, not more than twenty-five or thirty feet away.

Just when she was sure they were about to be discovered, someone called out to Mr. Holloway from the hall, and both he and the man with him stopped and turned back. Chris's entire body sagged in relief, but she knew they'd only been granted a temporary reprieve. Sooner or later Mr. Holloway and his guest would continue on into the garage, and she and Max would be caught red-handed. She had to think of something, and fast.

When she turned her head to see how Max was holding up, inspiration was waiting to smite her right between the eyes. Shoving at his shoulder, she frantically indicated with wild hand gestures and jerks of her head that he should climb into the coffin on the shelf in front of him. Unlike some of the others, the lid of this one wasn't divided into sections, which would make it easier to get into and out of. Even better, the lid was already partway open, propped up with a small wooden dowel. It would make a perfect hiding place.

Max didn't seem to share her enthusiasm. He shook his head, winced at the pain the movement caused him, then frowned fiercely and mouthed the word "No." Chris frowned right back at him and gave his shoulder another shove. Apparently realizing he wasn't up to a boxing match, he gave in with another frown that promised retribution.

The coffin lid rose smoothly and noiselessly, and as Max eased himself inside Chris retrieved the wooden dowel before it could fall to the floor and give them away. Before he had time to suspect what she had in mind, she dropped her purse in beside him and then slithered over the edge of the coffin herself and stretched out on top of him.

Max grunted in surprise. "What the hell—"

Chris poked him in the ribs and he pinched her fanny in retaliation.

"That's just a down payment on what you really deserve. Now watch your head," he whispered as he started to lower the lid. Chris wedged the dowel back in place just as the overhead lights came on.

As the men's voices drew nearer, she cautiously turned her head on Max's chest to peer through the crack between the coffin and the lid. He gave her a gentle nudge, as if to ask if she could see anything, and she moved her head in a negative response. All she could see was a couple of feet of garage floor and a few inches at the bottom of the opposite wall. But she could *hear* plenty.

"And Tony's sending the shipment the same way as last time?" The question came from the man with Mr. Holloway.

"That's correct. In fact, it should already be on the way. I expect to take delivery by the end of the week, at the latest."

"Has it been five or six months since we got the last batch? I forget."

"Closer to six than five, I'd say."

"Then this shipment will be even bigger than usual. I don't like it. I tell you, we're pushing our luck."

"You worry too much," Mr. Holloway soothed in his irritating semiwhine. "Everything will go according to plan, just like always. Come over here and let me show you the casket I chose for this delivery."

Casket? Chris almost stopped breathing. She suddenly remembered something she'd heard on the phone yesterday, when she'd called Holloway's from the airport.

The man who'd answered the phone at the funeral home had apparently turned away for a moment to speak to someone else, but Chris had still been able to hear what he said: "It wasn't supposed to be here till the end of the week, was it?"

Of course! When she'd called about Cy Gollum's coffin, they must have assumed that this shipment they were expecting had arrived ahead of schedule. No wonder Mr. Holloway had sent a hearse out to the airport right away. She was fairly bursting with the need to share her revelation with Max, unconsciously squirming against him in her excitement.

And then she saw two pairs of shoes enter her limited field of vision and head straight for their hiding place, and her fingers dug into Max's shoulders as she froze in breathless horror.

"It's exactly like this one," Mr. Holloway said as the shoes stopped directly in front of the coffin where she and Max were hiding.

"Which one—the one on the bottom?"

Chris closed her eyes and prayed that she wasn't going to faint.

"Heavens no, that's one of our most expensive models. There, on the second shelf. It's not a top-of-the-line model, of course, but very attractive nonetheless, don't you think?"

"Oh, very." The drawled response contained a trace of sarcasm, as if "attractive" wasn't a word the other man would personally apply to a coffin.

Once again Chris was struck by the conviction that she'd heard his voice before. If only she could see his face.... When he and Holloway entered the garage the light from the hall sconces had been at their backs, so she hadn't been able to see his features clearly. And since then her observation had been limited to his shoes—oyster Topsiders—and about an inch and a half of what looked like white carpenter's jeans above them. He wasn't wearing socks.

"Let's get out of here," he said as she stared at his shoes. "This place gives me the willies."

It was something of an anticlimax when the men suddenly turned and walked away. The sounds of their steps receded, and just before they reentered the funeral home the garage lights were switched off.

Chris collapsed against Max's chest, trembling in delayed reaction. She felt one of his hands administer a couple of awkward pats to her back.

"You okay?" he whispered.

She nodded, her chin pressing into his collarbone. "Fine. If you'll hold the lid up, I'll get out and then help you."

"We'd better wait a couple of minutes just to make sure the coast is clear," Max advised. There was a brief silence, and then he added anxiously, "You don't suffer from claustrophobia, do you?"

Chris grinned. "If I did, you'd have known about it before now. How's your head?"

"Don't ask," Max muttered. Actually at the moment his head was in far better shape than a couple of other parts of his anatomy. His right leg was beginning to cramp, and the way her pelvis was snugly nestled against his was causing him more than a little discomfort in that area, as well.

"Poor Max," Chris murmured. Shifting a little, she pressed a soft kiss on the underside of his jaw. His throat worked convulsively in reaction. It was all the encouragement she needed. Gripping his shoulders, she pulled herself up until she could reach his mouth.

Max had to stifle a groan when her slender body slid along his, rubbing against him in a way that made his stomach lurch. And then suddenly her lips were settling softly on his, and he couldn't have stopped his instantaneous response if his life had depended on it.

His mouth opened beneath Chris's, his fingers splaying over her back as he returned the gentle caress of her lips with a barely controlled hunger. A tiny voice at the back of his mind mocked him for his pathetic lack of self-control, but he ignored it as easily as he ignored the pain in his head and his leg. Self-control be damned, he needed this—to feel her sweet warmth, the soft, comforting touch of her hands and mouth . . . to revel in the fact that she actually *cared*.

When his tongue plunged past her teeth, a shiver scampered up Chris's spine, leaving goose bumps in its wake. Her hands slid over his shoulders and around to the back of his neck, her fingers restless yet careful to avoid the knot behind his right ear. When Max's tongue retreated, hers instantly gave chase. He moaned weakly into her mouth.

His chest was heaving, his breath came in short, labored blasts, and there was an unmistakable bulge beneath her stomach that hadn't been there a couple of minutes earlier. Chris was surprised that she'd aroused him so quickly with just a kiss—surprised, and very definitely pleased.

Still, she reminded herself, it was hardly the time or place for this kind of thing. And no matter how aroused Max might be, she had to remember that only an hour or so ago he'd been lying in a hospital bed, which was probably where he still belonged. She reluctantly eased her mouth from his and rested her head on his shoulder for a moment, struggling mightily to get her own libido under control.

Max cleared his throat softly before he attempted to speak. "Whew! I almost passed out for a second there. I really don't think I'm up to this."

Chris couldn't resist. "No?" she murmured silkily as she wriggled her hips against his.

Max groaned. He tried and failed to prevent his body from lifting toward hers in response. His right knee immediately screamed at him in complaint. "Stop that," he ordered tautly. His hands grasped her hips to still their tormenting movements. ''You know that wasn't what I meant.''

''I'm sorry,'' Chris said, and she sounded as if she truly was. ''It's cruel of me to tease you.''

''Yes, it damn well is,'' he agreed with a trace of amusement. ''I think it would be safe to get out of here now.''

''Okay.'' Sliding her arms from around his neck, Chris waited for him to raise the lid, then clambered out of the coffin. In the process she had to move against him again rather intimately. She heard Max suck in a strangled breath as her leg grazed the front of his jeans. ''Sorry,'' she said again as she scrambled to her knees. ''Did I hurt you?'' His reply was unintelligible. She suppressed a grin and reached into the coffin to retrieve her purse.

''Do you need help getting out?''

Max had serious doubts that he'd be able to get out even with help. He wasn't sure his damned knee would bend at all, and between Chris's attentions and the concussion, he was feeling distinctly light-headed.

''Max?'' Chris said softly, and the note of concern in her voice prodded him to action.

His right leg *would* be the one he had to lift out first, he thought grimly as he grasped the side of the coffin to pull himself up. He gritted his teeth and thought he was doing a pretty fair job of concealing his agony until Chris suddenly leaned forward to wrap her arms around his chest.

''Stop trying to be so damned stoic,'' she said impatiently.

Max would have laughed if he'd trusted himself to unlock his jaw long enough. She was really something else.

Chris gently eased his leg to the floor. The rest of him quickly followed, and she reached around him to lower the lid of the coffin, not bothering to replace the wooden dowel. "How you doing?" she asked in obvious concern.

"Don't ask," he said between clenched teeth.

Her shoulder was at just the right height to prop under his arm, and Max didn't object when she offered herself as a crutch. Without some kind of support, he doubted he'd be able to make it as far as the door.

Chris half guided, half carried him down the short alley to the street, turning them both toward Jess's car when they reached the sidewalk. She was surprised to see Max's truck parked behind the Civic. He must have picked it up from the motel before coming here. She felt a brief surge of irritation. He'd been in no condition to drive; it was a wonder he hadn't killed himself.

Jess jumped out of her car and hurried to meet them, flinging Max's left arm around her shoulders so that he was sandwiched between her and Chris. When Max chuckled softly, both women looked up at him in question.

"I was just imagining what the three of us must look like." His voice sounded a little slurred.

Jess frowned up at him. "He isn't, is he—inebriated?"

"No. Just woozy from the concussion and in a lot of pain. We really ought to take him back to the hospital."

"Forget that," Max growled. "Don't even think it. Just take me home and throw me down on the bed. All I need's a good night's sleep, an' I'll be fine."

The women exchanged a resigned look and reluctantly agreed. But when they reached Jess's car and he realized they intended to put him in it, Max rebelled again.

"Uh-uh. No way am I gonna ride with Jackrabbit Jessie. I've had enough excitement for one day." Squinting down at Chris, he mumbled, "You c'n drive my truck. Keys're in my right pocket."

The only thing that kept her from arguing with him was the fact that he was obviously ready to collapse. She dug the keys out of his pocket and with Jess's help managed to boost him up into the cab. Then she had to figure out the idiosyncrasies of the pickup's ancient transmission. By the time she realized that first gear was missing, they were only a block from Jess's apartment. Chris jerked the gearshift around until she located neutral and let the truck coast into the parking space beside the Civic.

She had assumed that Max would stay at Jess's apartment for the rest of the night, but both mother and son soon set her straight about that.

"Goodness no, he can't stay with me," Jess said, as if only a lunatic would even suggest such a thing. "And even if I wanted him, where would I put him?"

Max roused himself from his apparent stupor to claim that he'd sooner spend the night in the drunk tank.

"But..." Chris stared from one of them to the other in dismay. "Jess, you surely don't intend to make him stay out here in his truck all night!"

Jess reared back as if she'd been slapped. "Of course not! What kind of mother would do a thing like that to her own son? His apartment is right above mine. All we have to do is get him up one little flight of stairs, and he'll be home. You can stay with him tonight," she added as she put out a hand to steady Max, who was attempting to descend from the cab.

"Me?" Chris squawked.

"He'd probably pitch a fit if *I* offered to take care of him," Jess told her dryly.

Max grimaced at the very idea. But then his mouth slipped sideways in a cockeyed grin as he gazed down at Chris. "Looks like you're elected to play nurse," he said cheerfully.

He was punch drunk, Chris decided as he swayed and she hurried to wrap an arm around his waist. He definitely shouldn't be left alone tonight, and it *had* been Jess's idea for her to stay with him.

That "one little flight of stairs" might as well have been Mount Everest, she thought when they finally reached Max's apartment. Of the three of them, he was the only one who wasn't huffing like a steam engine. Fortunately, Jess had a key. She let them in, led the way to the bedroom and then announced that she was bushed and intended to go home and get some sleep.

Chris walked her to the door. When she returned to his bedroom she found Max sprawled facedown on the bed, still fully dressed. Heaving a weary sigh, she climbed onto the mattress and started pulling at his shoulder to turn him over.

"Max. Come on, Max, you can't sleep in your clothes."

"Sure I can," he mumbled into the pillow. "Do it all the time."

"Well you're not doing it tonight. Come on, darn it, give me a little help. I intend to undress you, anyway," she warned when he just lay there like a log.

"You wouldn't." He sounded drugged, but confident. "You've prob'ly never undressed a man in your life."

Chris tugged at his shoulder again. "I've got four younger brothers. Now roll your ass over."

He grinned and flopped onto his back. "Tut, tut. Such language."

Chris glanced up at him as she eased his shoes off. His eyes were closed, his hair tousled, his clothing rumpled. He looked like a little boy who'd stayed up way past his bedtime and fallen asleep in front of the television. "You're supposed to be helping."

"Can't," Max mumbled. "I'm too far gone." Which was truer than she could possibly know. He suddenly flung an arm over his eyes, and the action produced exactly the result he'd hoped for.

"Does the light hurt your eyes?" Chris asked in concern.

"A little."

The mattress bounced as she jumped to turn it off, and he winced. In truth, the single hundred-watt bulb in the ceiling fixture didn't generate enough light to bother him, especially with his eyes closed. Nor was he stalling to keep Chris from undressing him. He was looking forward to it, actually, provided he didn't fall asleep first. But he preferred that she do it in the dark. He wasn't sure how she'd react to his scars. She would probably still feel them—they were pretty hard to miss—but at least she'd be spared the shock that first sight of them was sure to give her. And he'd be spared the horror and sympathy he knew she wouldn't be able to conceal. He didn't want to see that look. Not on her face, not tonight. He was too weak to pretend it didn't matter.

He helped her not at all, but Chris didn't complain as she struggled to remove the snug jeans and faded T-shirt he'd put on before checking himself out of the hospital. His mouth twitched when he realized she wasn't going to peel off his boxer shorts, too. You might know she'd leave covered the one area of his body that wasn't in any way disfigured or flawed.

When Chris had folded his clothes and stacked them on the dresser, she tugged the corded bedspread and top sheet out from under him and covered him with both. "I'll sleep out on the couch," she whispered as she bent to lay a soft kiss on his forehead. "If you need anything, just yell."

But as she started to withdraw, Max's hand darted out from under the covers, his fingers curling around her wrist. "Stay. Please."

Chris didn't speak, nor did she hesitate as she slipped her arm from his light clasp and stepped back from the bed to take off the hot pink jumpsuit. She carefully folded it and placed it beside his clothes on the dresser, and when she turned toward the bed Max had thrown back the covers on her side. She heard his breath catch, and was grateful for the semidarkness that concealed her hot blush.

"Are you one of those militant feminists who doesn't believe in wearing a bra?" he said in a harsh murmur.

Chris smiled as she slid into bed beside him. "No, I'm one of those underdeveloped feminists who doesn't need one."

Without warning his hand slid over her breast, cupping it lightly. She jumped in surprise. "Where did you ever get such a crazy idea?" he asked incredulously. "Underdeveloped you are definitely not."

Chris pushed his hand away, not sure if she was more embarrassed or pleased. "Cut it out." She tried to make her voice stern. "Don't start something you can't finish."

Max sighed and shoved one arm beneath her to pull her against him, then wrapped the other one around her in a relaxed but firm embrace. "Much as I'd like to take exception to that slur, I suspect you're probably right," he said drowsily. "Are you comfortable?"

"Very," Chris whispered, snuggling closer to the warmth of his chest. "Are you?"

"You've got to be kidding," he mumbled. "If the concussion doesn't kill me, the frustration probably will."

She smiled and tipped her head back to kiss his chin, and in less than a minute they were both sleeping soundly.

It was several hours later when his hoarse voice woke her. Chris realized at once that he was having a nightmare, but her attempts to wake him only seemed to increase his agitation; in fact, he threw out an arm as if to fend her off and almost knocked her out of bed.

Whatever the dream was about, it was obviously causing him a great deal of torment. His fiercely muttered words were for the most part incoherent, but the anguish in his voice wrenched at Chris's heart. He couldn't seem to break free of whatever dark horror had seized his mind, twisting away from her violently when she tried once more to wake him. She eventually decided to try comforting him, as she had in the hospital. She stroked dampened tendrils of hair from his forehead and spoke tenderly in his ear, her voice low, calm and soothing. Later she couldn't remember exactly what she'd said. It didn't matter. At that moment the only thing that mattered was giving Max peace, bringing him back from whatever hell he'd fallen into.

After a while her soft touch and gentle voice seemed to penetrate his pain. He stopped thrashing, and finally relaxed with a shuddering sigh, turning toward her, reaching out for her with a mumbled plea that caused Chris's eyes to fill with tears as her arms closed around him in a tight, protective embrace.

He slept peacefully for the rest of the night, cradled securely in her arms, his head resting just beneath her chin. It was some time before Chris managed to get to sleep again, though. She was too aware of—and disturbed by—the intense emotions Max aroused in her, without even seeming to try. He could make her laugh one minute and want to slap him the next; he brought out her latent maternal instincts, made her worry about him as if he were a child; and yet he also stirred a passion in her the likes of which she'd never known.

It was too soon to know if it would last, but she was fairly sure she was falling head-over-heels in love with him.

CHAPTER EIGHT

MAX HAD ALWAYS BEEN a slow starter. He wasn't one of those lunatics who wake up all at once, bound out of bed and do fifteen minutes of calisthenics before they even head for the bathroom.

So he didn't immediately comprehend that he wasn't alone in his bed. His first clue came when he went to gingerly straighten his right leg and realized that something was lying on top of it. The object was warm, smooth and silky, and whatever it was, it definitely felt good—especially when he became aware that it wasn't just lying on his leg, but was in fact wedged between his thighs. And pretty far up, at that.

He pried one eye open to see what the devil he'd dragged into bed with him last night and nearly jumped out of his skin. Chris! Naked! *In his bed?*

The shock alone was enough to start his head pounding. He closed his eyes and forced himself to draw a deep, steadying breath.

What...? How...? Good Lord. Holding his breath for fear he might wake her, he lifted the covers and sneaked a quick look under them. The air whooshed out of his lungs in relief. They both had on underwear, which would seem to indicate that nothing had happened... wouldn't it? But if nothing had happened, what in blue blazes was she doing in his bed, virtually stark naked, with her knee making itself at home in the crotch of his shorts?

He eased himself out from under her with extreme care, then slid to the edge of the bed and got up. He frowned down at Chris's sleeping form. When she woke, somebody was going to be expected to come up with some explanations. He fervently hoped that somebody wasn't going to be him.

Chris stretched luxuriously before opening her eyes to see if Max was awake yet. He obviously was; his half of the bed was empty. A tender smile touched her mouth as she reached out to trail her fingers over his pillowcase. Then she threw off the covers and rolled out of bed in a sudden, excessive burst of energy.

When she emerged from the bedroom, Max was sitting at the table in his tiny dinette, munching on a cherry Pop Tart. He didn't look up when she pulled out a chair and helped herself to a seat beside him.

"Good morning," Chris said cheerfully.

Max stared at the Pop Tart as if he were totally fascinated by it. "Morning," he muttered in response.

"How does your head feel today?"

His head? Frowning, he lifted his right hand to cautiously probe the tender area behind his ear. His head! Of course, his head! A big chunk of his memory suddenly returned, and he felt a weakening rush of relief. Still, there was a lot that remained blank. He continued to avoid Chris's eyes.

"It's okay. Still a little sore is all." *What the hell were you doing naked in my bed this morning?*

"That's good. Can I have a sip of your coffee?" Not waiting for permission, Chris picked up the mug in front of him and helped herself. Her mouth immediately contorted in a grimace. "Coke!" The way she said it made it sound like something far worse. "You drink Coke for breakfast?"

Max shrugged. "I'm out of coffee."

Frowning, she got up and went to open his refrigerator. Max watched her out of the corner of his eye. "Good grief, Max, how do you stay alive? There's nothing in here but junk food," she said in disgust.

"I thrive on junk food," he retorted a little defensively. "There should be some milk. Glasses are above the sink."

Chris opened the quart carton and sniffed suspiciously before pouring herself a glass. When she returned to the table, she leveled a disapproving frown at him. "You don't even have any orange juice. Can't you get run out of Florida for not having orange juice in your refrigerator?"

Max felt the beginning of a smile and quickly brought it under control. Dammit, why was she acting so... normal! He didn't believe for a second that she made a habit of spending the night with men she'd known barely two days. What the hell had happened last night? Had *anything* happened last night?

Chris sipped her milk and wondered why he seemed so reserved this morning. Could it be that he was embarrassed about the nightmare he'd had, or the vulnerability he'd displayed afterward? She suspected that Max Decker would despise any sign of weakness in himself, and maybe he saw either the nightmare or his reaction to it as a weakness. If that was the case, she'd just have to set him straight.

She cleared her throat softly. "Listen, Max, about last night," she began. His head snapped up immediately. His grim expression was a little daunting, but Chris pressed on doggedly. ‘‘I don’t want you to feel . . . well, embarrassed or ashamed.’’

Ashamed? What was left of the Pop Tart crumbled in Max’s fist. What could he possibly have done that was so awful she’d expected him to be ashamed this morning? He realized with a sick feeling of dread that he was going to have to ask.

‘‘Uh, well. . .’’ His gaze shied away from Chris’s, but he grimly forced it back. ‘‘To tell the truth, I don’t seem to remember much about last night,’’ he admitted miserably.

Chris stared at him in surprise. And then she suddenly understood the reason for his unexpected reserve. He didn’t remember *anything* about last night, and consequently he wasn’t sure how to behave with her. She quickly ducked her head to hide her amusement. When she lifted it again, there was a pleading, almost stricken look in her eyes.

‘‘You don’t remember?’’

Max swallowed, or tried to, and shook his head. ‘‘I . . . no,’’ he said gruffly. He’d never felt crummier in his life.

Chris couldn’t conceal her amusement any longer. She suddenly grinned and leaned forward to plant a hard, enthusiastic kiss on his mouth. Max reacted with a startled jerk. Then he saw the laughter in her eyes and scowled at her fiercely.

‘‘That wasn’t a damned bit funny,’’ he growled.

‘‘It was so. You just don’t have any sense of humor,’’ Chris retorted. ‘‘If you could have seen the look on your face . . .’’

"You're just asking for it," Max told her, maintaining his frown with an effort. "Aren't you?"

Her grin became lascivious. "I got more than I asked for last night."

His eyes narrowed, but she could still detect the amused gleam in them. "I don't want to hear it," he said. "You'd probably just make up a pack of lies, anyway. You're a cruel, heartless woman, Christine Hudson."

"Now *you're* asking for it," she told him sweetly, and gulped down the rest of her milk. When she set the glass back on the table, Max's soft chuckle caused her to glance at him in question.

"You've got a white mustache," he remarked. "Here, let me wipe it off."

He reached out to take hold of her arms, and the next thing Chris knew she was sitting on his lap. He stroked the milk from her upper lip with his thumb, his expression soft as he gazed into her eyes. She lifted one arm and draped it around his neck.

"Did you get it all?" she asked huskily when his thumb stilled at the corner of her mouth.

"No," Max whispered as he leaned toward her. "I missed a little right here." His tongue administered a light, teasing caress, and Chris's breath caught audibly.

"Max." His name was little more than a sigh as she moved her head the half inch necessary to capture his parted lips with hers.

It was always the same, Max thought as his arms closed around her. Every time he touched her, he caught fire, and this time was certainly no exception.

He pulled her closer, wishing they were back in his bed, yet knowing that he wasn't going to suggest it.

He wanted her. Lord, how he wanted her! But he was totally wrong for her, even if Chris didn't seem to realize it. If he asked, he knew she would make love with him—right now, this minute.

But he couldn't do that, he told himself grimly. He was no more prepared to commit himself than he'd ever been. He could offer her nothing but a brief affair that would leave her hurt and disillusioned. She didn't seem to understand that, or maybe she just didn't want to accept it. Like it or not, he had to assume the responsibility of protecting her, from both him and herself. And if there was one thing he still did well, it was accept responsibility. He stopped kissing her and rested his cheek alongside hers.

"Mmm," Chris murmured in his ear. "I hope you're around the next time I eat barbecued ribs."

Max pulled back with a reluctant grin. "I was just making up for what I missed last night."

"You said you couldn't remember!" she accused.

"I couldn't. Not at first."

She gave him a skeptical look. "I get it. Your next line is 'Oh, yeah, it's all coming back to me now.' Right?" Max merely smiled. Chris shook her head at him, but then the skepticism suddenly left her eyes and she sobered.

"Do you remember having the nightmare?"

Max's smile abruptly vanished, his features going stiff with shock. He felt as if he'd been punched in the stomach. "Nightmare?" he repeated woodenly.

"Yes. It must have been around two or three this morning. When I tried to wake you, you nearly knocked me out of bed. You were throwing your arms and legs around and swearing...you really had me worried for a few minutes."

Max could imagine. He was stunned, hardly able to comprehend that he'd had the dream and had not woken from it in a cold sweat.

"You really don't remember?" Chris asked.

He shook his head dazedly. "No."

"It's probably just as well. That must have been a lulu of a nightmare."

"It was," Max replied without thinking.

Chris gazed at him intently. "You've had it before, haven't you?" His mouth thinned, but he didn't answer. He had; she was certain of it. Placing her hand on his chest, she asked softly, "Does it have anything to do with this?"

Max inhaled sharply. He looked down at her delicately shaped hand resting so casually over that grotesque memento of his past and wanted to pluck it away before it could become contaminated.

"Max?" Chris coaxed gently, as if she'd read his mind. "It's all right. I know about the liquor store robbery, that you were wounded in the line of duty. Jess told me. And I saw the scars on your chest and your leg last night...not clearly, because it was too dark, but I know they're there. Is that what the nightmare was about?"

Max tried to analyze the emotion that came and went in her low-pitched voice, listening closely for revulsion or maybe pity. He detected neither. What did come through, loud and clear, was the same gentle compassion she'd shown him more than once before. He felt his tensed muscles relax.

He hesitated, then placed his hand over hers as he answered her question. "Yes. That's what it's always about."

"Will you tell me? If it bothers you to talk about it—"

"No." He was amazed to realize that he *wanted* to tell her. He just wasn't sure how to. The only other person he'd ever talked to about it had been the staff psychiatrist at the hospital, and that had been six years ago.

"No," he said again. "It's all right." And he suddenly knew that it would be.

"Then let's go in the living room," Chris suggested. "We'll both be more comfortable on the couch."

When they were settled on the sofa Chris silently took his hand in hers, and he began to speak—stiffly at first, and then, as he gained confidence, more naturally. He'd been working a stakeout of the liquor store from a shoe repair shop across the street on the day of the robbery. A usually reliable informer had named the liquor store's owner as a fence for stolen merchandise, and Max and two other detectives were assigned to keep a twenty-four hour watch on the place. They'd already had the store under surveillance for a week, and so far they hadn't come up with anything in the way of evidence.

Max's shift was to start at ten that morning. It was Jess's birthday, and he'd promised to take her out to dinner that night. He'd impulsively decided to surprise her with a bottle of champagne. He'd stopped by the liquor store before going to relieve his partner across the street.

"It was just my rotten luck to walk in right behind the two guys who intended to rob the place," he said with a cynical twist of his mouth.

"Jess said you tried to stop them," Chris said.

Max nodded grimly. "Tried and failed."

Her fingers tightened around his. "Is that when you were shot?"

"Yeah. It was stupid—*I* was stupid," he said in disgust. "If I'd been using my head, I'd have slipped back out the door and gone across the street to get Marty. One of us could have called for assistance while the other one covered the liquor store. That's the way I should have played it—by the book. Instead, I reacted like some hotshot rookie. My gun was out before I even realized I was reaching for it."

Chris thought he was being unnecessarily hard on himself, but for the moment she refrained from saying as much. Though she wasn't sure she wanted to know the answer, something compelled her to ask, "Did you shoot them...the men who were holding up the place?"

"I wounded one of them," Max answered, and the bitterness in his voice made her suspect he wished he'd killed them both. She had to force herself not to judge him.

"We nailed each other at the same time," he continued in a flat voice. "I got him in the arm, and he blew my right leg out from under me. After I was down, his buddy opened up on me with a shotgun."

The blood drained from Chris's face, and her fingers closed on his like a vise. She was dimly aware that Max's hand was gripping hers just as tightly.

"That's not all," he said quietly. For the first time, his voice faltered. "There was a customer in the store."

Oh, God, Chris thought desperately. *No. Please, no.*

"He'd stopped in to buy some champagne, too. He and his wife had just had their first baby, and they were going to celebrate."

"Max," Chris said in an anguished whisper. She knew what was coming, but she didn't want him to say it. Not because of what hearing it would do to her, but because she knew the agony reliving it would cause him. She wrested her hand from his grip and wrapped both arms around him tight, wanting to protect him, spare him any more pain.

"They killed him." His voice was totally devoid of emotion, as coldly remote as the look in his eyes.

"Don't," Chris pleaded tearfully. "Stop, Max. Please stop."

He didn't seem to hear her. "Just blew him away... as if he were no more important than a fly on the wall. God, those sons of bitches!" His voice shook with six years of accumulated rage, and his next words were so ravaged by guilt that Chris thought her heart would break.

"It was my fault. Those bastards might have fired the shots, but I'm the one who caused him to die."

"No!" Chris denied fiercely. Tears trickled from her eyes, but her voice was strong and sure. "No, Max!"

He turned his head to give her a sad, heart-wrenching smile. "Yes," he said softly. "Yes, I did." He lifted a hand to gently wipe the moisture from her cheeks. His hazel eyes were clouded by regret.

Chris realized that trying to convince him he hadn't been responsible for the other man's death would be an exercise in futility. The guilt had begun six years ago, and by now it was too much a part of him to be routed with reasonable arguments. She concentrated on bringing her emotions under control and not letting him see how much his story had upset her.

"Jess said you almost died in the hospital." Despite her best efforts, her voice wavered slightly.

Max released a heavy sigh. "God knows I tried to," he said as he drew her against his chest and wrapped his arms around her. "Actually, I did die. Twice, in fact, while they had my chest open in emergency surgery. But they gave me a jump start and managed to get the old carburetor working again both times."

Chris realized that he was attempting to lighten the mood. She hugged his chest and murmured, "Just goes to show, you can't keep a good man down. Jess also said you had some kind of complications after the surgery."

He sighed again. "Jess talks too much."

"Were they serious?"

Max hesitated, but he sensed that she wouldn't let up until she'd wrung the whole story out of him. Besides, he thought ruefully, if he didn't tell her, Jess probably would. Still, he was reluctant. In some ways the part he'd left out—deliberately—was more appalling than what he'd told her.

"Max," she coaxed softly, and he tried to steel himself for the shock he fully expected to see in her eyes when she heard the rest.

"It depends on your definition of 'serious,' I guess," he said, his voice carefully controlled. "I cracked up."

"Oh, Max—"

He heard the dismay in her voice and kept talking to drown it out. "Went right over the edge, around the bend, came unglu—"

Chris quickly pressed two fingers over his mouth. "Hush," she urged softly. "Don't."

Max trembled, overwhelmed by a potent combination of relief and gratitude and some as yet unidentified emotion even more powerful than the other two. For the first time in six years, he realized there was a very real possibility that he might break down and cry. And then the absurd thought occurred to him that if he did, Chris would probably produce a handkerchief and tell him to blow his nose.

At first Chris thought the sound Max made was a sob, and her hold on him tightened. But then she recognized the way his shoulders were shaking beneath her hands and realized that he was laughing. She went as limp as an old dishrag in his arms. Max pulled back a little to gaze down at her, his lips twitching uncontrollably.

"Are you cracking up again?" she said, and then held her breath for his reaction.

His eyes crinkled at the corners, and his spontaneous smile bared the most beautiful set of teeth she'd ever seen. "I was just asking myself that same question."

Chris relaxed again. "And what answer did you get?"

His smile disappeared, though his eyes remained warmly amused. "That I shouldn't worry," he said soberly. "Because there's only one crazy person on this couch, and it's not me."

Chris produced an offended frown. "I take exception to that remark. I'll have you know I'm a perfectly normal, well-adjusted person."

"Who breaks into funeral homes and hides out in coffins," Max added dryly.

Chris suddenly lurched upright, twisting out of his arms as if she'd just discovered they were coated with swamp slime. Max stared at her in stupefied silence as she jumped to her feet and took several agitated paces away from him. Was this some kind of delayed reaction to what he'd told her?

"I'd forgotten all about that!" she cried, whirling back around to face him. Her face was flushed and animated, her eyes glittering feverishly. "What do you think it is?"

Max's mind grappled with the question for a moment, but he finally had to ask, "What?"

Chris frowned at him as if she suspected him of being deliberately obtuse. "The shipment they're expecting—the stuff they're smuggling into town inside a coffin, of course. What could it be, do you think?"

Max shrugged. "Almost anyth—"

"Drugs!" she interrupted, then nodded as if to confirm her own guess. "Holloway and the other guy are smuggling drugs. Of course that's it—I should have realized it right away. Everybody knows Florida is full of drug smugglers."

"Everybody knows that, do they?" Max drawled as he leaned back and folded his arms over his chest.

"Well..." The mocking amusement in his voice caused her to hesitate. "You don't think it's drugs?" She sounded so disappointed that Max had to squelch a smile.

"Could be. Then again, it could be watches or records or designer jeans...just about anything." He unfolded his arms and stood up. Chris noticed that his right leg only seemed a little stiff this morning. "But whatever it is, the police have to be informed. I'll go see Quinn and tell him about the conversation we 'overheard' last night," he said as he headed for the door.

When Chris realized he meant to leave without her, she hurried after him. "Hey, wait a minute! What about me?"

One corner of Max's mouth lifted a centimeter as he gazed down at her. "You can wait here, if you want," he offered.

"I don't want to wait here! I want to come with you."

He shook his head firmly. "Absolutely not. You can wait here till I get back, or go down and stay with Jess. Take your pick."

Chris's chin stuck out obstinately. "I was there last night too, and *I* wasn't suffering from a concussion. I might remember something you've forgotten."

"I'll just have to take that chance," Max said dryly. "It's going to be hard enough explaining what you and I were doing in the funeral home after business hours, without having to worry that you'll make some insulting remark about Quinn's intelligence every five seconds."

Chris opened her mouth to deny that she would, but before she could utter a single syllable Max bent and gave her a brief, hard kiss. "Stay put," he ordered sternly. "And try to keep yourself and my mother out of trouble, all right?"

Jess was waiting at the door when Chris arrived at her apartment. "I just saw Max leave. You didn't have a fight, did you?" she asked anxiously. "Did he chew you out about last night?"

"No, to both questions," Chris answered. "At least, he hasn't chewed me out yet. He's going to see Quinn Vincent to tell him what we overheard last night, while we were hiding in the coffin."

Jess's mouth fell open. "While you were *what*?"

"That's right, I didn't get a chance to tell you last night," Chris said as she took a seat at the table. "Have you got coffee made? There's nothing in Max's refrigerator but milk and Snickers bars, and he's out of coffee."

"How about some tea," Jess suggested as she set the kettle on to heat. While she was at it, she took jam and a couple of eggs from her own refrigerator. "Snickers bars!" she said in disgust as she closed the door. "All right, now tell me how you and Max came to be hiding in a coffin, before I die of curiosity."

MAX WAS STILL IN Quinn Vincent's office when the call came through. Quinn had to interrupt the lecture he'd been delivering about private citizens interfering in police investigations to answer it. As he listened and made notes, the frown that had already taken up residence on his smooth forehead deepened to a scowl. That wouldn't have bothered Max, except that Quinn kept shooting him irritated, suspicious looks all the time he was on the phone.

"You'd better come along on this one," he said curtly as he rose from behind his desk. "I've got a feeling it just might have some connection with your new client." Max didn't care for the sarcastic inflection Quinn gave the word "client," but he judiciously refrained from saying so.

"Where we headed?" he asked when they were in Quinn's car and pulling away from the station.

"The manager of one of the motels on Atlantic found a little surprise in his swimming pool this morning," Quinn said tersely.

The abrupt answer didn't surprise Max. Since he'd moved to Daytona Beach, he'd heard of cars, motorcycles and once even a small camper being dumped in motel pools during spring break. Two things did surprise him, though, and also made him more than a little uneasy: first, normal procedure would have been to send a uniformed officer to investigate the call from the motel; and second, Quinn had said he suspected that whatever had been dumped in the pool had something to do with Chris. Max's brows scrunched down over his nose and he slumped in his seat, his mouth grim as he anticipated what they were going to find when they arrived at the motel.

He'd been right. Resting on the bottom of the pool, around which a sizable crowd had already gathered, was a seven-foot coffin. Fastened to it by a piece of fishing line tied to one of the rails was a small Styrofoam paddleboard. The board was bobbing lazily on the surface of the water, directly above the coffin, and on it a message had been printed with bright red paint: "To the management, with the compliments of David Seitz, Stanley Gallagher, Melvin Braverman, Kevin Miller and Roger Sloane."

"MAX ISN'T GOING to like this," Jess warned as she gunned the Civic through a yellow light at the intersection of Atlantic and Silver Beach.

Chris clutched the side of her seat with one hand and braced the other against the dash, stifling a gasp as they barely missed sideswiping a delivery van. "He said to stay out of trouble. What kind of trouble could we possibly get into at the airport? Besides, I won't be ordered around by Max Decker or any other man," she added mutinously.

"Atta girl," Jess approved with a grin. "All the same, it might be a good idea to get back as soon as we can. If we're lucky, we might even beat him home. When he and Quinn Vincent get together they usually start reminiscing about the good old days and completely lose track of time. Right now they're probably shooting the breeze in Quinn's office."

Chris grinned back at her. "Well, let's hope they keep 'shooting the breeze' for a couple more hours, at least."

CHAPTER NINE

MAX PARKED HIS TRUCK in its usual spot, then went straight to Jess's apartment. When there was no response to his insistent knocking, he used his key to let himself inside. There was no sign of either his mother or Chris.

"Dammit," he said as he locked the door behind him on his way back out. He did not favor his stiff leg as he jogged up the stairs to his place. Chris had better be there. He distinctly remembered telling her to stay put until he got back.

His apartment was as empty as Jess's.

He stood in the living room, hands on his hips, and glared at the couch. He thought about what a pain in the butt stubborn, hardheaded women could be. And then he thought about the things he'd told Chris on that couch only a couple of hours before, and the totally unexpected effect it had had on them both. He'd felt freer, somehow, lighter—as if he'd finally managed to shed some of the load that had weighed him down for the past six years.

And Chris... He had expected her to look at him as if he'd just slithered out of a sewer. Instead, she'd held him and kissed him.

"Max? Max, are you home?"

He recognized her breathless, excited voice at once, and was annoyed at the rush of pleasure hearing it gave him. He was supposed to be ticked off at her for not staying put as he'd told her to, he reminded himself as he went to the door.

"Where the hell have you been?"

Chris ignored his obvious irritation as she breezed into the apartment, a flushed and equally excited Jess right behind her. "Out at the airport," she answered in an impatient rush. "And just wait till you hear what we found out! Well, what Jess found out, to give credit where credit's due. She was terrific, Max! Absolutely fantastic! You'd have been so proud of her—she ought to be on the police force herself."

Jess beamed at the enthusiastic praise and apparently decided to ignore Max's ominous glower. "It was nothing, really."

"Nothing!" Chris repeated, sounding incredulous. "Why, you were brilliant, Jess, positively brilliant." Turning to Max, she explained, "She found a baggage handler who remembered seeing a pickup truck in the cargo unloading area Monday, at about the same time the coffin disappeared. Then she kept after him until he also remembered that the truck had a rental plate. Now I ask you, was that brilliant detective work or not?"

Max's frown never wavered. "Brilliant," he said dryly as he folded his arms over his chest.

"Anyway," Chris hurried on, eager to tell him the rest, "we found out that the truck didn't come from one of the rental places at the airport. It was rented from a car dealer a couple of miles up the road. We went there to check it out, and look what we got."

Digging into her shoulder bag, she located a piece of paper, which she thrust into Max's hand. "The name, address and social security number of the guy who rented it, *and* the number of miles he put on it! How's that for good, solid detective work?"

Max was impressed, but he wasn't about to congratulate them for snooping around on their own. There was no telling what that kind of encouragement might lead them to do next.

"Francis David Markowic," he read aloud.

"Who just happens to live in Evansville, Indiana," Chris added. Her smug tone earned her a hard look from Max, which didn't do a thing to dampen her enthusiasm.

"The two of you just walked into the auto dealership and asked for this information?" he asked, deliberately keeping his voice flat and disapproving.

"Well, not exactly." Chris slid a nervous glance at Jess, who smiled encouragement at her. "The salesman we spoke to didn't want to give us the information. So Jess pretended she was thinking of trading her car for a new one and lured him outside to look hers over and tell her what he thought it would be worth."

Jess made an indignant huffing sound. "Those people should be arrested for highway robbery. He only offered me fifteen hundred for my Civic, can you imagine?"

Max forced his lips into a stern line and didn't reply.

Chris finally noticed his intimidating stance and the disapproval in his eyes. "Anyway," she continued hastily, "while they were outside, I sneaked a peek at the list of cars and trucks that had been rented or leased this week. The truck this Francis Markowic rented Monday had just been returned. That's why I was able to get the number of miles he'd put on it. It might help us figure out where he drove it, don't you think?" she asked hopefully.

"It might," Max said with an utter lack of enthusiasm. This only made her dig her heels in further.

"Of course it will!" she told him with a trace of defiance. "ALL we have to do is get a map of the area and—"

"Wrong," Max interrupted. "All we have to do is turn this information over to Quinn Vincent."

"Vincent!" Chris pulled a face. "He's the enemy."

"He's a duly authorized officer of the law," Max corrected. "Who happens to be in charge of investigating the alleged theft of the alleged Cy Gollum's alleged coffin. As law-abiding citizens, we have a duty to turn any information pertaining to the case over to him. Besides which," he added when Chris started to object, "if Quinn even *suspects* that I've been delibierately withholding evidence, it could cost me my license and possibly get me charged with obstructing justice."

"All right, all right!" Chris conceded resentfully. "I get the message. But you could at least give us a pat on the back for all the work we did, couldn't you—before you go running off to hand the results of our sweat and toil over to your buddy Vincent? Would it kill you to say 'nice job,' or 'way to go,' or even 'not half bad'?"

One of Max's brows formed a surprised arch. "I'm supposed to compliment you for harassing airport personnel and then deliberately deceiving a legitimate businessman in order to gain access to his company's records?''

''Has he always been such a stuffed shirt?'' Chris asked Jess in disgust.

''It's that overdeveloped sense of responsibility I told you about. His father, God rest his soul, was exactly the same.''

Max heaved a long-suffering sigh. ''Could we forget about me for a minute?'' he said dryly. ''Or maybe you're not interested in hearing what happened when I went to see Quinn this morning?''

He told them about the coffin, the message attached to it, and the five students from UE who just happened to be staying at the motel where it had been left sometime during the night. Chris immediately stated her intention of paying them a visit.

''You'll do no such thing,'' Max told her firmly.

''But I just want to find out if any of them know or have ever heard of another UE student named Cy Gollum,'' she protested. ''What harm could it do to *ask*, for heaven's sake?''

''Forget it, Christine,'' he growled. ''You'd just antagonize Quinn even more than you already have.'' Hoping it might distract her and make her forget about the students for a while, he added casually, ''Speaking of Quinn, he ran a routine check on deCosta's friend Marchand yesterday and came up with one piece of information that's particularly interesting...especially in light of what the two of you turned up this morning. Dear Freddie evidently got his start making cheap horror flicks. Then a couple of years ago he moved up to producing bigger budget movies, and decided to change his name, along with his image."

"You mean Frederick Marchand isn't his real name?" Chris asked with a frown.

"It is now. He had it legally changed a year or so ago. But he started life as Frederick Markowic, of Chicago, Illinois. Should be interesting to see if he had any relatives named Francis or Frank, huh?" he added with a grin, waving the paper Chris had handed him under her nose.

They all trooped down to Jess's apartment for lunch, during which the women speculated nonstop about the possible connection or connections between Frederick Marchand, Francis Markowic, the five UE students and the late Cy Gollum.

Max watched and listened from Jess's sofa while they moved around the tiny kitchen. He'd always heard that two women in the same kitchen was one woman too many, but they worked in perfect harmony.

He leaned back, linking his fingers behind his head and stretching both legs out in front of him, feet crossed at the ankles. This was nice—he experienced a brief twinge of regret that it couldn't always be like this. For some inexplicable reason a lump formed in his throat, and he was horrified to feel the sting of tears at the back of his nose. He swallowed hard, pasted a smile on his face and called himself ten kinds of fool as he joined Chris and Jess in the small dining area.

As soon as he'd finished eating, Max pushed his chair back and got to his feet, driven to escape, to put some distance between himself and all this suffocating domesticity.

"Think I'll take a quick shower before I go see Quinn," he announced as he turned for the door. When he reached it, one of the other tenants in the small apartment block was standing outside, his hand raised to knock.

"Hi, Bill. You want to see Jess?" he said loudly as he opened the door and stood aside to let the other man in. Bill Ferguson was eighty if he was a day, and almost stone deaf.

"Just for a minute, if she ain't busy," Bill shouted back at him. "I brung back the tape measure she loaned me last week."

Max smiled and nodded, gesturing for the old man to go on into the kitchen, then opened the door again to leave. Bill's booming voice made him halt and glance back with a crooked grin.

"Well, hello there, little lady!" the old man hollered as he spotted Chris. "Fancy seein' you here. Say, did the police ever find the pervert who stole yer dead horse?"

Max slipped out while Chris was trying to get across to Bill that it was a human corpse she'd thought had been stolen, not a dead horse. He was chuckling softly as he climbed the stairs to his own apartment.

After half an hour, Chris gave up. Leaving Jess to make things clear to her neighbor, she went after Max, intending to convince him that she should go see the five UE students and question them about "the alleged Cy Gollum."

He didn't answer the door when she knocked. Thinking he was probably still in the shower, she tested the knob. The door wasn't locked, so she opened it and stepped into the living room, then paused to listen for the sound of running water. Except for the distant hum of the central air-conditioning system, the apartment was as quiet as a tomb.

"Max?" she called softly as she crossed to the door of his bedroom. He must be here; his truck was still parked outside. When she reached the door she halted, her heart swelling with tenderness.

He was lying facedown on the bed, wearing nothing but a clean pair of boxer shorts. His head was turned sideways, his cheek resting on one hairy forearm, his left foot dangling over the edge of the mattress. His hair was tousled and still damp from the shower, and a few drops of water sparkled like beads of glass between his shoulder blades.

Poor baby, Chris thought as she tiptoed to the bed and gazed down at him. He must have conked out from sheer exhaustion. She couldn't resist the urge to reach out and lightly stroke his shoulder before reminding herself that he was still recovering from a concussion and needed his rest. She took a reluctant step backward.

When her fingertips trailed over the point of his shoulder and he sensed her imminent withdrawal, Max reached up blindly, finding her wrist and capturing it to stop her. Her arm twitched in surprise, but she didn't attempt to pull away. His fingers slid down to clasp hers as he rolled onto his right side. He opened his eyes and found that she was smiling down at him. He murmured the only two words in his vocabulary at that moment, his voice just a little uncertain.

"Don't leave."

Chris had no intention of leaving now that she knew he was awake. Neither did she hesitate. She stepped out of her shoes, and two seconds later she was lying beside him, her arms wrapped around his waist. Her eyes were level with the scar tissue that covered a large part of his chest. She impulsively pressed her lips to his warm, clean-smelling skin, and heard his soft, startled gasp.

"Oh, Max," she whispered against his skin. She felt his fingers tangle in her hair, and then clench into a fist. Her eyes misted as she gently pushed him onto his back and began covering every square inch of his chest with soft kisses.

When her mouth abruptly ceased ministering to him, Max felt abandoned. But then he realized she was only moving lower on the bed, and suddenly he felt the same butterfly caresses against the outside of his right leg. He closed his eyes, grappling with some alarmingly powerful emotion that was totally alien to him. He felt disoriented, confused. For a moment he wondered if he might be experiencing some kind of delayed reaction, if maybe these unsettling feelings might be a result of the concussion.

Her soft, soothing lips continued to move over his leg, from just below the knee, where she'd started, up the outside of his thigh. Halfway to the hem of his shorts she suddenly changed direction, laying a string of the light, fleeting kisses across his tensed muscles as she transferred her attention to the inside of his leg. And suddenly Max wasn't at all confused about what he was feeling.

He reached down to grasp her arms and urge her up to him, his hands shifting to her head as she came willingly. Neither of them spoke, each half afraid that words would break the spell. His hard palms cradled her jaw as if he thought it was made of crystal, as if he feared his touch might shatter her fragile bones. When she felt his strong, capable fingers tremble against her skin, Chris's breath caught, and she closed her eyes against a wave of nearly overwhelming emotion. Tears collected under her lids, and as he pulled her down to him a couple of them leaked out and left glistening tracks down her cheeks.

Their mouths met in a gentle, slightly tentative caress. For timeless moments the only movement they allowed themselves was the soft brush of one pair of lips against another, testing, sampling, relishing the delicacy of the contact. But eventually Max needed more. He slipped one of his hands into Chris's hair, and the other began an agonizingly slow quest down her back.

His hand closed on her hip and he shifted her over him, fitting them together like interlocking pieces of a puzzle. When she felt the hard insistence of his arousal, a sighing moan escaped her. She opened her legs, tucking her feet under his calves as her pelvis surged against his.

Max rolled carefully, still handling her as if he expected her to disintegrate at any second. Their mouths never lost contact as he wrestled with the knot holding the bottom of her blouse together. He was suddenly impatient, frantic to feel her breasts against him. His hands shook as he peeled the fabric away; and when he felt her aroused nipples nudging his chest, his arms became conduits that carried the tremors to the rest of his body.

Literally the second he'd dispensed with the barrier between them Chris wrapped herself around him, arms and legs contracting fiercely to clasp him to her. His ravenous kisses communicated his urgency, the need raging inside him. He was shaking with it; she could feel his involuntary shudders beneath her hands.

When she moaned his name, making it a husky plea, Max thought his heart would explode. He was ready to burst into flame, so aroused that a single spark would be all it took to ignite him, and she just kept egging him on—returning his kisses with a fire and passion that drove him wild, moving beneath him in deliberate invitation, making sure he knew how badly she wanted him, needed him.

He wanted to give her more pleasure than she'd ever known before, drive her out of her mind with it. He pulled away, moving his mouth to the taut rosy peaks of her breasts. At the first tormenting flick of his tongue Chris arched wildly, her fingers clutching at his hair. A sound that was part gasp and part sob broke from her lips. Max gloried in that sound. It exhilarated him, made him feel young and vital, ten feet tall and strong as an ox, king of the world. His fingers curled to tenderly hold her breast as his mouth opened over her, oh, so very gently.

The thumping noises gradually penetrated the passionate haze fogging Chris's senses, and she moaned in protest as her mind reluctantly identified them. A second later Max lifted himself away from her and sat up with a muttered oath.

"Somebody's at the damned door."

"Ignore it," Chris urged as she reached for him.

He let her wind her arms around his waist, and his hand came up to stroke her head in an instinctive, comforting gesture. But then her lips tugged at the line of hair bisecting his stomach, and the urge to comfort was instantly replaced by a much more basic and compelling urge.

"Chris! Don't," he said hoarsely. "It might be Jess."

Chris's hands climbed his chest to clasp his shoulders, and she slid her body up his in a provocative caress. "But it might not be," she murmured as her mouth settled on his. "Forget about the door, Max," she whispered between soft, beseeching kisses. "Forget about everything but making love to me. I want you so much."

He trembled, and as his arms closed around her a deep, disturbed groan rumbled up from his chest.

"Max! Dammit, I know you're in there!"

Max swore under his breath. "It's Quinn." He gave Chris a fierce hug, then reluctantly eased her from him. His mouth twisted as he pulled the sides of her blouse together and worked the buttons through their holes.

"Tell him to go away."

"Wouldn't do any good." There was another burst of impatient rapping, and he raised one brow at her. "See?" Turning toward the living room, he yelled, "All right already! You don't have to break it down! I'll be there in a minute."

He left Chris to retie the dangling tail of her blouse, while he hastily collected the jeans he'd stripped off and discarded on his way to the shower. Quinn Vincent's voice carried to them clearly as Max jammed a foot into the wrong leg, swore, yanked the jeans off and started over again.

"What's keeping you, buddy? I haven't got all day."

Max muttered a disgusted, "Hell," then raised his voice and shouted irritably, "Hold your horses, dammit!"

"Need some help?" Chris offered in amusement. He had his left leg in the jeans and was awkwardly hopping in the general direction of the living room, stabbing at the empty leg with his right foot. "Those jeans were already pretty snug, and now... I just wondered if you were going to be able to fit everything inside without seriously injuring yourself."

Max scowled and didn't deign to reply. He glared at her as he grimly stuffed himself into the jeans and carefully eased the zipper up its track. He seemed to hesitate for a moment, then muttered something to himself and stepped back to the bed. Grasping her chin firmly, he tilted her head back.

He was still frowning, but his eyes held a devilish mirth Chris had never seen in them before. He kissed her hard on the mouth, ordered, "Stay here till he's gone," and gave her a light shove that sent her sprawling backward onto the mattress. As he left the bedroom, he pulled the door firmly closed behind him.

Chris couldn't hear what Max and Quinn Vincent were saying, even when she pressed her ear to the door, but she'd bet anything it had something to do with the coffin that had been discovered in the motel pool that morning. She made a hasty trip to Max's bathroom, where she used his brush on her hair and did her best to smooth the wrinkles out of her clothes. Returning to the bedroom, she took a deep breath, opened the door and casually strolled out to join them.

"Hello, Sergeant Vincent," she said, making an effort to keep the antagonism she felt out of her voice. She hurried on before either he or Max could recover from her unexpected presence. "Have you managed to learn where that coffin that appeared so mysteriously this morning came from?"

Quinn Vincent gazed at her steadily for a moment before answering. If he was more than mildly surprised that she'd just emerged from Max's bedroom, he didn't show it. "Hello, Miss Hudson," he said. "Yes, as a matter of fact, we have. I was just telling Max that it appears to be the coffin that was stolen from the Deihl Funeral Home in Evansville last weekend."

"You don't say!" Chris's brows shot up in exaggerated surprise. "Would that be the same coffin you accused me of plotting to smuggle a criminal out of the country in? *That* coffin?"

"Christine." Max's voice held a cautioning note, but she ignored him.

"And did you happen to find this Peters person, or whatever his name was, inside the coffin, Sergeant?"

Quinn released a frustrated sigh. "No. It was empty. Look, Miss Hudson, I'm just trying to do my job."

"Right," Chris said curtly. "Well, if you don't mind my saying so, you seem to be going about it ass backward."

"Chris!" Now Max sounded exasperated, but also just a tiny bit amused. "Leave well enough alone, for Pete's sake. Quinn hasn't 'accused' you of anything . . . yet.'' Taking hold of her arm, he ushered her to the front door. ''We're going to run a computer check on this Francis Markowic, see if we can turn up any connection between him and Marchand. You and Jess wait at her place—and I mean *wait* there. I'll call as soon as we know anything.''

He opened the door for her, but Chris didn't seem in any hurry to leave. Max recognized the obstinate expression in her eyes, and when she opened her mouth he quickly placed two fingers over her lips.

''Don't argue,'' he said firmly. ''Just do as you're told for once, all right?''

For answer she ran the tip of her tongue over his fingers. His breath caught at the brief but erotic caress, and her lips twitched as she hastily backed out the door. ''Try not to be gone too long,'' she said in a low, throaty tone. And on that parting shot, she turned and ran down the stairs to Jess's apartment.

Jess was on the living room floor doing sit-ups. ''I think I finally got Bill straightened out,'' she said as she dipped to touch one elbow to the opposite knee. ''He's the salt of the earth, but I do wish he'd give in and buy a hearing aid. Did Max leave to go see Quinn Vincent?''

''No,'' Chris said, taking a seat on the couch. ''Quinn Vincent came to see him. They're going down to the police station to check for a connection between deCosta's producer friend and Francis Markowic.''

Evidently having completed her quota of sit-ups, Jess rolled to her feet and began touching her toes. ''And I suppose Max wants us to be good little girls and stay at home until he gets back,'' she said without missing a beat.

''Right,'' Chris replied.

''Are we going to?'' There was a teasing challenge in the question which surprised Chris.

''We probably should, but...'' Her gaze suddenly fastened on Jess's baggy green sweatshirt and white running shorts. ''Back in a minute,'' she said as she jumped up and headed for the bedroom. A few seconds later she called out, ''Do you have a pair of tennis shoes I could borrow?''

''Certainly, if you can wear a size six. Are we going to play tennis?''

''Nope,'' Chris said as she came back into the living room dressed in her cutoffs and yellow T-shirt. ''We're going jogging. I've always heard that running on sand is really good for the leg muscles.''

''Oh, it is,'' Jess confirmed with a twinkle in her eye. ''And our beach is so nice and wide...people walk and run up and down it all day long.''

''Even in front of the motels?'' Chris asked hopefully.

''Especially there.'' Jess was smiling her fairy godmother smile again. ''We'd just be two more faces in the crowd. I doubt anyone would even notice us.''

CHAPTER TEN

JESS HAD BEEN RIGHT: no one seemed to be paying them any attention as they mingled with the throngs of people moving along the wide, hard-packed white beach. It would be a couple of hours yet before the tide started to turn, and all the students who'd come south for spring break seemed to be out taking advantage of the glorious weather.

Several motels had set up nets on the stretch of beach they fronted, and quite a few ferocious volleyball games were in progress. Every fifty feet or so some enterprising citizen was doing a brisk business selling hot dogs, ice cream cones, soft drinks, Sno cones or some other tasty delight that the vacationing students might acquire a sudden craving for.

They jogged passed two more motels, then abruptly slowed their pace to a brisk walk. "That's the one, isn't it?" Jess asked, nodding furtively at the place they were passing.

Chris read the name painted on the sea wall in big block letters. "Yes, that's it all right."

"What now?"

"Keep walking. Act casual."

"Right." There was a brief silence before Jess asked, "Are you going to try to talk to them . . . the students, I mean?"

"I don't know yet." Chris was surveying the motel's layout, trying to figure out what would be the best approach. Should she just go straight to their rooms and start asking them questions, or might it be better to lie back and just keep an eye on them for a while?

"If you do, Max will have a fit," Jess said bluntly. "When he finds out, and you can bet he will, he'll murder us both."

"Mmm. I think first I'd better go to the office and make sure they're still registered. The management could have kicked them out by now."

They stopped walking and turned to look back at the motel. Jess pursed her lips thoughtfully. "I doubt it. Max said all five of them had airtight alibis for last night. Whoever put that coffin in the pool, he and Quinn agreed that it doesn't seem likely it was one of them. I'll bet it was somebody they knew, though."

"Yeah," Chris agreed grimly. "Maybe a supposedly dear departed friend named Cy Gollum. Come on, let's go see if they're still here."

By casually leaning over the desk while the clerk checked his computer terminal, Chris managed to find out not only that the five students were still registered, but also what rooms they were occupying.

"One oh eight and nine," she whispered to Jess as they walked away from the desk. "Let's check 'em out."

All the rooms on the ground floor were entered from outside, which made it easy to find the two they were looking for. Chris started toward them with a brisk, determined stride. Suddenly Jess clamped a hand on her arm and spun her around in the opposite direction.

"What are you doing?" she demanded in surprise.

Jess shook her head and practically dragged her back toward the beach. "Don't turn around, but there's an unmarked police cruiser down at the end of the parking lot, with two plainclothesmen in it. Quinn probably has them there to keep an eye on the five students from Evansville."

"Darn," Chris said. "How am I going to talk to them in privacy with two cops watching their rooms?"

"If I were you, I'd forget about talking to them at all," Jess told her. "At least for the time being. But we *can* still keep an eye on them, if you want."

"How?" Chris grumbled. "If we hang around here for very long, Sergeant Vincent's watchdogs will start to suspect we're up to something."

"Not necessarily." Jess suddenly smiled. "Look what's going on right across the parking lot."

Chris looked. She frowned in bewilderment. "They're building a new hotel or something next door. So? How's that going to help us keep tabs on the five students?"

"Simple," Jess said as they reached the beach and started back down it in the direction they'd come. "We're going undercover."

Chris blinked at her. "We're what?"

"Going undercover," Jess repeated with a mischievous grin. "Haven't you ever wondered what it would be like to be a construction worker?"

Chris was silent as she matched her pace to Jess's. Undercover work? The two of them? She suddenly grinned. "You're really something else, Jess."

Jess gave her a beatific smile. "Thank you, dear. So are you."

Two and a half hours later they returned to Jess's apartment, hot and sweaty, exhausted and thoroughly dejected. Chris yearned for a long, cool shower, immediately followed by a long, cool drink. What she had to face instead was Max's ominous frown as he looked up from Jess's sofa, where he'd been lounging with a can of beer while he watched a ball game on her television set.

"What in the name of— What the devil have the two of you been up to now?" he demanded. "Good Lord, you look like refugees from a labor camp."

Chris frowned at him as she unzipped her coverall and started to peel it off. Max's eyes widened until he realized she was wearing more clothes underneath.

"We've been working undercover," Jess announced before Chris could think of a way to answer his questions without incurring his wrath.

Max leaned forward to deposit the can of beer on the floor. He inhaled a deep, calming breath and tried to count to ten. He made it to eight, which was an indication of the remarkable self-control he possessed.

"I don't think I heard that right," he said. His voice was deceptively soft.

"Yes you did," Chris responded uneasily. There was a dangerous light in his eyes, and every muscle in his body seemed to be tensed, as if he was forcibly holding his anger in check.

"Let's have it," he said through gritted teeth. "All of it."

Chris shifted from one foot to the other, but before she could work up the nerve to tell him how they'd spent the past three and a half hours, Jess started talking. Jess didn't seem aware that she was damning them both as she obediently reported every single thing that had happened that afternoon.

"So the two of you have been passing yourselves off as construction workers," Max commented when his mother had finished her incriminating testimony. His voice was too mild; he sounded much too calm. "And how did the guys who were working on that building react when the two of you suddenly infiltrated their ranks for your 'undercover work'?"

Chris sighed and plopped down beside him on the couch. "Jess told them right off the bat what we were doing so they wouldn't make a fuss. They gave us each a hard hat and a tool belt and put us to work hauling stuff around for them so it would look like we really belonged there.

"I thought I'd die, or at least collapse from heat exhaustion. And it was all for nothing," she added disgustedly. "In the entire two and a half hours we were there, we only saw one guy go into each of the motel rooms and another guy leave as soon as he got there—almost as if they were changing shifts, or something. Nobody else even came near those two rooms." She glanced at Max and caught the corner of his mouth twitching. "So help me, Max, if you laugh—"

Max quickly controlled his amusement. "Laugh?" He made his voice cold and disapproving. "I don't see anything to laugh about, Christine. What you did today was criminally irresponsible, not to mention the fact that you could have put yourselves in danger with your ridiculous snooping. We still don't know what those students might be involved in. What if they'd spotted you and decided you were some kind of threat to them?''

He saw a momentary flicker of apprehension in her eyes, and was glad. If it took a good scare to keep her from unintentionally putting herself in jeopardy, he was perfectly willing to scare her witless. The idea of Chris being harmed, in any way, shape or form, was something he found he simply could not tolerate.

''They're just a bunch of harmless college students,'' she protested. ''You make it sound as if they're members of the mob, or something.''

''Do you know that they're not?'' he challenged. Now that she'd finally started to question her own impulsiveness, he wanted to make sure she'd think twice before behaving so rashly in the future. He decided it wouldn't hurt to saddle her with a little guilt while he was at it. ''If you're not concerned about your own safety, you might at least consider Jess,'' he accused. ''I don't much care for the way you've involved my mother in all this, Christine.''

Chris drew back in indignant offense. ''The way *I've* involved *her*! For your information, it was her idea for us to 'go undercover' today!''

Max turned to Jess with an astonished frown. ''Is that true?''

''Well, I couldn't just let her hang around the motel all afternoon. Either Quinn's men would have eventually spotted her, or she'd have found some way to get in and talk to those students without them knowing about it. And as you pointed out a minute ago, there's no telling what kind of dirty business they might be mixed up in.''

Chris's mouth fell open. ''Jess!''

"I'm sorry, dear," Jess apologized, only she didn't sound the least bit sorry. "But I felt it was my duty to look after you, keep you out of trouble. Max would have had my scalp if I'd let anything happen to you, not to mention the fact that I'd never have forgiven myself. I think I'll go take a quick shower before I get dinner started. You two just sit there and relax for a while."

She'd disappeared into the bedroom and closed the door behind her before Chris could untangle her tongue. Max allowed himself a small smile when he glanced down and saw the dazed look on her face. He casually slipped an arm around her shoulders.

"That crafty old fox," Chris remarked. He was amused by the note of admiration in her voice. "She really snookered me, didn't she?"

"Don't feel too bad," Max told her dryly. "She's a past master. She led Dad around by the nose for thirty-seven years, and he never suspected a thing."

She tipped her head back to smile up at him, and his heart thumped uncomfortably against his ribs. It was happening again, and there wasn't a damned thing he could do about it. His fingers curled around her shoulder, his free hand lifting to brush a few damp, curling tendrils of hair off her face.

"Are you still mad?" Chris whispered, catching his hand to press a soft kiss against his palm.

"Darn right I am," he growled. At the touch of her lips his heart had given another agitated leap and then started pumping double time. How could she do this to him, have this effect on him, without even trying?

"You're not as mad as you were, though," Chris murmured against the heel of his hand. "For a minute there, you looked ready to explode."

She was only teasing, trying to replace the troubled expression in his eyes with a smile. She wasn't prepared for the intense compassion that replaced it and made him suddenly seem so vulnerable.

"I was only concerned for your safety. If anything happened to you, I'd never forgive myself. I never even told you how much I—" He didn't falter. There wasn't so much as a second's hesitation or indecision. He cut off the word before his treacherous tongue could push it past his lips. He looked appalled, horrified. His hands were a little rough as he pushed her away and in almost the same movement launched himself off the sofa and toward the door. He heard Chris say his name, her voice a soft entreaty, but he didn't stop until he was upstairs in his own apartment.

Even then he couldn't relax. He shuddered to think what might have happened if he hadn't come to his senses when he did. Lord, what had come over him? What on earth was he going to say to Chris the next time he saw her? What was she going to *expect* him to say?

Forty-five minutes later Chris followed Max up the stairs. She hesitated, wiping her palms down the legs of Jess's light blue slacks before she lifted her hand to knock on his door. She knew he'd been shaken by what had almost slipped out of him, and she wasn't sure how he would react to seeing her again so soon. The uncertainty made her tense and anxious.

He answered the door promptly, which eased her anxiety somewhat. But then she noticed the guarded expression in his eyes and the slightly taut set of his mouth. The smile she gave him was a little strained.

"Jess sent me to tell you supper's ready."

Max seemed to hesitate a moment. "Okay." He stepped outside, turning back to pull the door shut behind him and check the lock. Chris was aware that he was finding it difficult to meet her eyes for more than a second at a time. Without allowing herself time to second-guess the impulse, she reached out and caught hold of his hand as she turned for the stairs.

"We're having some fish she said you caught last week. Do you go fishing often?"

Max was encouraged by the casual way she'd taken his hand and the light tone of her voice. "At least once or twice a week." His fingers impulsively closed around hers, and halfway down the stairs he tugged gently to draw her to a halt. Chris turned and lifted her face to him, her eyes softly questioning.

"I just wanted to say I'm sorry. For that little scene at Jess's, I mean. I don't know what came over—"

"Stop right there," she said curtly. "Before you go any further, tell me exactly what it is you're apologizing for."

She was staring straight into his eyes, almost as if she were challenging him.... Max floundered in confusion for a moment, and in the brief silence that followed, he had the irrational feeling that those huge, intensely blue eyes of hers could see right through all his carefully constructed walls and into his soul. In an astonishing flash of intuition, he realized that the answer he'd been about to give would be totally unacceptable.

"For bolting out of the room like that?" He hoped that was the correct response.

Apparently it was. Chris's slow smile warmed him all the way to his toes. "In that case, apology accepted," she said softly. Stretching up, she placed a light kiss on his cheek. "Now that that's out of the way, let's go eat. I'm starved."

Over dinner Max told them what he and Quinn Vincent had learned that afternoon—that Frederick Marchand just happened to have a nineteen-year-old nephew named Francis David Markowic. Markowic's official address was Chicago, but he was presently attending school in Indiana.

"Don't tell me," Chris said eagerly. "He's a student at the University of Evansville, right?"

"Right," Max confirmed. "He's a sophomore." He paused for effect, then added just before he stuck a forkful of coleslaw into his mouth, "As are all five of the young men at the motel you two staked out today."

Jess drummed her fingers on the table as she speculated out loud. "It would appear that young Mr. Markowic is up to his ears in whatever's going on. We've already established that he collected the stolen coffin from the airport in a rented truck. Do you and Quinn think he's also responsible for leaving it in the motel swimming pool?"

Max shrugged. "So far, he's the most likely candidate. Quinn's working on the assumption that Markowic and the other five know one another, and that dumping the coffin in the pool might have been nothing more than a practical joke."

Chris shook her head with a dubious frown. "Uh-uh, I can't buy that theory. If it was a joke, it was the most expensive one I've ever heard of. Markowic might have stolen the coffin, but he still had to pay the air freight to ship it down here. And let's not forget the cost of my round trip ticket and the charge for my motel room, plus whatever Elliott charged him for my services. I can't believe that the average college sophomore would have that kind of cash lying around, much less be willing to spend it on a dumb practical joke."

Max slanted her a wry glance. "One other possibility did occur to Quinn, but I eventually managed to convince him it was too farfetched to pursue," he said dryly. "They still haven't located the guy who was set to go on trial for operating the credit card scam. Now *he* no doubt would have had the kind of money you're talking about."

Chris looked outraged. "He doesn't still suspect me of plotting to smuggle that creep out of the country! Why that's the most ridiculous, idiotic . . ."

"Preposterous," Jess put in stoutly.

"Thank you. Preposterous thing I've ever heard of. What is the man using for brains, anyway?"

"He's just trying to cover all the possibilities," Max said mildly. "Try to see it from his point of view." He ticked off the items on his fingers as he enumerated them.

"First he's got you and your missing coffin, which turns out to have been stolen from a funeral home back in Evansville. Next, he's got a bail-jumping credit card thief who just happened to take a walk the same day you left town with said coffin. And *now* he's got five college students from Evansville staying at a local motel, and our famous disappearing coffin suddenly turns up at the bottom of that same motel's swimming pool." Spreading his hands, he concluded flatly, "It would be asking a bit much to expect him to chalk all that up to coincidence, Chris. Even you must see that."

She made a disgruntled sound and dropped her chin into her palm. But then she suddenly brightened. "You left something out." At Max's questioning frown, she elaborated. "Holloway. Remember the conversation he had with the other guy last night, about some kind of shipment they're expecting? Something came back to me at the time—something I overheard on the phone when I called Holloway's funeral home from the airport—but what with one thing and another I forgot about it again until just now."

She repeated the remark she'd heard that "It wasn't supposed to be here till the end of the week," and then flashed a smug grin. "What does that suggest to you, Mr. Private Investigator?"

Max stared down at his plate in silence for a moment, his expression somber. "When you called about the hearse you were expecting to meet you, they assumed *your* coffin was the one containing this shipment they're waiting for. That's why Holloway went ahead and sent the hearse to the airport."

"Even though he wasn't expecting a shipment that day," Chris added with barely controlled excitement. "This morning you said that Holloway and his partner could be smuggling almost anything into town inside a coffin.'' She paused to make sure she had his full attention, then asked quietly, ''‘Almost anything’ would include stolen credit cards, wouldn't it?''

CHAPTER ELEVEN

IT WAS CLEAR TO CHRIS that Max wasn't thrilled with the possibility she'd just raised. She couldn't decide whether it was because the idea sounded so wildly improbably, or because he hadn't thought of it himself.

She had no way of knowing that he was proud of her for spotting the possible connection between Holloway and the credit card scam—a wrinkle both he and Quinn had somehow missed. But he was also concerned. A group of vacationing college students was one thing, but Holloway and his pals were obviously professionals. If *they* started to see her as a potential threat . . .

He ought to get her out of Daytona Beach—just drive her to the airport and put her on the first plane home. Two things stopped him from doing exactly that: one, he suspected she'd fight him tooth and nail; and two, he wasn't at all sure he'd be able to let her go, even if she was willing.

While Max worried and stewed, Jess reminded them of their first priority. "Let's not get sidetracked by Holloway and his shenanigans. If it's important, Max, you can tell Quinn later. Let him worry about it. In the meantime, I say we get back to the problem at hand." She suggested they all go out that night, make the rounds of the vacationing students' favorite haunts and see if they could pick up any information about the five UE sophomores, "the alleged Cy Gollum," Francis Markowic or a prank involving a coffin. Judging by Chris's reaction to the scheme, Max figured the two of them would probably take off the minute his back was turned, anyway, so he might as well go along to keep them out of trouble.

They spent three hours mingling—or trying to—with vacationing students at some of the more popular spots. They hit Finky's, Mac's Famous Bar, the Ocean Deck and the pool deck of Checkers, then moved on to several oceanfront motels where parties were in progress around the pools or in the lounges.

So far their little excursion had been a colossal waste of time, Max thought as they arrived at the last place on Jess's list. The only one of them the students had been interested in talking to was Chris; and he didn't for a second believe that the dozen or so jocks who'd approached her had wanted to tell her about a practical joke involving a stolen coffin.

At the entrance to the motel's lounge, a perky young waitress greeted them and showed them to a table. A few minutes later a strapping young man sporting a bushy mustache and an assortment of muscles approached their table. He flashed a smile at Chris and then proceeded to ask Max whether his "daughter" could join some other "young people" out by the pool for a while. The glare Max leveled at him and the blunt remark that followed sent him hurrying back outside to rejoin his friends.

"You were rather rude to that young man, Max," Jess said in mild reproof.

Max scowled at her and took a long drink of his beer.

Catching Jess's eye across the table, Chris slipped her a wink. "Have you noticed how some people lose their sense of humor as they get older?" The comment earned her a scowl, as well. She laughed softly, then suddenly grabbed Max's hand and jumped up. "Come on, Gramps, dance with me."

"I don't dance," he muttered. All the same, he let her pull him onto the minuscule dance floor.

"That's okay," she said with a soft, coaxing smile. "This is a slow one. Just put both arms around me and shuffle your feet once in a while. Think you can manage that?"

"I'll give it my best shot," Max assured her solemnly.

Some time later Chris realized that the music had changed to an up-tempo, top forties song. She didn't bother to point that out to Max, though. As far as she was concerned, they could go on shuffling around the floor like this all night—pressed closely together, her arms wound around his neck and his hands spread possessively over the gentle slope where her waist ended and her derriere began. She sensed that he wanted to move them lower, and she certainly wouldn't have objected.

But she knew Max well enough by now to know that he would be uncomfortable with any such public display. In truth, he wasn't all that comfortable with private displays. Not yet, but he was getting there. The thought made her smile against his shoulder.

"Share the joke?" he murmured close to her ear.

Chris shook her head. "There isn't any. I was just thinking that you're an old-fashioned kind of guy."

"How do you mean?" His breath fanned her cheek, soft and warm and smelling faintly of beer.

"Well . . ." She smiled again. "For instance, unlike some of the people on this dance floor, I suspect you prefer to do your lovemaking in private."

Two deep grooves appeared between Max's brows. Was she saying she thought he was too square or something? He'd been making love to her in his mind for the past half hour. But apparently she hadn't noticed. His hands abruptly pressed her closer. He felt a purely masculine thrill of satisfaction when a soft, surprised little gasp escaped her.

"Max!" His name was a shocked, breathless whisper. Holding her against him, he rocked his hips suggestively. If it was public demonstration she wanted, by damn that was exactly what she'd get.

"Max!" Chris made a valiant but futile attempt to wedge some space between them. The pressure of his arousal against her stomach was having an alarming effect on her respiration, not to mention her equilibrium. "For heaven's sake!" she hissed. "We're in the middle of the dance floor."

Max's mouth lifted into an incredibly sensual smile. "So who's being old-fashioned now?" he taunted huskily, and his strong fingers tilted her pelvis forward to meet his gentle thrust.

Chris moaned weakly and arched against him in helpless, instinctive response, and suddenly Max couldn't remember what he'd been trying to prove, or why.

"God, I want you," he said softly. Chris moaned again. "I want to be inside you...all of me, filling you up."

He suspected the rasping declaration had shocked Chris almost as much as it had him. He felt a shudder ripple through her body, and his arms contracted in remorse.

"Chris." His voice cracked like an adolescent's. He swallowed and tried again. "I'm sorry. This isn't the time or place to—"

"Take me home."

For a moment Max forgot how to breathe. "What?"

"I asked you to take me home. Now." She pressed a heated kiss just beneath his ear, and then he felt the tip of her tongue flick across his skin. "Please," she whispered. "I want that, too, Max."

He closed his eyes and inhaled a deep, painful breath. At the moment, he didn't think there was a chance in hell he could make it all the way back to his apartment with her.

"What about Jess?" He sounded like a bullfrog with a bad case of laryngitis.

Chris lifted her head to stare at him blankly. "Jess?"

Max swallowed again, hard. Her eyes were soft and unfocused, fogged by the intensity of her own arousal. "You remember—my mother, the white-haired lady you're staying with."

Chris blinked as if he'd just shaken her out of a deep sleep. "Oh." Casting a guilty glance past his shoulder, she saw that Jess was frantically flapping her hands to get their attention. "She's waving at us. I think she wants us to come over there."

Max stifled a groan as he reluctantly allowed her to slip out of his arms. As they returned to the table he was careful to keep Chris slightly in front of him, so that neither his mother nor the elderly gentleman with her would see the unmistakable bulge at the front of his jeans.

Jess introduced Chris as "a friend of Max's," and then announced that she and Josh—her banker friend—were leaving to join some people from their arts and crafts club for an all-night Victor Mature film festival in Port Orange.

"You don't mind, do you, dear?" she asked of Chris as she collected her purse. "I'm sure Max will be happy to look after you."

"No!" Chris blurted with embarrassing eagerness. "Er, I mean, no, of course I don't mind. Don't worry about me—I'll be fine."

Jess ducked her head to fish in her purse for the keys to the Civic. "Yes, I'm sure you will. Here, Max, you take my car. Josh can bring me home. I'm sorry to rush off like this, but if we don't hurry we'll miss the beginning of the first movie." She met Max's eyes briefly as she added, "And you know how I adore Victor Mature."

Max and Chris watched the older couple depart, then slowly turned to look at each other.

"One of us must be living right," Max said with a crooked grin.

Chris grinned back at him. "She did say it was an all-night film festival, didn't she?"

He nodded. "All night." His voice was a soft rasp. He jerked his head toward the table. "Grab your purse and let's get out of here."

He didn't touch her as they walked across the lot to Jess's car. Nor did he open her door for her. As Chris slid in beside him, she noticed that his hand trembled when he inserted the key in the ignition. She impulsively leaned over to lay hers on top of it. Max jerked away as if she'd branded him.

"For God's sake, don't touch me," he said fiercely. "I'm already about to explode."

Stunned by the uncharacteristic outburst, Chris instantly sank back into her bucket seat. What had become of the cool, self-contained ex-cop who con sidered any show of emotion a weakness? Had *she* done this to him?

By the time they reached the apartment block, Max had managed to tamp down his lustful urges. He switched off the ignition and reluctantly turned to Chris, half expecting to find her cowering against the door like a cornered animal. When their eyes met, she flashed a mischievous grin.

He felt unaccustomed heat climb his neck. "I'm sorry I snapped at you like that," he said gruffly.

Chris's grin disappeared. "It's all right. I guess the chemistry between us is pretty. . ."

"Explosive," he furnished in a voice that wasn't quite steady.

Suddenly Chris couldn't seem to draw anything but sharp, shallow breaths. "Yes," she whispered. "Explosive. And a little scary."

Max wanted to admit that he knew exactly what she meant, but the words lodged in his throat. He hesitated, then lifted one hand to her cheek. Her skin felt like warm velvet. His thumb drifted slowly across her lips. "Are you scared now?" he whispered. He wanted her to say that she was as terrified of what was happening between them as he was, though of course he knew she couldn't possibly be.

The hint of uncertainly in his voice tugged at Chris's heart. "Yes, a little. I've never wanted anyone this... desperately. I feel as if I don't have any control—of my emotions, my body...anything." Her soft smile was slightly apologetic. "So yes, it scares me a little." Her voice lowered and became husky as she admitted, "But it excites me, too."

Max stared at her in speechless wonder. She'd described his own confused feelings and anxieties so perfectly that she might have been reading his mind. He forgot that he was all wrong for her, and that she'd be going home in a day or two. He forgot everything but the way she felt in his arms, and the way she made him feel when she wrapped hers around him. His hand slid to the back of her head, and he urged her forward to meet him as he leaned across the space between their seats.

"*You* excite me," he whispered as his mouth closed softly on hers.

A few minutes later Chris pulled away a little to ask breathlessly, "Max, are we going to make love in your mother's car?"

He smiled and forced himself to release her, but when they met in front of the Civic he had to reach for her again. They climbed the stairs slowly, arms fastened around each other, pausing on every fourth step for a long, intoxicating kiss, deliberately drawing out the heady sense of anticipation. Max kept one arm around her as he opened the door, and as soon as they were inside he swept her into a hard, enveloping embrace.

"You feel so good," he breathed against her lips. "Smell so good." His mouth dropped to her chin and he nibbled gently. "Taste so good. I want to taste you all over."

Chris shivered at the image his words conjured up. The urgency he'd displayed earlier was gone now; she'd felt it dissolve and fade away while they were sitting in the car. Now there was a new tenderness in his touch, his voice, the way he looked at her, and also a patient restraint that let her know he wasn't going to allow either of them to rush.

She moved back to remove her blouse. When a ribbon of moonlight floated through the window and draped across her breasts, she heard Max's breath catch softly, but neither of them spoke. Chris stepped out of her shoes, then pushed her slacks and panties down to her ankles and stepped out of them, as well. Before he could reach for her, she bent to collect the clothes and fold them neatly before placing them on the coffee table. Then she turned to Max with a provocative smile.

"Did you say something about wanting to taste?"

He started with her face and worked his way down her body, eventually sinking to his knees on the floor. He sampled every part of her, slowly and with obvious enjoyment, kissing and licking, nipping and nibbling, his soft growls of pleasure muffled against her skin.

By the time he started back up, Chris was barely able to stand. When he reached her knees she grasped a fistful of his hair to steady herself. His hand slid between her thighs, nudging her legs farther apart, and then she felt his hot breath on the only part of her he hadn't yet touched. Her wobbly knees suddenly locked. Her fingers clenched in his hair. His agile tongue was one second aggressive, the next tenderly persuasive. Chris's head fell back, and a long moan was released from the very core of her being.

"Max!" The way she gasped his name made it a plea. She wanted him to continue, to give her body the fulfillment she craved. But more than that, she wanted to know that he was with her totally when she reached the final climactic peak.

"No. Stop." When she succeeded in pulling him away, a part of her wanted to cry out at the sudden deprivation.

Max rocked back on his heels to look up at her. The sight of her made everything inside him contract, and then just as suddenly go slack and loose. He reached up to grasp her waist, using her for leverage as he rose to his feet. There was so much he wanted to say to her, to tell her, but he knew none of it would come out right. So he just took her hand and led her into the bedroom.

Chris started to undress him, but Max was just as impatient to be out of his clothes as she was to have him out of them, and he ended up helping her. She scattered hot, eager kisses over his neck and shoulders and chest, her palms flattened on his back as if she thought it was possible to pull him even closer.

He somehow managed to move them both onto the bed without prying Chris away from him. As he settled himself between her legs she was reaching for him, her slender fingers enclosing him in a strong, sure grip to guide him to her. Her touch nearly undid him. The tattered remnants of his control began to ravel around the edges, and he groaned in despair. He wanted so badly to take things slow and easy, to make it perfect for her.

As if she'd read his mind—again—Chris murmured, "Don't hold back, Max," as she arched to bring him deep inside her. The sensation was so devastating that they moaned in unison.

Their lovemaking was all that Chris had known it would be: uninhibited, totally honest and wholly satisfying. Max didn't set out to impress her with skill or technique; nor did he insist on playing any of the conventional male-female games to assert his dominance. When it became obvious that they were both headed for a too-rapid climax, he altered their position so that they lay face-to-face on their sides.

Chris had never made love this way. When she told him so, Max grinned and asked her how she liked it. Her answer must have pleased him, because he took her with him to a level of ecstasy she'd never imagined it was possible to achieve.

When he had regained enough strength to move, Max shifted again so that Chris was sprawled across him, her head nestled in the curve of his shoulder. He hoped she wouldn't expect him to talk, especially about what had just happened. It was too soon to express what he was feeling with words. He wasn't sure he'd ever be able to, or if the words even existed. If they did, he didn't think he knew them.

At the moment, the only thing he *did* know for sure was that the woman whose weight felt so incredibly good against him had managed to completely alter his life in the space of two and a half days. He'd suspected as much before they made love. Now he was certain, and the knowledge both disturbed him and made him feel foolishly, recklessly exhilarated.

The exhilaration was dangerous because he sensed that it might cause him to unlock doors that would be better left sealed, dream of walking paths he knew were off limits to him.

He experienced a brief but sharp pang of regret. Chris had already forced the locks on a couple of those doors, and in the process exposed the most private and well-guarded corners of his soul—the dark places where the scars had never completely healed.

He couldn't hold it against her, though, because the pleasure of just being with her more than compensated for whatever pain she'd unintentionally caused him. She was so *alive*, so bursting with energy and enthusiasm. And when he was with her, some of her natural exuberance seemed to rub off on him: he felt young and strong and damned near invincible.

She was a wonder, an absolute wonder; and knowing he had absolutely nothing to offer that she could possibly want in no way diminished his desire to keep her as close to him as he could, for as long as he could.

"Have you gone to sleep?" Chris teased softly.

Smiling, he lifted a hand to stroke her hair. "No. I'm just recuperating."

She propped an arm on his chest to raise herself above him. "Mmm, I guess when a man gets to be a certain age—ow!" She frowned and reached back to massage the spot on her fanny that he'd just pinched. "That hurt."

Max was unrepentant. He hadn't pinched her that hard. "You asked for it."

A slow, utterly wanton smile curved her mouth. "And would you give me anything I asked for?"

"Within reason," Max said judiciously. "But remember my advanced age and state of decrepitude before you ask for anything really big."

Chris collapsed against him with a throaty chuckle and then gave him a long, lusty kiss that took his breath away and made his stomach do flip flops.

"You're something else," he gasped, shaking his head with wonder.

Chris said, "I know," sounding quite sincere, and settled back down on his chest. Max's soft chuckle reverberated against her ear. "What?" she mumbled drowsily.

"You sounded like Jess."

Chris grinned and replied, "I'll consider that a compliment. Speaking of Jess," she continued, "I suppose I should get dressed and go down to her place, before I fall asleep."

"No, you shouldn't. You're spending the rest of tonight right here." *Where you belong,* he added silently.

"Oh, Max, I wish I could. But what will she think if I'm not there when she gets home in the morning?"

"I can only imagine," he drawled in amusement. "But I can tell you what she'll think if you *are* there. She'll figure her sacrifice was all for nothing."

"Sacrifice?" Chris repeated, lifting her head with a frown. "What sacrifice?"

He grinned. "She can't stand Victor Mature. Right about now she's probably wishing she was anywhere else in the world but at that movie theater."

"You're putting me on!"

Max shook his head. "I'm not, I swear. Believe me, she'd rather take a dose of castor oil than sit through even one of those movies."

Chris closed her eyes with an embarrassed groan, but the next second she fell against him in helpless laughter. "Why that devious, conniving old busybody!"

"Tell me about it," Max said. "Since she moved in downstairs, I haven't had a minute's peace—or privacy, either. She took that apartment just so she could deep tabs on me twenty-four hours a day."

"She was worried about you," Chris told him gently. "Because she loves you."

He released a heavy sigh. "I know. And I'd be the first to admit she had reason to worry, at least in the beginning. When I first came down here I was a mess, both physically and emotionally. But that was six years ago. I'm okay now."

Chris thought she detected just a trace of defensiveness in his voice. She laid a soft kiss on his collarbone.

"Jess knows that, Max," she said quietly. "If she seems a little overprotective at times, try to remember that you're the only family she has left. Besides," she added on a lighter note, "mothers are supposed to worry. After nagging, it's what they do best. My mother spends most of her waking hours worrying about one or another of her children."

"If your brothers are anything like you, I can understand why," he replied in wry amusement. "But I understand what you're saying—I should make an effort to be a little more tolerant, right?"

"Right. And it would be nice if you could show her a little affection now and then, while you're at it."

"Are you trying to reform me?" Max asked suspiciously.

"Well, you don't seem to have any trouble showing *me* affection."

"Is that what you thought I was doing—showing affection? That's nice, Christine. You really know how to shoot a guy down."

Chris raised herself to grin down at him. "Don't be a horse's behind, Max. You know perfectly well what we were doing. And whether you're ready to admit it or not, you also know there was quite a bit of affection involved, on both sides." Before he could respond to that, she dipped her head to give him a brief but erotic kiss. "Now, about Jess. I think we should do something to show our appreciation for her 'sacrifice,' don't you? I know—we'll take her to dinner. What's her favorite restaurant?"

"The Asian Inn," Max answered automatically. "She likes Cantonese food. You feel . . . affection for me?"

"You could say that," Chris replied as she snuggled down on his chest again. "I'm in love with you."

CHAPTER TWELVE

BY THE TIME Max recovered from the shock, Chris was sound asleep on his chest.

God!

She couldn't be in love with him. How could she have said such a thing? Nobody had ever been in love with him. How on earth was he supposed to deal with this . . . ? How was he supposed to react?

He felt as if she'd reached down his throat and yanked him inside out.

It was almost dawn before he managed to come up with a rationalization that allowed him to fall sleep. Chris was a person whose emotions were very close to the surface. She probably fell in and out of love three or four times a month. Sooner or later this infatuation she felt for him would pass, or wear off... whatever. He'd give it another day or two. Three, tops.

And just to be on the safe side he wouldn't make love to her again. First thing in the morning he'd escort her downstairs and turn her over to Jess for safekeeping, and then do his level best to stay away from her until she decided to go back home. Convinced that he'd solved his problem, he relaxed and was almost instantly sound asleep.

Barely an hour later he was catapulted back to wakefulness by Chris's tongue, as it leisurely caressed a particularly sensitive area of his anatomy. The sensation was so exquisite that he moaned.

"Thank goodness," she whispered as she pulled herself over him. "I was beginning to wonder what it would take to wake you up. Know what time it is?"

Max tried to get his brain to function independently of his libido. He didn't have a lot of success. "No," he said breathlessly. "What time is it?"

Chris answered in a husky murmur against his lips. "It's time for me to taste you."

By the time she'd finished "tasting" him, Max could barely remember his own name, much less his resolution not to make love to her again. When she finally moved to straddle him, he felt every muscle in his body clench in anticipation. But when his hips lifted toward her, Chris suddenly retreated, denying him access. A frustrated groan was torn from his chest. He needed to be inside her more than he'd ever needed anything in his life.

"Lie still," she ordered huskily. "Please, Max. Let me give you what you gave me last night." She leaned down in slow motion, filling his vision, the tips of her breasts teasing him unmercifully as she feathered a kiss across his parched lips. "Let me show you how much I love you," she whispered against his mouth.

The soft promise was repeated in her smile, and the tender, glowing light in her eyes. For a moment Max's stomach churned violently. He experienced a spurt of blind, dumb panic. Then she sank down to take him inside her, enveloping him, welcoming him, and the panic was supplanted by an overwhelming desire to have the promise fulfilled.

It was. With exhaustive, painstaking care. And afterward he slept like a baby.

The next time he woke Chris was nestled close at his side, one arm flung across his waist and a slender leg wedged snugly between his thighs. She looked sweet and vulnerable and so damned beautiful that the sight of her made his chest hurt.

The gentle caress at her nape caused Chris to stir and murmur a sleepy, incoherent question.

"Good morning," a gruff voice breathed in her ear.

She moved toward him, eyes still closed, her mouth finding his by instinct alone. "It certainly is," she agreed as she rolled onto her back and pulled him with her.

He kissed her in a way he'd never kissed her before—slowly, leisurely, as if nothing in the whole wide world was as important as this one single wake-up kiss between Max Decker and Christine Hudson. Chris had never felt so cherished, so adored. She reveled in the sensation, rejoicing that it was Max who was making her feel this way. Inhibited, reticent Max. Her Max. Her lover and her love.

"You are so nice to wake up to," she whispered as she circled his chest with her arms.

Max rested his chin on the top of her head and tenderly stroked her face. They stayed like this for several moments, quietly absorbing the miracle they had discovered in each other's arms. After what seemed like ages, Max sighed deeply and spoke.

"Much as I'd like to, we can't spend all day in bed."

"Sounds like a good idea to me," Chris suggested as she nuzzled his neck.

Carefully and reluctantly, Max disentangled himself and managed to shove himself up until he was sitting on the edge of the bed. He raked both his hands through his hair with a wry smile. "Don't tempt me," he said, pushing himself to his feet.

"Hey!" Chris said, sitting up. "Where are you going?"

Max threw the answer over his shoulder as he entered the bathroom. "To take a shower and then to see Quinn Vincent."

"Can I come?"

His head poked back out the door. "To Quinn's office, no. But you're welcome to join me in the shower, if you promise to behave yourself."

Chris stifled a disappointed sigh. "That doesn't sound like much fun," she grumbled as she scrambled off the mattress.

Max shrugged. "Suit yourself."

She waited until she heard the water running in the shower stall, then tiptoed into the bathroom and yanked open the frosted door to join him under the spray.

"Christine!" Max growled. He tried and failed to sound stern. "I told you you'd have to behave."

"But I didn't promise, Max," she pointed out reasonably.

"You didn't?"

"No."

"Oh. Well, that's okay, then. Want me to wash your back?"

Chris grinned. "Actually, I'd rather wash your front."

WHEN CHRIS ARRIVED at Jess's apartment, the older woman was evidently preparing to leave. She tossed the nylon tote she'd just brought out of the bedroom onto the sofa and gave Chris her sunniest smile as she plopped down beside it to retie the laces of her lavender tennis shoes.

"Good morning, dear. Have you had breakfast?"

Chris felt her cheeks grow warm. "No." *Not unless you count Max.*

The negative answer seemed to please Jess. She glanced at her watch, but refrained from commenting on the fact that it was almost nine, for which Chris was grateful. The knowing gleam in those shrewd brown eyes made her uncomfortable enough as it was.

To put an end to the awkward silence, she asked, "How was the film festival?"

Jess pulled a face. "Dreadful. At least, what I saw of it. Thankfully I managed to sleep through most of the last two movies. Did you get around to telling Max that you're in love with him last night?"

Chris was momentarily dumbfounded. She managed to utter a stunned, almost inaudible "Yes."

Jess nodded in approval. "And how did he take it?"

Chris pursed her lips thoughtfully, considering. "I think he's decided to pretend I didn't say it. Or that if I did, he didn't hear it."

"It figures," Jess remarked. She scooped up her tote and got to her feet. "Max would go a mile out of his way to avoid an emotional confrontation. The trick is not to let him get away with it. Keep telling him until you convince him it's true. And whatever you do, don't let his bullheadedness make you give up on him." Glancing at her watch again, she frowned and hurriedly made for the door.

"Goodness, I'm going to be late for my aerobics class. Fix yourself some breakfast, dear, and then try to catch up on your sleep. I should be back in about an hour."

After Jess left, Chris sank down on the sofa and just sat there for several minutes. This had to be the weirdest romance on record. She was in love with a man she'd first set eyes on three days ago, a man who was terrified of making an emotional commitment. And that's no exaggeration, she thought. Max wasn't even comfortable with his own emotions; he certainly didn't want to have to deal with hers, as well.

And now, as if the situation wasn't already complicated enough, Max's mother had apparently decided to move things along by playing Cupid. Chris was touched by Jess's desire to help, but she seriously doubted she'd take the advice Jess had just handed out. She'd always had an instinctive aversion to the idea of setting out to "win" a man, as if he were the prize in some kind of contest.

She heaved a sigh and pushed herself to her feet. Sitting around and brooding wasn't going to get anything accomplished. She fixed herself two slices of toast and a cup of instant coffee and then went out in search of some public transportation.

She found it, in the form of the Votran bus system. Twenty minutes later she was standing across the street from the motel where the five UE students were staying, trying to convince herself that she'd be able to talk

Max out of strangling her for what she was about to do.

"The hell with it," she mumbled as she stepped off the curb. She'd had enough of sitting by while he and his pal Vincent called all the shots. Where had their combined expertise and professional investigative techniques gotten them, anyway? They were no closer to knowing who'd sent her down here with that coffin, or why, than they'd been three days ago.

She looked for but didn't see any sign of the unmarked police cruiser that had been parked in the lot yesterday. Relieved that Vincent seemed to have called off his watchdogs, she went straight to the door of room 109 and repeatedly applied her knuckles to its surface.

The young man who opened the door was only a couple of inches taller than Chris, and so thin that he almost looked malnourished. He peered at her from behind a pair of gold wire-rimmed glasses.

"Who is it?" an eager voice called from inside before Chris could state her business. "Is it him?"

"No." The word was impatiently flung over his shoulder before the young man turned to face Chris again. "Yes? Can I help you?"

She wasn't sure what she'd expected, but it certainly hadn't been a soft-spoken, well-mannered young man who looked as if he might still sleep with a teddy bear. Somehow she couldn't see this guy having anything to do with stolen coffins, much less being involved with a gang of interstate credit card thieves.

"My name is Christine Hudson," she said briskly as she advanced through the doorway, forcing the startled young man to back into the room. "I'm down here on business, from Evansville. I need to talk to you and your friends about another UE student I believe you may know. His name is Cy Gollum."

The youth looked as if he was about to swallow his tongue. Beyond him, a second young man suddenly leaped into the doorway connecting the two rooms. He was of medium height, with a headful of bright orange curls and a complexion that was probably pale at the best of times. At the moment his face was the color of wallpaper paste, which made the million and one freckles on it even more noticeable.

"Gollum?" the new arrival asked in a strangled voice. "Did you say Gollum?"

Chris struggled to contain her excitement. *Bingo, old girl. Looks like you've hit the jackpot.*

"That's right. Cy Gollum. Do the two of you know him?" The question was unnecessary, of course. It was as plain as day that they did.

The student gaping at her from the doorway started to answer, but before he could, his friend blurted, "No! We don't know anybody by that name, do we, Roger?"

Fifteen minutes later Chris was tempted to throttle them both. They were lying their heads off—she was certain of it. They *did* know Cy Gollum—their reactions to hearing his name had established beyond a shadow of a doubt that they did—but for some reason Stanley had decided to deny it and Roger had followed his lead.

She glared at Stanley. He was the troublemaker here. The only information she'd managed to pry out of him had been their full names—Stanley Gallagher and Roger Sloane—and the fact that they were both sophomores at the University of Evansville, which she'd already known. Stanley returned her glare with stubborn stoicism that made her want to turn him upside down and shake some honest answers out of him.

She reluctantly amended her original assessment of the youth. He might look like a young Fred MacMurray, but Stanley Gallagher was undeniably one sharp cookie. She heaved a disgusted sigh and rooted around in her bag until she located a pen and a scrap of paper.

"Okay, you win. But just in case either of you should suddenly remember that you *do* know someone named Cy Gollum, you can get in touch with me at this number." She scrawled Jess's phone number on the back of a cash register tape and handed it to Stanley. Both he and Roger remained mute as she gave them one last reproachful stare and let herself out.

When it rains, it pours, Chris thought half an hour later, as she stood on an unfamiliar corner waiting for a bus to come along. When she left the motel, she'd gotten on the wrong one by mistake, only she'd been too preoccupied to realize it right away. Fortunately the driver and several passengers had been eager to help by giving her directions. She'd been instructed to catch a certain bus at this corner in about ten minutes, then transfer to another one four stops later. Everyone assured her that—provided she didn't goof up again—she'd be back at her original starting point in no time flat. Now if she could just remember all the directions.

It was because she was scanning the oncoming traffic so intently—afraid she'd either miss the bus when it stopped or else that it would drive right by her—that she noticed the car that turned into a parking lot barely a dozen yards away. Even so, she might not have looked at it twice if it hadn't been such a distinctive car. You didn't see a De Lorean rolling down the street every day of the week.

From her unobstructed vantage point she enviously ogled the sleek, low-slung vehicle as the driver parked it. He deliberately centered the beautiful machine on top of the yellow line separating the two parking spaces at the end of a row. Chris didn't blame him; if she owned a De Lorean, she wouldn't take chances with it, either. The distinctive gull wing door on the driver's side swung up, and the car's lucky owner stepped out onto the pavement.

"Wouldn't you know," Chris muttered. Of all the people in Daytona Beach, she should have figured the De Lorean would belong to Julio deCosta.

He left the parking lot and started down the sidewalk in her direction. Chris hastily smoothed a hand over her hair. Would it be too presumptuous to ask him for a ride back to Jess's? Yes, of course it would, she thought with a sigh. And anyway he hadn't even noticed her. He was approaching the entrance of the building behind her.

When he came back out fifteen minutes later, there was still no sign of the bus she was supposed to catch. Chris impulsively hurried after him as he headed for the parking lot.

"Mr. deCosta! Yoo-hoo, Mr. deCosta!"

He stopped, then turned toward her. His wide forehead was creased with what looked like mild impatience. "Yes?"

When Chris reached him, she was embarrassed to realize that he didn't even recognize her. "I, uh, just wanted to say hello." She smiled self-consciously. "I spoke with you at your producer friend's house the other day," she reminded him when he just stared at her blankly. "I was with a friend of mine who's a private detec—" she caught her own error and automatically corrected it. "A private investigator. We were looking for a Mrs. Gollum."

DeCosta's shaggy brows rose in acknowledgment. "Ah, yes. Miss Hudson, isn't it? And did you and your friend, Mr..."

"Decker," Chris supplied. "Max Decker."

Two rows of large, perfectly aligned teeth flashed in a blinding smile. "Yes, of course. Max Decker. Did you and Mr. Decker ever find the lady you were looking for?"

"I'm afraid not. In fact we'd almost decided that she probably doesn't even exist. But then just today I—"

"That's too bad," deCosta interrupted before she could finish. "It was nice seeing you again, Miss Hudson, but I'm afraid I'm rather rushed." His smile flashed again for an instant. "Please give my regards to your friend Mr. Decker."

"I will," Chris replied, but he had already turned away and was striding briskly toward the parking lot. With a pensive frown, she watched him climb back into the De Lorean. Strange. On Monday he'd given every indication that he was fascinated by everything about her, yet just now he couldn't even be bothered to pass the time of day.

She was so preoccupied with Julio deCosta and his inconsistent behavior that she almost missed the bus she'd been waiting for. She waved wildly as it passed her, fortunately managing to catch the driver's eye, and dashed for the designated stop at the corner. As the bus pulled away from the curb, Julio deCosta pressed his right foot—which was shod in an oyster Topsider—down on the De Lorean's accelerator and changed lanes to pass it.

WHEN CHRIS ARRIVED back at Jess's, both Jess and Max were waiting for her—both curious to know where she'd been. In fact, Max demanded to know the second she came through the door.

"Mostly I've been riding buses," she said as she sank down on Jess's sofa. "I think I managed to ride on every bus in Volusia County today."

Max sat down beside her with a resigned expression on his face. "Okay, let's have it. From the beginning."

"You mean from the time I woke up this morning?" Chris asked innocently.

He leveled a menacing look at her. "I mean from the time you took off on your own... presumably to do some more 'detective work.'"

Chris's mouth turned down at the corners. "I went to see the five UE students," she confessed. "And before you start, let me say that I felt I had a perfect right to go talk to them."

"Oh, you did, did you?" Max growled.

"Yes, darn it, I did!" Chris snapped at him. "And I'll thank you not to use that sarcastic tone of voice with me, Max Decker. Just because you're a big-time private detective—"

"Investigator," Max corrected in a deliberately bland tone. He didn't know why he got such a kick out of baiting her. It probably had something to do with what happened to her eyes when she got all worked up. Blue sparks seemed to shoot out of them.

"Stop interrupting me!" Chris said between clenched teeth.

There was a sudden burst of determined rapping from the front door. "I wonder who that could be," Jess reflected as she went to answer it.

It was Quinn Vincent. A scowling Quinn Vincent. Compared to him, Max looked slaphappy. "Oh, great," Chris said. "Just the person I was dying to see."

"Hush," Max growled softly. "Mind your manners. He's probably here to see me."

But Quinn soon disabused him of that notion. It turned out that the two plainclothesmen he'd assigned to watch the motel had seen Chris arrive and enter room 109. He wanted to know precisely what she'd been doing there and why she'd stayed inside with two of the UE students for approximately seventeen minutes.

"Where were they?" Chris asked curiously. "I didn't see their car in the parking lot."

"Across the street" was the terse reply. "Posing as a couple of construction workers."

Jess suffered a sudden coughing fit. Chris's mouth fell open and Max made an enormous effort not to laugh out loud.

"Well?" Vincent said with an impatience he didn't try to hide. "I'm waiting, Miss Hudson. What's your connection to those five students? Did you know one another before you all came to Florida, and if so, how well?"

Chris stared at him. "Does the city pay you some sort of bonus if you manage to cram more than one dumb question into a sentence?" she retorted acidly.

There must have been a particularly offensive air-borne irritant in the room, because Max suddenly succumbed to a fit of coughing even more violent than Jess's had been. When he'd recovered, he tried to intervene in the role of mediator.

"Now listen, you two—"

"Stay out of this, Max," Quinn Vincent ordered sternly.

"Yes, Max, stay out of it," Chris seconded as she jumped to her feet. "I don't need any help."

Deciding she was probably right, Max folded his arms over his chest and subsided against the arm of the sofa to watch.

"After all," she began mildly, "it's not Detective Sergeant Vincent's fault. Why he's just a public official who's so determined to carry out his job 'by the book' that he seldom if ever exercises any judgment!"

Quinn bridled at that. "Now hold on just a min—"

"No, *you* hold on," Chris told him. She'd built up a good head of steam, and she wasn't about to quit now. "Three days ago you were insinuating that I was some kind of pathological liar getting her kicks by pulling a fast one on the police department. Would you say that was a fairly accurate analysis of your attitude?''

Vincent glanced at Max, as if looking for some kind of assistance. Max merely smiled. God, she was something when she really got rolling!

''Considering the circumstances,'' Vincent began stiffly, then sighed and gave Chris a grudging nod of affirmation. ''Yes, that's exactly what I thought.''

''But since then you've changed your mind.'' Though it wasn't phrased as a question, she pointedly waited for a response.

''Obviously, I have,'' Vincent said dryly.

''Obviously. Otherwise you wouldn't be hounding me as if I were some kind of criminal.'' He would have objected to that claim, but Chris didn't give him the chance.

''Listen carefully, Sergeant Vincent, because I only intend to say this once. I have done nothing illegal. I'm only attempting to clear my good name and find out what kind of crazy goings-on I seem to have unintentionally become involved in. To my knowledge I have never met any of the five students staying at that motel I visited today. I can't swear to that, because only two of them were there when I arrived.''

''Stanley Gallagher and Roger Sloane.'' Vincent provided the names in a calm, businesslike tone. His frown had disappeared. He seemed to be listening closely to everything she said and taking it seriously, which made for a nice change.

''That's right. I went there to find out if any of them knew another UE student named Cy Gollum. Both Stanley and Roger nearly flipped when they heard the name . . . and then they both emphatically denied ever knowing any such person.''

Vincent pursed his lips and stuck his hands into his trouser pockets. ''You think they were lying.''

''I *know* they were,'' Chris said with conviction. ''What I can't figure out is why.'' She hesitated, her gaze swinging to Max as she added in frustration. ''Especially since Cy Gollum—if he ever actually existed—is supposed to be dead. Why on earth would they feel the need to lie about whether or not they knew someone who's dead?''

CHAPTER THIRTEEN

AFTER QUINN VINCENT LEFT, Chris remembered her chance meeting with Julio deCosta. When she told Jess and Max about it, Max didn't see anything odd about the incident, but Jess disagreed.

"For goodness' sake, Max, you admitted that when the two of you saw deCosta on Monday he played the 'Latin lover' to the hilt," she pointed out. "Yet today he didn't recognize Chris until she jogged his memory. Even then he didn't show any personal interest in her. Don't you find that strange?"

"Not if he's gay," Max drawled, slanting a wickedly amused grin in Chris's direction.

"Oh, my," Jess said. "I hadn't considered that possibility. Do you suppose he is?"

"Not a chance," Chris said dryly. "Max is just being cute."

"Cute?" he repeated with another lopsided grin. He wasn't taking either of them seriously, which irritated Chris. Quinn Vincent had finally started to take her seriously; why wouldn't Max? "You think I'm cute?"

She chose not to dignify the question with a reply. In fact, she ignored Max entirely and continued speaking to Jess. "I've got a funny feeling about deCosta. I can't say why, but I'm positive he's not what he appears to be."

"Of course he's not," Max said. He didn't seem aware that he was being ignored. "He's an actor. He earns his living pretending to be something he's not. And he's probably 'on' even when he isn't in front of a camera. Julio deCosta is exactly what you called him the other day—a phony. Nothing more and nothing less."

Chris shook her head. There was an obstinate look in her eyes that meant trouble.

"No, it's more than that," she insisted. "I'm telling you, I have a deep-down feeling about the man, Max."

"Feminine intuition," he said heavily. "Lord save us."

Chris's voice sharpened with annoyance. "How is it that when *I* have a gut reaction to something, it's 'feminine intuition,' while *your* feelings qualify as 'instincts'?" Not giving him a chance to respond, she turned to Jess. "I'm going back to check out that building where I saw deCosta. Want to come along?"

"Whoa! Hold it right there," Max growled. He might as well have saved his breath.

"I think I'll pass," Jess said with an apologetic smile. "I really ought to take a short nap. You're welcome to use my car, though."

"She won't need to use your car, because she's not going anywhere," Max stated flatly.

He suspected even as he said it that Chris had already made up her mind, and that short of cuffing her to a table leg he didn't have much chance of stopping her.

"I beg your pardon, Max. I am going," she told him as Jess handed her the keys to the Civic.

He could tell from the chill in her voice that she was irritated. He discovered that he didn't like having her use that tone with him. It hurt.

The realization that she could hurt him at all was stunning. Knowing she could do it with so little effort made him irrationally angry. Dammit, didn't she understand that he was only trying to look after her, keep her out of harm's way?

Evidently not. She collected her purse and started for the door without another word or even a glance in his direction.

"Then I'm going with you." The resentment she heard in his voice made Chris stop and turn toward him in surprise. She thought he favored his right leg just a little as he started forward. Concern instantly replaced her annoyance.

"That isn't necessary, Max," she said hastily. "I won't do anything foolish, I promise." If his leg was bothering him, he ought to stay off it. He certainly didn't have any business running all over town keeping an eye on her, which was exactly what he had in mind.

Max's lips formed a grim, implacable line. She obviously didn't want him anywhere near her. Well, that was tough. "I said I'm going with you. Give me the keys. I'll drive."

Chris shook her head. If he insisted on coming, she would at least make sure he could stretch his leg out and be comfortable. "No, I'll drive," she said firmly. She hurried out of the apartment before he could argue, and was already seated behind the wheel of the Civic when he reached it.

Neither of them spoke as Chris tried to locate the corner where she'd run into deCosta. She was silent partly because she was concentrating on not getting lost, and partly because she was worried about Max. Was he in pain? He looked as if he might be—there was a strained, tense look around his mouth and his jaw was clenched. *Stubborn man,* she thought with equal amounts of irritation and tenderness. Even if he was in agony, she knew he'd never admit it. He had much too much pride for his own good.

Max sat and steamed while Chris drove the Civic down one street after another in her pigheaded determination to find the exact spot where she'd met deCosta. So now she was going to give him the silent treatment, was she? Well, two could play at that game, dammit.

What had he done, for crying out loud, to make her so mad? She's the one who'd called him "cute." Babies were "cute." Cocker spaniel puppies were "cute." But a woman didn't call a man she'd made mad, passionate love with not so many hours ago "cute" unless she was being deliberately insulting. Max hunched down in the bucket seat with a fierce scowl.

But maybe it had been his remark about "feminine intuition" that had ticked her off. Or maybe he'd sounded just a little too bossy when he'd objected to her taking off on her own again. He released a dejected sigh. He wondered if all women were as hard to figure out—much less please—as his mother and Miss Christine Hudson.

"There it is! That's it!"

Chris's excited announcement was the only warning he got before she made an abrupt left turn across two lanes—which fortunately were clear of traffic—and into a parking lot across the street. Max barely had time to brace himself against the door. Jess must have been giving her driving lessons, he thought as the Civic's left rear tire bounced over the curb. They just missed clipping the corner of a sign that read in big red letters: Parking for Doctors' Patients Only. All Others Will Be Towed Away.

"You can't park here," he said as Chris squeezed the Civic into a space between two full-size cars. He turned toward her to repeat the message, but she was already climbing out.

"You can't park here," he said again when she came around and opened his door. "It's reserved for patients."

"Oh, Max, don't be such a fussbudget. We won't be staying that long."

"We?" he muttered with a wary frown.

"We'll just run inside and see if we can find out what deCosta was doing here. It should only take a minute or two. Do you need help getting out, or would you rather just wait for me here?"

Let her go inside alone? Fat chance. Heaven knew what kind of mess she'd get herself into. "I'll come with you," he grumbled as he lifted his right leg out of the car. The damn thing was stiff again, probably because the only exercise he'd gotten so far today had been in a horizontal position. He swore irritably as he stood, flexing his knee a couple of times to loosen it up.

"Darn you, Max," Chris said fiercely. His head jerked around in surprise. What had he done *now*? "I knew your leg was bothering you. If you had any sense, you'd have stayed at home. Here, lean on me."

She hurried to pull his arm around her neck and wedge her shoulder under it. Her unexpected show of concern threw Max for a moment. But then his lips quirked in a crooked smile.

"Not mad at me anymore?"

Chris frowned at him. "Of course I'm mad at you. You're a proud, stubborn fool and an arrogant chauvinist on top of it. Can you walk all right? Maybe you should just stay out here and wait for me."

Max felt as if something had lodged at the base of his throat. He thought it might be his heart. "I'm sorry," he heard himself say in a strange voice. Chris's frown turned questioning. "For acting like an arrogant chauvinist."

The slow warmth that entered her eyes was like a caress. "What about acting like a proud, stubborn fool? Aren't you sorry for that?"

"Yeah," he said gruffly. "But I doubt there's much I can do about it. I've always been a proud, stubborn fool."

A tender smile joined forces with the warmth in her eyes, and Max had to forcibly restrain himself from sweeping her up in his arms right there in the parking lot and kissing her deaf, dumb and blind.

"We'll have to work on that," she said softly. And then *she* stretched up on tiptoe to kiss *him*. Full on the mouth. Right in front of God and everybody, with traffic streaming by not more than eight feet away. Somebody tooted his horn in salute as he passed. *Eat your heart out, buddy,* Max thought as his arms slid around Chris and he started kissing her back.

"Wow," Chris said breathlessly when she finally pulled away. "And here I've been thinking you didn't go in for public displays." She was grinning as she took his hand and started pulling him toward the building adjacent to the parking lot.

The building housed the offices of two doctors: an ear, nose and throat specialist and a cosmetic surgeon.

"One guess which of them deCosta was here to see," Chris said as she tugged Max toward the cosmetic surgeon's office.

She breezed into the waiting room before he could ask what she had in mind. Except for a pretty blond receptionist sitting inside a glass-fronted cubicle, the room was empty. The receptionist looked up and flashed a bright professional smile when they entered.

"Good morning. May I help you?"

"I certainly hope so," Chris replied in a tone that sounded slightly desperate.

Max glanced at her suspiciously. What on earth was she up to?"

"My fiancé would like to see the doctor," Chris explained, and Max quickly stifled an astonished gasp. "To see what can be done about his nose," she added earnestly.

The receptionist hurried out from behind the partition, offering to check with the doctor and see if it would be possible to work in an appointment for a consultation that day.

Max watched with a frown as she disappeared through a door at one side of the waiting room. He resisted the urge to reach up and feel his nose. The way the girl had reacted, she must think he qualified as an emergency case. He turned to ask Chris what was so terribly wrong with the way his nose looked, but discovered that she was no longer at his side.

"What are you doing?" he whispered in disbelieving horror. It was a brainless question if he'd ever heard one. What she was doing was sneaking into the receptionist's cubicle. "Are you nuts? Get the hell out of there!"

She scowled at him and pressed a finger to her lips, cautioning him to be quiet. Max was tempted to turn on his heel and walk right out of the office without her. Either that or march into the cubicle and yank her out of it by her hair. Now she was riffling through some papers on the desk. He gritted his teeth and gestured furiously for her to come out, at the same time keeping a frantic eye on the door for the receptionist.

Just as he decided he'd have to go after her, Chris darted out of the cubicle. She grabbed his elbow as she passed him, and dragged him out of the waiting room with her. By some miracle, the receptionist didn't reappear.

"He came about his hair transplant," Chris said as they fled the building. She sounded amused and also exhilarated. Breaking the law had that effect on some people, Max thought grimly. He could have strangled her. He told her so.

"Don't be such a stuffed shirt," she replied as they reached the Civic and climbed inside. "We didn't get caught.

"We didn't get caught!" Max glared at her incredulously. "Is that all you have to say—'We didn't get caught!' My God, you're a menace."

"It didn't take."

Max closed his eyes and prayed for self-control. "What!"

"DeCosta's hair transplant. It didn't take. It's starting to fall out." Her laughter filled the car. "Don't you think that's hilarious? He's going bald."

Max tried to hold on to his anger, but the rich, throaty sound of her laughter made it next to impossible. Lord, he loved to hear her laugh. "Dammit, Christine," he sputtered in annoyance. "What am I going to do with you?"

Another laugh gurgled out of her. This one was husky, sexy as sin. The hair on Max's arms lifted in response. She suddenly reached over to give his thigh a gentle squeeze. "I'm sure you'll think of something," she said in a provocative murmur. "But before you do anything with me, you have to feed me. I'm starving."

They ended up parking the car and walking barefoot along the beach. Max bought them each a footlong hot dog and a soft drink from one of the vendors for their lunch. Chris seemed perfectly happy with his choice of cuisine. She even demanded an ice cream cone when her hot dog was gone.

"Want a lick?" she offered, holding the dripping cone in front of Max's mouth. The temperature had already reached eighty-six balmy degrees, and the habitual stiff offshore wind blew a couple of vanilla drops onto his cheek. Ice cream had to be practically inhaled in weather like this. He stuck out his tongue and removed most of the messy stuff from around the outside with one circular swipe.

"Hey!" Chris objected. "Leave some for me."

Max laughed and wrapped an arm around her as they started walking again. Chris took a few more licks, but eventually decided she'd rather hold Max than a sticky, melting ice cream cone any day. She dumped what was left of it in one of the trash barrels they passed and snuggled close to his side, circling his waist with her right arm.

A second later Max glanced down at his side. "Stop wiping your fingers on my shirt."

"But they're all sticky."

He heaved a long-suffering sigh and released her to pull her arm around in front of him. He then proceeded to slowly lick the ice cream off her hand, one finger at a time. "Better?" he asked as he replaced her arm.

Chris tipped her head back to gaze up at him. She knew by the way his breathing faltered that he recognized the desire in her eyes. "Well, I don't feel sticky anymore," she told him solemnly. "But now I've got another problem."

Max decided to play along. "You don't say. Is it a bad problem?"

"Awful. Want to know what it is?"

Max glanced around in sudden impatience. Damn. There had to be at least five or six hundred people sharing this stretch of beach with them. His restless gaze suddenly lit on a shadowed alley between the motel they were passing and the one next to it. He turned Chris and started steering her away from the ocean.

"Come up here and whisper it in my ear."

As soon as they were out of the sun and hopefully concealed from prying eyes, he put his back against the motel wall and pulled her between his legs. Chris stretched up, her hands at the back of his head to guide him down to her. But when his lips were within centimeters of hers, she suddenly twisted to place her mouth against his ear. Max shuddered at the husky words she murmured and the images they evoked in his mind.

"God," he groaned. He urgently sought her mouth, intending to silence the erotic words spilling from it before she managed to drive him out of his mind.

"Chris!" Her name was a ragged plea as she continued to elude him. "Please. Stop tor—"

The rest was lost in the sweetness of her mouth as it finally mated with his. There was no more teasing, no more playful evasion. She gave, and then gave some more, opening to him with an eager generosity that melted Max's bones. His hands slid down her back to cup her firm, perfectly shaped bottom, lifting her to him for an even tighter fit. It wasn't enough. No matter how close he held her, it wouldn't be enough. He lifted his head with a harsh, sobbing breath, fighting desperately for control.

"Oh, lady, what you do to me," he said in a shaken whisper.

Chris rubbed her cheek against his chest. Her arms remained fastened around his neck, and she continued to rest against him, needing the support his body provided.

"You do the same thing to me." The husky throb in her voice told him it was so. "If we weren't a dozen feet from a crowded public beach, I'd show you how badly I want you right now, this minute."

A hoarse, hungry sound broke from Max's throat. "You don't have to show me," he said as he shifted his hands to the safer territory of her back. "I can feel it."

"I'm glad," Chris whispered. She leaned back to gaze up at him solemnly. "I want you to feel how much I need you, and how much I love you. I don't want you to ever know a moment's doubt about either."

An expression almost like pain flickered across Max's face. His head dropped back against the wall and he squeezed his eyes shut. "Don't," he said roughly.

"Don't say that I love you?" Chris asked. In contrast to his, her voice was soft, gentle, endlessly patient. "But I do, Max."

"No." His head moved in denial. "You want me. We both know that. But you aren't in love with me. You can't be."

"Please give me credit for knowing the difference between wanting you and loving you." Though her voice was soft, it was filled with conviction. "I know the difference, Max. I want you, yes, but it happens to be a part of loving you. Why can't you accept that?" She hesitated, giving him a chance to respond. When he didn't, she pressed on. Each word was filled with husky sincerity.

"Are you afraid that if you do, I'll start to make demands? I won't, I give you my word. All I ask of you for now is that you accept the fact that I love you...get used to the idea, let it grow on you," she added persuasively. "Who knows, you might decide you like it."

Like it? Max thought bitterly. If she only knew the idea already thrilled him beyond belief. That was the trouble. He had to make her understand what a terrible waste it would be to give her love to him. Somehow he had to make her see how utterly *wrong* it would be. He lifted an unsteady hand, pressing her head to his chest as he began to speak. "My earliest memories are of watching Jess watching the clock, worrying—would my father come home at the time he was supposed to... would he come home at all? She tried not to let me see what it was like for her, but fear for a person you love isn't something you can easily hide.

"When I was still in my teens, even before dad was killed, I'd made up my mind never to put another human being through that kind of misery. I knew what I wanted, even then. I wanted to be a cop—a good cop, like my dad had been—and I knew that I could be. But I also knew it would have to mean forgetting about marriage or any kind of long-term relationship. So I made the choice and I never regretted it all the years I was on the force."

"Do you mean that you were never... romantically involved with anyone, in all that time?" Chris murmured. Was he telling her that in his entire adult life he'd never had a close personal relationship with a woman? The possibility stunned her.

"That's right. I'm not saying I never had sex," he added dryly. "But I made sure that it was never more than that. The few women I allowed into my life had to understand that our 'relationship' ended at the bedroom door. Then, too, the nature of the assignments I usually drew tended to... isolate me, I guess you'd say.'' He hesitated for a moment, not sure how to go on, or even if he should.

''I think I'm beginning to understand,'' Chris murmured against his chest. She moved her head a little to press a soft kiss on his neck. ''Please don't stop. I want to hear the rest.''

Max took a moment to draw a deep, fortifying breath. Did she really understand what he was trying to tell her? He wanted to look at her, see if he could read the expression in her eyes, but he couldn't bring himself to do it. So he just started talking again.

''When you work undercover most of the time, as I did, you can't afford to let many people get close to you. You learn to exercise caution—about who you trust, what you say and who you say it to...everything. You're constantly on guard. Eventually you find yourself holding back even with people you know are your friends. You put up walls, and then you can't figure out how to take them down again. You forget how to...communicate.''

He didn't realize that his voice had hoarsened, couldn't see the distress in his own eyes. When Chris suddenly stretched up and placed her mouth on his, his first, fleeting reaction was confused surprise. But then the feel of her, the taste of her, broke through, and his arms contracted to mold her to him. He kissed her as if she was his salvation, as if her sweet, clinging warmth held the secrets to the universe, the answers to every question he had ever asked, or would ever want to.

''Oh, Max,'' Chris breathed when his lips shifted to her temple, and then her cheek. Her eyes shimmered with tears, but the tremulous smile on her lips couldn't have been sweeter. "You silly, foolish man. You communicate just fine. And I love you more than I can ever say."

Max closed his eyes and rested his forehead against hers. A despairing sound emerged from his throat. "No. You don't."

"Yes, dammit, I do. Stop telling me I don't."

Max groaned. He could feel himself weakening. "You shouldn't. God, Chris, you shouldn't."

She snuggled deeper into his arms and kissed the underside of his jaw. "Why shouldn't I, Max? Give me one good reason why I shouldn't love you."

"Because... because I wouldn't know what to do with your love—how to take care of it. It would be like giving a priceless china vase to a gorilla." The frustrated anger in his voice was the only thing that prevented Chris from laughing at the analogy. "And because, dammit, I can't... I can't love you back!"

"Horsefeathers," Chris said clearly. "You already do love me back—you just don't know it yet."

Max's head snapped up at that. He felt as if she'd just plunged a knife into his chest. "No." It was inconceivable, beyond the realm of possibility... utterly terrifying. "No," he said again. The denial was a hoarse rasp. "You don't understand. I can't. I don't know how."

Chris shook her head at him the way an indulgent adult might shake her head at a child who was beginning to try her patience.

"Max, loving isn't something you learn to do, like riding a bike. It's something that just *happens*, like... like breathing. You think you don't know how to love because you've never let yourself love. You've never let it just happen. That's all you have to do, darling,'' she assured him softly. ''Just let it happen. Stop fighting it, stop hiding from it, and you'll see how wonderfully easy it is.'' She suddenly grinned. ''A baby could do it, it's so easy.''

Max stared at her in helpless, bewildered silence. Hadn't she heard a word he'd said? He drew a long, slow breath, then released it in a rush. ''One of us,'' he said with conviction, ''is definitely crazy.''

Chris's rich, throaty chuckle astonished him. ''Maybe we both are. Love has that effect on people, I'm told. Come on.''

''Where are we going?'' he asked as she tugged him back onto the beach. Not that he really cared. At that moment she could have led him over a bed of hot coals, and he didn't think he'd have felt a thing.

''To see Julio deCosta,'' Chris answered. ''After talking to Stanley and Roger this morning, I'm convinced that Cy Gollum does indeed exist—or at least did. And if he wasn't just a product of someone's fertile imagination, it stands to reason that neither was his mother.'' She grinned up at him as she lifted his arm and hung it around her neck. ''Wasn't it clever of me to work that out?''

Max tried not to smile, but only for a moment. ''Brilliant,'' he agreed. ''Have you ever thought of becoming a private detective?''

''Investigator,'' Chris corrected as they crossed the street to where Jess's Civic was parked.

THE FIVE YOUNG MEN WERE ASSEMBLED in room 108. Mel was sprawled on one of the beds, David and Kevin were seated on the other and Stanley and Roger were pacing back and forth between them.

"You're sure she said Gollum?" David asked, with an unhappy frown.

Stanley nodded grimly. "You think I'd make a mistake about something like that? I almost fainted. It was Gollum, all right . . . *Cy* Gollum."

"Cy as in cyclops," Mel said under his breath. He didn't sound any happier than David looked.

"Cyclops," Kevin repeated in disgust. "It's him, all right. Damn, he's done it to us again."

"Not necessarily," David interjected. "Even if he's here—"

"What do you mean, *if* he's here?" Mel challenged as he rolled off the bed. "That girl told Stanley and Rog that Cy Gollum's 'remains' were shipped to Daytona Beach from Evansville on Monday. Wednesday morning a coffin just happened to turn up in the swimming pool out there, with a note fastened to it listing all five of our names! You think that was coincidence, David? He's here, all right, and he's making sure we know it."

David remained calm. "All right, so he's here." He glanced around, making sure he had everyone else's attention before he continued. "But getting here was only a third of the bargain. He still has to complete the other two-thirds. The question is, are we going to just stand by and let him?"

Four male voices shouted, "Hell, no!" in unison.

CHAPTER FOURTEEN

CHRIS WAS DISAPPOINTED that there was no sign of the De Lorean when they arrived at deCosta's; she'd been hoping for a closer look at it. But there was another car parked in the rear drive—a plain, dark blue Chevy four-door.

"Looks like the superagent has company," Max remarked as they passed it on the way to the front of the house. He instinctively glanced down and filed a mental note that the car bore a Volusia County license plate.

When deCosta answered the door, Chris was certain she saw stark fear flare in his eyes for an instant. The look was gone almost before she could register it, though, and a second later the actor had pasted a wide, toothy smile on his handsome face.

"What a pleasant surprise, Miss Hudson. And I see you have your friend Mr. Decker with you."

A tiny crease appeared between Chris's brows as deCosta practically shouted the greeting. Did he think she'd gone stone deaf in the past couple of hours?

"Yes. We're sorry to intrude on you again, but if it's not too much trouble we'd like to talk to you for a few minutes. It's about Mrs. Gollum, the lady we were trying to find when we were here before."

Almost before she finished speaking, deCosta had started to explain that he was in the middle of an important business meeting. He was polite and charming, even slightly apologetic, but all the same he managed to close the door in their faces less than two minutes after he'd opened it.

As they turned to leave, Chris thought she detected a movement at one of the windows along the front of the house. Probably deCosta's business associate, she thought, checking to see who had interrupted their meeting.

"That guy missed his calling," Max commented as they rounded the corner. "He should have gone into politics."

"Or used car sales," Chris agreed dryly. "Did you see the look on his face when he opened the door?"

They'd reached the Civic. Max gave her a sharp glance as he automatically opened the door on the passenger's side for her. "You mean that panic-striken, totally terrified look? Yeah, I saw it. For a second I almost turned around to see if Godzilla was wading out of the ocean behind us. But then he started pouring on the charm, and I decided I must have imagined it."

"You didn't imagine it," Chris told him. She handed him the keys and folded herself into the car without suggesting that she drive. His leg seemed fine now. She was watching him walk around the front of the car when another movement at one of the rear windows caught her eye.

"Don't look," she said as Max slid behind the wheel, "but somebody's watching us...peeking out from behind the drapes there at the corner of the house.''

Max didn't raise his eyes above the dash as he inserted the key in the ignition. ''Can you see who it is?''

''No, darn it. All I can see is a hand holding the drapes back a couple of inches.''

''A man's hand, or a woman's?'' As he asked, Max twisted to look back over his shoulder while he reversed into the turnaround area in front of the garage.

''A man's, I think. Whoever it was, he's not watching anymore. I hate it when people do that,'' she said angrily. ''What did he think we were going to do—make off with dear Freddie's shrubbery, or something?''

Max grinned and shifted into first gear. ''Maybe Godzilla really did follow us.''

''Right,'' Chris said sarcastically. ''I'm telling you, Max, there's definitely something strange about that man...'' A pained groan from the other side of the car made her clamp her lips together without finishing. Darned if she'd give him ammunition for another snide remark about ''feminine intuition.''

When they returned to Jess's, she was waiting to inform Max that Quinn Vincent had phoned while he was out.

''Don't ask me what he was calling about,'' she added with an offended sniff. ''He didn't see fit to tell me.''

While Max returned Vincent's call, Chris told Jess about their trip to the cosmetic surgeon's office. By the time Max hung up the phone, his mother's normal good humor was back in evidence.

"Are you going to tell us why Quinn called you?" she asked as he handed her the keys to the Civic.

"He's turned up another interesting fact about Frederick Marchand. Seems he's the owner of that crummy motel Chris's boss booked her into."

"Actually, Mrs. Gollum made the reservation," Chris corrected. "At least, that's what Elliott told me. You say Marchand owns the place?"

Max nodded. "He bought it a little over four years ago, before he changed his name from Markowic to Marchand. That's why it took Quinn a while to discover that he's the owner. I'm going over there to talk to the manager, see if he can shed any light on Marchand or his nephew."

Chris made a derogatory sound. "Good luck. I'd be surprised if that pathetic little man could tell you the time of day. He practically went to pieces when he let us in and we found you out cold on the floor Tuesday morning."

Max's mouth settled into a grim smile. "That's one of the things I intend to question him about. From all indications, somebody let himself into that room with a key... twice. Either the key was stolen, or the manager was an accessory to two illegal entries in twenty-four hours."

After Max left, the women went over every detail of the events that had taken place in the last few days. Unfortunately their efforts didn't result in any stunning bursts of insight. They still had no idea who had sent Chris to Florida with a coffin, or why; who or what had been in that coffin; or how the five UE students and/or Mr. Holloway were involved...*if* any of them were involved.

"I've got a gut feeling that Julio deCosta is hiding something," Chris told her as she stirred the cup of tea in front of her. "And I'm not referring to his dumb hair transplant. Max can make all the smart-aleck remarks about 'feminine intuition' he wants, but I *know* that man got the shock of his life today when he opened the door and found us standing on his front porch. He was more than just surprised to see us, Jess, he was horrified. And then he yelled out our names, almost as if he was announcing—"

She suddenly broke off and bolted out of her chair. "Of course!" she exclaimed. "Of *course*! Why didn't I realize it before!" She whirled around to face Jess, who was standing at the sink. The feverish excitement in her eyes caused Jess to drop the cup she was rinsing and stare at her as if she feared for Chris's sanity.

"Jess, don't you see," he *was* announcing us—to whoever was inside the house. He's an actor, for God's sake," she explained when the other woman just continued to stare at her in mute concern. "His voice is one of the tools of his trade. He doesn't have to scream to make himself heard—in fact he's probably careful not to yell, to avoid straining his voice. Well, that does it!" she mumbled to herself, snatching her purse off the table.

"Come on," she said, already headed for the door. "Maybe that blue car is still there. If we can get the license number, Max can have Vincent find out who owns it."

"Oh, but..." Jess began anxiously. "Chris, I don't think it would be wise to go back to Mr. deCosta's house, especially if he really does have something to hide. And you know what Max would—"

"Don't worry," Chris interrupted as she scooped up Jess's purse. She thrust it into Jess's hands and started urging her toward the door. "We don't have to go up to the house, or even onto the property. If that car is still parked where it was, we should be able to read the license plate from Atlantic Avenue. We couldn't possibly be putting ourselves in any danger, so Max won't have any reason to be upset."

"Famous last words," Jess quipped as Chris pulled the door firmly shut behind them.

THE CUBAN MANAGER of the motel was more than merely cooperative. He couldn't wait to spill his guts. Not about Frederick Marchand—whom he'd seen in the flesh only once since he started to manage the place—but about Marchand's nephew, Frank Markowic.

Max shifted position, and the cheap plastic upholstery beneath his jeans made an embarrassing noise. "So young Frank called you last Friday morning, and made the reservation for Christine Hudson for Monday night?" He faced the motel manager across a battered metal desk. On the wall behind it was a nail-studded board holding three rows of keys.

"Yes, that is correct," the man confirmed at once. His eagerness to please took some of the fun out of questioning him.

"And then he turned up himself on Monday afternoon, claiming he needed another room?"

Cordero's head bobbed vigorously. "Yes. He has stayed here occasionally before, as I told you, but he has always made arrangements in advance. This time he said nothing about wanting a room for himself until he arrived. And—this was especially strange—he paid for Miss Hudson's room for Monday night, and also for his own . . . but for the entire week. In cash."

Max frowned. "Why was that strange?"

The Cuban spread his hands in an eloquent gesture. "Because I have never known him to have more than twenty or thirty dollars in his wallet. Two years ago young Mr. Markowic came down with some of his friends for spring break, and they ran out of money. He had to borrow fifty dollars from me—I mean from the motel, you understand—to get home."

Max's frown deepened. "Yet on Monday he paid you in cash for his room for the entire week?"

Senor Cordero was beginning to look like one of those plastic dogs people stick in the rear windows of their cars. His head was going a mile a minute.

"Yes. It came to more than three hundred dollars, including tax."

"And did you see how he arrived—by car, bus, taxi?" *Pickup truck?* Max added silently. *With maybe a hot coffin stashed in the back?*

Senor Cordero's head finally took up a different rhythm. "No, I am sorry, I did not. But I don't believe he was driving, because there has been no car parked outside his room all week."

"And which room is that?" Max asked as he rose from the rude plastic chair.

"Number six, two doors down from the room Miss Hudson was checked into."

The manager accompanied him to room number six, but there was no response to Max's insistent knocking. Senor Cordero seemed even more disappointed than Max that Frank Markowic wasn't available to rake over the coals. He offered to get the master key from his office and let Max have a look around, but Max scrupulously declined.

He got a description of Markowic—"tall and skinny, dark hair, horn-rimmed glasses, a bad complexion"—and a promise from Cordero to call him when the young man showed up, and then headed back to his apartment, intending to ask Chris for her boss's phone number and call the jerk himself. Good ol' Elliott had quite a bit of explaining to do...starting with why he'd told Chris that "Mrs. Gollum" had made the motel reservation for her, when in fact it had been Francis David Markowic who had arranged for her room.

THEY'D TAKEN OFF AGAIN, DAMMIT. No use telling himself they'd just gone out for groceries, or down to the cleaners. Knowing those two, they were probably out at the cemetery robbing somebody's grave.

"Hell," Max muttered as he stood in the middle of Jess's living room and raked a hand through his hair. When the phone rang, he snatched it up and growled, "Yeah, what is it?" into the mouthpiece.

"Max? Is that you? Oh, thank goodness. I tried your place, but there wasn't any an—"

"Christine, where the hell are you?"

"We're at a gas station." She named the intersection, and then mumbled, "Uh, Max, we've had a little accident."

His heart came up into his throat. He had visions of snipers, drunk drivers, redneck truckers.

"Accident? What kind of accident? Are you hurt?" The very thought made his voice crack. "Is Jess?"

"No, no, we're both fine," Chris assured him quickly. "The brakes went out and we had a little fender bender, that's all. But we're stuck here. Could you—"

"I'm on the way. Just stay put. I'll be there in five minutes." He started to hang up, then lifted the receiver again long enough to snarl, "And if you ever scare me like that again, I'll wring your gorgeous little neck."

The tow truck arrived just ahead of Max. When the driver crawled under the Civic to drop the transmission, Max ushered his mother and Chris to his pickup and installed them in the cab with orders not to budge an inch."

"You're sure you're both all right?" he demanded through the open window. "Maybe I should take you by the hospital for some X rays or something, just to be safe."

"We're both fine, Max," Chris assured him for perhaps the seventh time. "Stop worrying. When Jess realized the brakes had failed, she downshifted and steered the car straight into that planter." Max glanced around and shivered. *Straight into that planter*. The one made out of cement blocks. The one built like a damn bunker.

"We were both wearing our seat belts. We got jerked around a little, but that's all. We're fine, I swear, mostly thanks to Jess's quick thinking. Stop frowning like that, as if you're looking for somebody to beat up. It wasn't anybody's fault—it was just a stupid accident."

Max opened his mouth to tell her that this "stupid accident" couldn't have happened in the first place if they'd stayed at home where they belonged, but just then he felt a tap on his shoulder. He turned impatiently. It was the tow truck driver.

"Could I have a word with you, mister?" He jerked his head toward the Civic, which he'd already winched up and was ready to tow off to the garage. "Over here."

Chris watched curiously as Max accompanied the man back to his tow truck. The driver made a brief remark as he squatted beside a dark patch on the pavement under Jess's car. Chris saw Max stiffen in reaction. Next the young man stuck his already grimy finger into the pool of liquid, then lifted it to Max and said something else, gesturing to the underside of the Civic.

"What's going on?" Chris asked in confusion. She turned to Jess, and was startled to see that the older woman was pale. "Could the car have had some kind of leak?"

Jess shook her head firmly. "I just had it serviced two weeks ago. The mechanic said it was in A-1 condition."

When Max returned to the pickup, he wore a grim expression. Jess waited until he'd climbed inside and closed the door before asking calmly, "Was it the brake line?"

He gave a curt nod. "Somebody took a nick out of it."

"What?" Chris gasped.

Max turned his head toward her. The look in his eyes chilled her blood. "Somebody cut the line. Not all the way through, just enough for the brake fluid to leak out slowly."

"But who . . . ?"

"That's the question of the hour, isn't it?" Max said. His voice was flat and hard. Chris had never heard him use that tone before. He sounded . . . dangerous.

"Do you have any ideas?" Jess asked.

"A few," he answered tersely.

He didn't say anything else until they reached Jess's. Then, still in that same unnaturally flat voice, he ordered them to stay inside the apartment and not open the door to anyone until he told them it was safe to do so.

"Nobody, and I mean nobody, gets past that door," he emphasized. "You don't open it to old Bill, the paper boy, not even Quinn Vincent unless I tell you it's okay. I don't care if the Pope comes around in person to collect for world hunger relief, he doesn't get in. Got it?"

"Got it," Jess replied firmly.

"The Pope?" Chris repeated, sounding dazed, but Max didn't hear her.

He spent a couple of minutes checking locks, then left in such a hurry that he didn't even say goodbye. Chris stood in the living room and stared at the door he'd slammed behind him. For an instant she wondered whether she might have dreamed the past half hour.

"I could use a cup of tea. How about you?" Jess asked behind her. Chris turned toward the kitchen.

"How can you be so calm?" she demanded incredulously. "Hasn't any of this shaken you up at all?"

Jess smiled as she filled the kettle with water. "Of course it has. But I'm so relieved to see Max acting like himself again that the rest of it just doesn't seem all that important."

Chris went to pull out a chair and sit at the dinette table.

"Acting like himself again?"

"Mmm. For the past six years, he's just sort of... gone through the motions, almost as if he was sleepwalking. Oh, he functioned all right, but he didn't really *care* about anything. Nothing seemed to touch him, affect him on more than a superficial level." She smiled as she took a seat next to Chris.

"But everything started to change on Monday, when you came into his life. All week he's been emerging from his shell, without even realizing it. I suspect it's been a little frightening for him now and then, and more than a little painful. But I could tell from his behavior just now that he's almost back to normal." The teakettle started to whistle. Jess slipped Chris a wink as she got up to remove it from the burner. "You just had a glimpse of the man who used to be known as 'Mad Max' in certain areas of his precinct."

"Mad Max?" Chris tried to swallow, but her mouth was suddenly dry. "Jess, he wouldn't do anything...uh, rash, would he? I mean, he's not going to suddenly turn into some kind of one-man vigilante force, or something?"

Jess laughed in genuine amusement. "Heavens, you do have an active imagination, don't you? Don't worry, Chris. My son might be as hardheaded as they come and have an independent streak a yard wide, but he's *never* rash. He's always had the ability to maintain absolute control, even in the most tense situations."

Just as Jess finished speaking, the apartment door flew open and Max stormed through it.

"Where the hell is my gun?" he demanded. "I just tore my bedroom apart, and the damn thing's not there. Come on, Jess, I know you've got it. Hand it over."

As Chris looked on in stunned amazement, Jess jumped up and started rummaging in the kitchen cabinets. Max waited with barely contained impatience for her to locate the missing weapon. Meanwhile he directed an accusing frown at Chris.

"You didn't even put the damn chain on the door."

"Stop that swearing, Max," Jess instructed from inside a cabinet, "or you can find your own gun."

"What on earth is she doing with your gun?"

"Why didn't you chain the damn—the blasted door? I just opened it and walked right in. I could have been some kind of psychopath!"

"I'm not sure you're *not* some kind of psychopath," Chris retorted. "I forgot, okay? I'm sorry. Skin me and nail my hide to the wall. What is Jess doing with your gun?"

"God knows," he said irritably. "She probably sneaked up and took it the last time I tied one on. I think she's got some crazy idea that one of these days I might decide to use it on myself."

Jess withdrew her head from the cabinet under the sink to glare at him. "I don't think and never have thought any such ridiculous thing," she told him firmly. "I admit from time to time I've brought the gun down here, but only because you leave it lying around just any old place, and I was afraid that some night you'd come home, trip over it and blow your foot off or something. Honestly!" Still grumbling, she returned to her search.

Chris gave Max a sharp jab with her elbow. "I apologize," he told his mother gruffly. "And I'm glad you've never thought I would do myself in, because there's no chance of that. But listen, Jess, I know da—darn well the gun was under my bed last week. When did you come up and get it?"

Jess backed out of the cabinet again. "Tuesday, when I was collecting your things to take back to the hospital. After you'd been hit on the head and knocked unconscious, I thought you might want to start carrying it, so I brought it down to clean and oil it for you. With all the excitement since then, I forgot I even had it." Turning away again, she muttered under her breath, "they say forgetfulness is the first sign of senility, Jessamyn."

"And talking to yourself's the second," Max added dryly. "Have you looked in the cookie jar?"

"The cookie jar?" Chris asked with a grin.

Jess popped up like a jack-in-the-box. "The cookie jar! Of course!" She sounded thoroughly disgusted with herself for not having remembered.

"She always used to hide her household money in the cookie jar," Max explained to Chris as he reached up and brought it down from the top of the refrigerator. "She said it was the last place a burglar would go looking."

"Unless he had a sweet tooth," Chris remarked. "Where did you keep the cookies, Jess?"

Jess smiled ingenuously. "In the bread box, of course."

Max's hand disappeared into the cookie jar and a second later came out holding the gun. He checked to make sure it was loaded, then stuck it at the back of his belt, under his shirt.

"Remember what I said about not letting anybody in," he reminded them as they both walked him to the door. When they reached it, he stopped, seemed to hesitate, and then added, "I don't want anything to happen to either of you." His voice was a little rough, and there was a smear of brick red across each of his cheekbones.

"We don't want anything to happen to you, either," Chris told him softly. "Right, Jess?"

"We certainly don't. Be careful, Max."

Jess opened the door for him, but on the verge of stepping through it he suddenly bent to dab a quick, slightly awkward kiss on her cheek. Chris didn't know which of them looked more stunned by the gesture.

"Hey, what about me?" she said into the astonished silence. "Don't I get a goodbye kiss?"

Max turned to her with a slightly sheepish smile. "Only if you promise to put the chain on the door this time."

Chris promised, and got her kiss. It didn't last much longer than the one he'd given Jess, but the fierce hug that went with it made up for the total lack of passion or tenderness in the brief caress of his lips.

MAX LOCKED HIS GUN inside the glove compartment of his truck, and then went after the only solid lead he had. He returned to the motel and informed Senor

Cordero that he'd changed his mind about having a look at Frank Markowic's room. Fortunately for Frank, he was still out.

There was an assortment of men's clothing strewn around the room. "Did Frank have anybody else with him when he checked in?" Max asked as he examined two knit shirts he'd picked up off the floor.

"No," Senor Cordero said in surprise. "He was alone. Why do you ask?"

"Because there are two different sizes of clothes here. It looks like somebody's been sharing the room with him."

Moving to the closet, he found a cheap terry robe and, on the hanger beside it, a blue windbreaker with a designer label. The robe was a small, the Windbreaker an extra large. He knelt to look for shoes.

"Bingo," he said softly. He picked up one of the two brand new white leather high-tops lying on the floor of the closet. "Got you, you son of a bitch."

"These shoes are important?" Cordero asked eagerly. He'd crept up behind Max to peer over his shoulder. "You have seen them before?"

"Oh, yeah," Max replied. He dropped the shoe and stood up to go into the bathroom. "The guy who brained me with the phone down in number eight the other night was wearing 'em."

Cordero crossed himself and mumbled something in Spanish.

Max came out of the bathroom carrying a bottle of man's cologne. He unscrewed the cap to sniff it, and his lips thinned in satisfaction. "That's it," he said, depositing the bottle on the room's solitary chair. "I've seen enough."

Outside he paused to glance around the motel's parking area while the manager locked the door of number six. Things were finally starting to come together. Now if he could just get his hands on Frank Markowic for fifteen minutes...

His arm was suddenly seized in a frantic, sweaty grip. "Senor Decker, there he is!" Cordero yelled, gesturing wildly at a thin young man who had just crossed the street and was ambling toward them. "That's him...that's Frank Markowic!"

The young man stumbled to a halt, his mouth gaping in astonished terror for a moment before he spun around and started running in the opposite direction.

Max swore and took off after him.

CHAPTER FIFTEEN

"YOU'RE WEARING A HOLE in the rug, dear. Why don't you pace from east to west for a while."

Chris stopped and gave Jess's carpet a rueful glance. "Sorry. How long has he been gone now?"

"Not quite an hour. Would you like another cup of tea? A sandwich? I know, how about some cream of tomato soup?"

"No, nothing thanks. He should have come back by now, shouldn't he? Or at least have called. What if that Markowic guy was waiting to jump him? Max could be lying unconscious on the floor of one of those tacky rooms again, for all we know. He could have another concussion, or a fractured skull, or something even worse. What if Markowic had a gun?"

"I imagine Max would take it away from him," Jess said calmly. "Really, you mustn't worry so. Max can take care of himself, believe me. Why don't we both lie down and rest for a while. I doubt either of us got much sleep last night."

Chris's pacing came to an abrupt halt. Her eyes narrowed shrewdly. When she turned around to face Jess, she rolled her shoulders as if they were stiff, then patted a fake yawn.

"I didn't, that's for sure," she admitted with a sheepish grin. "And I've been going since I got up this morning. I guess I could use some rest, but I don't think I'd be able to sleep."

Jess was already heading for the closet where she kept the extra bed linen. "Of course neither of us will sleep until Max is safely home," she said as she carried a pillow and blanket to the sofa. "But there's no reason why we shouldn't prop our feet up and relax in the meantime. I wouldn't mind stretching out on the couch, if you'd like to use the bed."

"Oh, no!" Realizing how desperate she'd sounded, Chris quickly flashed a smile and refused the offer in a more normal tone. "No, I wouldn't dream of taking your bed. Anyway, I'd rather stay in the living room, by the door. Max can't get in until somebody unfastens the chain, remember?" As she lay down on the sofa and spread the blanket over her, she wondered guiltily what the penalty was for lying to your fairy godmother.

Fifteen minutes after Jess went into the bedroom Chris slipped on her shoes, picked up her purse and stealthily slipped out of the apartment, making sure the door was locked behind her.

When she reached the motel where the UE students were staying, she marched straight to room 108. She'd known better than to follow Max, but she hadn't been able to stay cooped up in Jess's apartment doing absolutely nothing for another minute. These guys knew something about what was going on, and she meant to find out what.

She knew before she raised her hand to knock that they were inside. They were making enough racket for twenty people. When her fist came down on the door it unexpectedly swung open. Chris only hesitated an instant before she stepped inside . . . into a scene of absolute chaos.

All five of the students were there, running back and forth between the two connecting rooms, apparently intent on tearing them both apart with their bare hands, pausing now and then to yell terse messages to one another. At first none of them even seemed aware of her presence.

"Did you find it?"

"Not yet. Try Mel's shaving kit. He was using it the other day."

"It's not there. I checked there already."

Roger Sloane suddenly noticed Chris standing just inside the door. He grinned sheepishly and started toward her, but before he made it halfway across the room one of the other students bawled in a wounded tenor.

"My Madonna tape's missing."

Roger whirled around with a scowl. "Oh, hell. Are you sure?"

"Positive. Hey, who's the fox?"

Three heads swiveled in Chris's direction and six eyes surveyed her appreciatively. Roger opened his mouth to identify her, but a hefty boy in a pair of patched cutoffs spoke up before he could.

"Who cares who she is. This is no time to be thinking about women, you birdbrain. What about my shampoo? Did anybody find my shampoo?"

"Screw your lousy shampoo," the one who'd lost his Madonna tape retorted. "That tape cost me $8.95, plus tax."

"For your information, airhead, that shampoo sells for $12.50 a bottle. There are only four places in Evansville that even stock it."

"In other words, if he got it he won't have any trouble proving it's yours. That's great. Just terrific."

Stanley Gallagher suddenly appeared at the connecting door. He looked as if he'd just swallowed a cyanide capsule. "I hate to even mention it, guys," he confessed miserably, "but I can't seem to find my prescription sunglasses."

There was a chorus of agonized groans.

Stanley and the fifth student joined the others in room 108, and they all collapsed onto the two beds. Their expressions displayed varying degrees of bitter defeat and angry frustration.

"Well, that's it," one of them said in disgust. "He's done it. We might as well pack it in and go home."

Roger suddenly bounded to his feet. "Go home! What are you, crazy? We've still got three days of vacation left, and there are still thousands of nubile, half-naked females out there looking for a good time."

"Awright! Now you're talkin'." One of the others jumped up beside Roger, and then another, and another. Chris barely got out of the way in time to avoid being trampled as all five of them rushed for the door like a herd of...like a herd of college students on spring break, she thought wryly.

She impulsively picked Stanley to follow. He wandered aimlessly down the beach, hands jammed in the pockets of his cutoffs, shoulders hunched in dejection. When he eventually stopped and turned to face the ocean, she walked up beside him. She knew he was aware of her, but he didn't speak right away. She was just about to start hurling questions at him when he gave her a lethargic, "Hello again."

"Hello." Chris didn't add more. Some instinct told her that if she just gave him time, he'd volunteer all the information she wanted.

"I guess you're wondering what that business back at the motel was all about."

"Well...yes, now that you mention it," Chris replied. "I gather each of you is missing some item he brought down here from Evansville."

Stanley nodded glumly. When he turned to face her, his crooked grin surprised Chris. "I'm afraid so, thanks to our mutual friend, Mr. Gollum. His real name is Steven Kline, by the way. He's a sophomore at UE, like the rest of us, and as you've probably figured out by now he's not dead...yet."

Chris drew a deep, calming breath. "I think we'd better find someplace to sit down," she suggested. "And then you can tell me all about this friend of yours...starting with why he apparently passed himself off as a corpse and shipped himself to Daytona Beach in a coffin."

MAX KNEW DAYTONA BEACH far better than Frank Markowic did, otherwise he knew he wouldn't have had a prayer of catching the young man. As it was, he was acutely conscious that if he took a single wrong step, put an ounce too much weight on his bum right leg, it might buckle and send him sprawling onto the pavement.

As he raced between two fast-food restaurants and then zigzagged through a parking lot, he promised himself he'd start a vigorous exercise program to build the damn thing up again—just as soon as he got this crazy mess straightened out for Chris and knew she wasn't in any real danger.

The shortcuts he'd taken brought him out of a service alley just as Frank Markowic came pounding past. Max caught hold of his T-shirt with one hand and swung him around, slamming the young man up against the building and knocking the wind out of him.

"Okay, hotshot," he panted as he hauled Frank into the alley. "Here's how it works. I ask the questions, and you provide the answers. Question number one: what were you looking for in Christine Hudson's room the other night, when you clobbered me with the telephone?"

Frank's eyes were nearly bugging out of his head as he gasped for air. "It wasn't me!" he cried frantically. "I swear, it wasn't me that hit you. It was Steven . . . Steven Kline. He did it."

Max's grip tightened on the young man's T-shirt. "And who, pray tell, is Steven Kline?" he asked in a menacing growl.

Frank looked as if he was about to faint. He gulped a sobbing breath and then blurted. "He's Cy Gollum."

CHRIS JUST STARED at Stanley as if he'd suddenly told her the moon was made of cheese.

"Let me get this straight," she began. "You mean all this—shipping himself down here, paying Elliott to have me escort the coffin, dumping the coffin in the swimming pool—it was all to win a stupid *bet*!"

Chris had never been so angry in her life. She thought that if she ever got her hands on Steven Kline, alias Cy Gollum, he would wish he'd held on to that coffin a little longer.

Stanley blushed and rubbed at the end of his nose. "I guess it must sound pretty juvenile."

"Juvenile doesn't begin to cover it, Stanley," she assured him. "It sounds like the most idiotic, tasteless..." She broke off and struggled to bring her temper under control. "And this isn't getting us anywhere. Okay, let's run over it again. Steven Kline bet the rest of you that he could sneak out of Evansville and into Daytona Beach without any of you catching him, filch one object from each of you—"

"A minimum of one object," Stanley interrupted. "I wouldn't be surprised if he managed to get more than one from a couple of us."

"And then beat you back to Evansville before the end of spring break. Does that about cover it?"

Stanley nodded unhappily. "Pretty much."

"*Why?* Why would anybody in his right mind make a bet like that to begin with? And why would the rest of you go along with it?"

The question clearly made Stanley uncomfortable. In quick succession he averted his eyes, cleared his throat and tugged at his earlobe. "Steven came up with the idea in the first place just to prove he could actually do it, and the rest of us went along with it because it seemed like an easy way to finally get the better of him at something," he mumbled. "I know that's petty and immature, but you'd have to know Steven Kline to appreciate how badly the five of us wanted to see him mess up at *any*thing, just once."

"I think I'm beginning to get the picture," Chris remarked. "He's a grade-A creep, right—the kind who cheats on his chemistry final, and then brags about it when he gets an A."

"That's Steven exactly," Stanley agreed. "He sees himself as some kind of daredevil or something. He's always getting into some kind of scrape, and his folks are always bailing him out. They're pretty well off, so they can afford to indulge him. Anyway, Steven thinks 'the rules' were made for everybody else, but they don't apply to him. He makes up his own rules as he goes along."

"It's probably just as well Mr. Kline and I never met," Chris said shortly. "All right, I understand why he used the coffin. It was a means of getting out of Evansville without being detected, and the phony name was probably just extra insurance. But he didn't need to hire me to escort the coffin down here, and there was no earthly reason for him to dump it in the motel swimming pool. That was just plain sick, Stanley."

"I think he did it to show us up. He probably thought one of us would figure out it was from him. Unfortunately, we didn't. It wasn't until you showed up this morning, asking if we knew anybody named Cy Gollum, that we finally put two and two together. You see," he explained, "we're all D&D freaks."

"Dungeons and Dragons?" Chris asked. She was familiar with the popular game; two of her brothers were D&D fanatics. "You mean the six of you play together?"

"Right. Steven's favorite character, the one he uses most often, is a cyclops. He's also a big fan of J. R. R.

Tolkien. He's read Tolkien's *Lord of the Rings* trilogy about a dozen times."

"Tolkien!" Chris felt like kicking herself. "Of course! Gollum is one of Tolkien's more obnoxious characters. So the Cy was for cyclops, and the Gollum was from Tolkien's books. And Steven knew that if any of you ever heard the name, you'd recognize it immediately, right?"

"Right. Except that none of us heard it until this morning, when you came to see Roger and me. By then it was too late for the information to do us any good, not that it would have, anyway. This time Steven pulled out all the stops. I'm convinced he must have had help at some point, though. I don't see how he could have done everything on his own. At the same time, I can't think of a single person dumb enough to let Steven talk him into going in on this crazy stunt."

Chris's mouth twisted as she met his eyes. "I may have the answer to that one, Stanley. Does the name Francis David Markowic ring any bells?"

WHEN SHE LEFT THE MOTEL and started toward the bus stop, Chris was still steamed at the way Steven Kline had manipulated her. She remembered how sorry she'd felt for the poor Cy Gollum and his elderly, semi-invalid mother, and felt like a fool. And as for Elliott . . . She clamped a lid on her temper before she ended up giving herself a stroke. She'd deal with Elliott when she got home.

The bus she needed to catch rolled up to the stop while she was still half a block away. Great. As if her day hadn't been lousy enough already. Hitching the strap of her shoulder bag higher to keep it from sliding down her arm, she broke into a brisk trot. She heard the screech of brakes behind her, but didn't look back to see if there'd been an accident. At the moment the only thing on her mind was reaching that bus before it pulled away. Heaven knew when the next one would come along.

Suddenly someone grabbed her from behind and roughly yanked her to a halt, then started dragging her backward down the sliver of sidewalk. For a moment Chris was too startled to resist, but that moment passed swiftly. It was anger more than fear that ignited her furious struggles to free herself. Darned if she'd let some purse snatcher make her miss that bus!

"Let go of me, you jerk!" she barked as she tried to dig in her heels. At the same time, she tried to tear the man's fingers loose from her arms. "Dammit, I said let *go* of me!"

She was released so abruptly that she nearly lost her balance and fell into the street. "Moron!" she spat furiously as she watched her bus pull away from the curb. "Now look what you've done." A car streaked by her with a squeal of tires, leaving the smell of burned rubber in its wake, but she didn't even spare it a glance. Damn, damn and double damn!

"Miss Hudson! Miss Hudson, are you all right?"

Whirling around to see who was shouting at her, Chris received yet another unpleasant surprise as she caught sight of the two men pounding across the street toward her from the motel parking lot. They were both young and athletic looking, both were dressed in slacks and lightweight sport coats, and they both had guns in their hands.

What next? she thought a little hysterically as she backed up a step in reflex.

"Did you get a look at the guy? He was too far away for us to see him clearly. He didn't hurt you, did he?"

Chris didn't—couldn't—respond for a moment or two. Then the men simultaneously lifted their jackets and slid their weapons into shoulder holsters, and her tongue finally came unglued from the roof of her mouth.

"No," she said. So her voice was a little shaky. It wasn't every day two men came tearing at her with guns in their hands, she told herself. "He didn't hurt me. He just made me miss my bus. Uh, listen, if you don't mind my asking...who are you guys, anyway?"

QUINN VINCENT'S MEN—whose names, Chris was amused to learn, were Chuck and Barry—insisted on driving her back to Jess's. When the three of them walked through the door, they found Max prowling the living room like a caged tiger. He took one look at the two plainclothesmen and threw himself down on the sofa. The glare he leveled at Chris told her he'd just about reached the limit of his endurance...and of his patience.

"I don't think I want to hear it," he said flatly.

Chuck told him, anyway. "Somebody tried to snatch her off the street in front of the motel where those students from Evansville are staying."

That hard, dangerous look came into Max's eyes again as he jerked forward. "I'm okay," Chris told him hastily. "I thought he was a purse snatcher or a mugger or something. He just grabbed me and started dragging me down the sidewalk, and I figured he was after my wallet. He made me miss my bus,'' she added crossly.

''He jumped out of a late model dark blue four-door,'' Barry explained. ''There was a second man behind the wheel. We were too far away to get a good look at either of them, but Chuck managed to read a couple of numbers from the car's plate, maybe enough to run a trace on the registration. We'll give it a shot, anyway.''

When the two officers had gone, Chris approached Max hesitantly. He had every right to be angry with her, she knew. She'd deliberately disregarded his instructions, tricked Jess and then sneaked out without letting anyone know where she was going. Still, when he heard what she'd learned from Stanley, maybe he'd be somewhat mollified.

''Max,'' she began in a soft, conciliatory tone as she sank down beside him on Jess's sofa.

''I don't think we'd better talk about it just yet.''

Chris took in the grim set of his jaw and decided he was probably right.

''Okay. Where's Jess?''

Max turned his head to give her a stare that made Chris wonder if she'd be able to squeeze herself under the sofa. ''In the bedroom, asleep. What did you do—slip her some knockout drops?''

She blushed guiltily. ''No. I didn't have to. It was her idea for both of us to lie down for a while. I pretended to go along with it, and after she went into the bedroom I sneaked out. I'm sorry if you're disappointed in me, Max—''

One of his brows lifted eloquently. "'Disappointed' in you?"

"All right, mad at me, but I just couldn't stay cooped up in the apartment another minute. I had to get out and *do* something."

"So you went back to see the students again. I guess I should be grateful you didn't decide to pay Julio deCosta another visit."

"I may be impulsive and stubborn, Max, but I'm not a complete idiot."

"I'll reserve judgment on that, if you don't mind. Well, did you learn anything new?" He obviously doubted that she had.

"Yes, I managed to pick up one or two new facts." If she sounded a little smug, Chris told herself she didn't care. There was no need for him to be so patronizing.

When she finished repeating what Stanley had told her, Max merely pursed his lips and gave a thoughtful nod, which wasn't exactly the reaction she'd been hoping for.

"Well, aren't you even going to congratulate me, or say nice job or something?" she asked indignantly.

Max surprised her by grinning. "Congratulations, Chris. Nice job. Now, would you care to hear what I found out from Frank Markowic?"

Frank had been assisting Steven Kline all along, even before the two of them had stolen a coffin from the Diehl Funeral Home in Evansville the previous week. Steven had chosen Diehl's because the owner happened to be a distant cousin of his father's. He'd figured that if they were caught, his dad would step in and smooth things over with the cousin to keep him out of jail.

Steven had already "borrowed" samples of the forms he would need to ship the coffin out of state, from the funeral home's files. After he'd made photocopies of the forms, he used white-out to delete all the information from the copies and *then* made several copies of the blank forms he'd created . . . which he filled out in triplicate for the fictitious Cy Gollum.

"Wow," Chris said in awe. "That kid ought to be working for the Internal Revenue Service, or maybe the CIA. It took a really devious mind to figure all that out."

"Apparently Steven Kline loves a challenge," Max told her dryly. "But this time he went too far. In the course of creating his fake documents, he forged several people's names. Add that offense to the theft of the coffin, interstate transport of stolen merchandise, and whatever charges the airline may eventually bring against him, and young Mr. Kline is going to find himself in some very hot water before all is said and done. But if you think it took a devious mind to figure a way around the necessary paperwork, wait'll you hear about the trouble they took to actually ship the coffin by air."

First, Steven had located a UE student who worked part-time in the airline's cargo department. He bribed the young man to see that the coffin would be loaded into one of the plane's pressurized cargo bins, which are normally used only to ship perishable items.

"What do you mean by 'perishable items'?" Chris asked curiously. "Food, rare plants, stuff like that?"

"Or animals," Max added. "Any cargo that would require a constant supply of oxygen and a regulated temperature."

"He had the guy he'd bribed open the coffin's lid before the plane took off from Evansville, so he wouldn't suffocate. Then, when you reached Atlanta, Frank sneaked into the cargo compartment to check on him."

"Frank was waiting at the Atlanta airport, then," Chris said.

Max shook his head. Chris thought the slight smile that touched his lips looked just a little sympathetic. "Actually, Frank was on the plane with you and 'the late Cy Gollum.' "

"What!"

"That's right. He came down on the same flight as you. In fact, he could have been sitting beside you during the trip."

"Well, if Frank was on the same plane, why did Steven have Elliott send me along, for Pete's sake!"

Max shrugged. "I guess because this way *you* were officially responsible for the coffin . . . if there'd been any kind of problem with it, the airline people would have come directly to you. Make sense?" Max asked her. Chris only nodded.

"Steven had arranged ahead of time to rent a truck from a Daytona Beach auto dealer. As soon as you had the coffin placed in the baggage area at the airport, Frank went back and let Steven out. They took a cab to collect the rented truck, drove it back to the airport and loaded the coffin—all in less than half an hour.

"They'd originally planned to stay in Frank's uncle's house while they were here—without his knowledge or consent, I might add. But when they arrived at Marchand's house, they discovered that somebody else was already staying there."

"Julio deCosta."

"Right. So they decided to get a room at the motel Marchand owns instead. Frank booked the room in his name. He didn't let on to the manager that Steven was with him. Steven had raided his savings account before they left, and cashed a couple of bonds. He gave Frank enough money to pay for their room for the rest of the week, as well as yours, and then the two of them scouted around town until they found out where the other five were staying."

"How did they do that?" she asked.

"The five of them made themselves easy to find." Max told her. "David Seitz left his car parked right outside their rooms, in plain view of anybody who happened to drive down Atlantic Avenue."

"Not very smart," Chris concluded. "Speaking of not very smart," she said with a fierce frown, "who knocked you out on Monday night—Steven or Frank?"

"Steven. He'd been interrupted before he could finish searching your room the first time. He had Frank follow us when we went out to get something to eat. When Frank saw us start back, he ran ahead of us to warn Steven we were on the way. Later they saw us leave with your suitcase, and Steven figured it would be safe to go back and have another look around, on the off chance you might have left the papers he'd forged to ship the coffin."

"*That's* what he was looking for? Why?"

"He originally intended to leave 'Cy Gollum's' paperwork with the coffin. He knew that when the other five read the name of the deceased, they'd realize not only that he was in town, but how he'd managed to get here undetected. If he'd taken the trouble to search me after he knocked me out, he'd have found the papers in the hip pocket of my jeans.

"By the way," Max added with a grim smile, "They kept the coffin in the rented pickup truck. The motel where the other five were staying was so busy that Steven and Frank didn't get a chance to unload it until late Tuesday night. That's why they didn't return the truck till Wednesday."

Chris slumped against the back of the sofa. "This is all so complicated it's giving me a headache. I'll probably be sorry I asked, but when and how did Steven gather the items he needed from the other five? Stanley said they'd been careful to make sure at least one of them stayed in each of the rooms at all times. How did he manage to sneak in and out without getting caught?"

"He didn't. The two who were 'on duty' Tuesday night apparently decided that since they couldn't go out to any of the parties, they'd throw a party of their own in their rooms."

"Don't tell me," Chris groaned. "Steven was one of the people at their party, right?"

"Right. He got a punk haircut, sprayed it purple, decked himself out in leather and chains, and wandered in with six other people. When he left, he had what he'd come after."

"Was this before he'd put the coffin in the motel pool, or after?" Chris asked sardonically.

"After. When he and Frank unloaded the coffin the party was already in full swing. That's when Steven got the idea to crash it." Max shook his head in grudging admiration. "You've got to give the kid credit for being inventive."

"Oh, yeah, I can see he's got a terrific future ahead of him," Chris muttered. "As a crime lord."

Max grinned. "Or maybe a United States senator."

"Or both."

He chuckled softly and lifted his arm, and Chris scooted under it to nestle against his side. "Did you really chase Frank Markowic across half of Daytona Beach?"

"It sure seemed like it," Max drawled. "I didn't realize until today how out of shape I've let myself get."

"But you caught him," Chris pointed out softly. "Your leg must have taken quite a beating. Does it hurt?"

"Not nearly as much as it should."

"Oh," she said with a disappointed sigh. Max gave her a questioning look. Her hand crept onto his thigh. "I was going to offer to massage it," she explained.

"On second thought, it does ache a little," he said with a devilish gleam in his eye. "It's sort of a throbbing ache, if you know what I mean."

"I know exactly what you mean," Chris whispered. "And I've got the perfect cure for that kind of ache."

Her hand inched higher. Max groaned. "I'll just bet you have."

He lowered them to lie full length on Jess's sofa, leaving room for both of them to caress and explore. Things were beginning to get really steamy when the wall phone in the kitchen started to ring.

"No," Chris protested when Max levered himself away from her. "Don't answer it."

He leaned back down to drop an apologetic kiss on her mouth. "If I don't, the noise will wake Jess, anyway."

It already had. Jess wandered out of the bedroom as Max plucked the receiver from its bracket. Chris hastily sat up and tried to straighten her clothing. "I must have dozed off," Jess said as she joined Chris on the sofa. "When did Max get back?"

"Uh, about an hour ago, I think. Did you have a nice nap?"

"Lovely. How about you? Did you manage to get any sleep?"

"Well..." Chris hesitated. She was reluctant to lie to Jess, yet equally reluctant to tell her the truth and cause her needless anxiety.

"She was too hyped up to sleep," Max said as he came into the living room. Chris glanced up at him in surprise. The gentle smile he gave her made her feel warm all over. "That was Quinn. He's taken Frank Markowic's statement. Now he wants us both to come down and give him ours. It looks as if your 'missing coffin' case is about to be officially closed."

CHAPTER SIXTEEN

AFTER SHE AND MAX HAD REPEATED their stories to Quinn Vincent, Chris asked him what would happen to Frank Markowic and Steven Kline.

"It depends," he said with a shrug. "Neither of them has been in serious trouble before. If the manager of the motel where they dumped the coffin decides to press charges, they could both have to come back to Daytona Beach for trial. Otherwise, we'll let the Evansville P.D. handle it from here. It's their headache now," he added with a boyish grin.

"Did Steven Kline ever show up?" Max asked. "And if he did, what are the chances I could have five minutes alone with him?"

"Sorry, Max," Vincent said. "We still haven't turned him up. He's probably back at his folks' house by now."

"Gloating," Chris added.

Vincent's somber blue gaze swung to her. "At this point I'm more concerned about you than Kline and Markowic. It's highly unlikely that any of the students from Evansville were involved in the attempt to abduct you this afternoon. Do either of you have any idea who those two men might have been, or what they were after?"

"Don't look at me," Chris said with a shake of her head. "I thought it was just your typical run-of-the-mill purse snatching. The guy grabbed me from behind. I didn't see him *or* the car."

Vincent picked up a folder from his desk and scanned the two reports inside. "The car was a late model dark blue four-door. Chuck thinks it was an Olds and Barry says it was a Chevy. Sound familiar?"

"Yeah," Max said. Chris glanced at him in surprise. "The car that was parked at deCosta's when we were there today," he reminded her.

"You're right! At least, it was dark blue," she said to Vincent. "And I think it had four doors, didn't it, Max?"

"Two in front and two in back," he confirmed. "And it was a Chevy, not more than two model years old."

Vincent made a note on the pad in front of him. "I guess you didn't happen to get the plate number?"

"'Fraid not," Max answered. "But it was a Volusia County plate, if that's any help."

"It is. Both reports claim it was a local plate."

There was nothing else to keep them at the police station, so Max and Chris left to return to Jess's.

JESS IMPATIENTLY DUMPED the contents of her purse out on the table. She knew good and well she'd paid that bill, but where was the silly receipt? She quickly located it, but as she sat back with a satisfied smile she noticed the black address book she'd found on the floor at Holloway's.

"Jessamyn, you're getting to be a forgetful old woman," she said as she picked it up. She had intended to ask around that night and see if she could find out who had dropped it, but in all the excitement it had slipped her mind.

Thinking the owner's name might be inside, she opened the book. Strange. All the entries were for businesses. Several of them were familiar to her, but some were located as far away as Charleston, South Carolina. Frowning, she closed the book and turned it over. On the lower right hand corner of the back, embossed in gold letters, was the name Vernon E. Holloway. She sat for a moment, absently tapping a fingernail against the book, then got up and went to the phone.

"Mr. Holloway, my name is Jessamyn Decker. I have something that I believe belongs to you. Yes, that's right. It occurred to me that you might need it to conduct your business. Yes, I'm at home. Mr. Holloway?"

Holding the receiver in front of her face, Jess gave it an annoyed stare. "Rude man," she sniffed as she hung it back on the wall. She started to turn away, then stopped, her eyes narrowing as she gazed down at the small black book in her hand. There had been something in Holloway's voice when he asked if it was the item she was referring to.... He'd sounded anxious—almost desperate, in fact. She impulsively reached for the phone again and dialed the number of the police department, thinking it would be a good idea to get Max's advice before she handed the book over to Holloway.

"DO YOU THINK IT'S TOO LATE to take Jess out to dinner?"

Max didn't answer for a moment. "I'd rather you didn't go out in public until Quinn finds those guys in the blue Chevy."

"That's ridiculous," Chris scoffed. "If I have to stay indoors like some kind of prisoner, I might as well go home."

"It might be best if you did," he said quietly. "In fact, I would have suggested it, but I figured you'd snap my head off."

"You were right," Chris said curtly. "I would have."

He sighed. "Listen, Christine—"

"Do you *want* me to leave? You're tired of me already, is that it? If it is, all you have to do is say so. Heaven knows I don't want to stay where I'm not wanted."

"Don't be an idiot!" Max growled impatiently. They'd reached the apartment block. He steered his truck into its usual place and cut the engine before he spoke again. "Why can't you be reasonable just once," he snapped, yanking the key out of the ignition.

"Why can't you answer my question," Chris retorted. "*Do* you want me to go home?"

"You know damned well I don't!"

The fierce response surprised them both, especially Max. He locked both hands around the steering wheel and stared through the windshield as if something on the rust-pitted hood of the truck had riveted his attention. He heard Chris's soft sigh, but he didn't turn to face her.

"You're still fighting it, aren't you?" she said gently. "Max, be honest, what do you feel when we're together? Just tell me...as simply and honestly as you can."

His forehead creased with concentration as he groped for an answer. There was no way mere words could describe how she made him feel. It was asking too much to expect him to be able to explain it. But because it was Chris who was asking, and because it seemed important to her, he tried.

"I feel . . . confident." He said it as if he was confessing to some heinous crime. "When I'm with you, I . . . believe in myself again."

Certain that hadn't been what she wanted to hear, he reluctantly turned to face her. The warm, loving smile on her face was as unexpected as the way she suddenly threw her arms around his neck and kissed him.

"What was that for?" he asked when she sat back, her hands still clasped at his nape. "Not that I'm complaining, you understand."

"It was my way of thanking you for the present you just gave me," Chris told him huskily. He frowned down at her quizzically, but she only laughed and kissed him again before releasing his neck to slide across the seat and out her side of the truck. Max stared after her in confusion for a moment before he joined her. Present? What present?

Chris reached out to take his hand as they walked to Jess's door. Knowing she was expecting them, Max used his key to let them inside. Lights were burning in the kitchen and living room, but there was no sign of Jess. Chris went to check the bedroom and bath.

"She's not here," she said as she joined Max in the dinette. His head was bent over a piece of the yellow notepaper Jess used to make out her grocery lists. "Maybe she went to visit one of the neighbors. Is that a note from her?"

When Max glanced up from the paper in his hand, she was stunned to see that he had gone pale. "It's a note, but not from Jess." He handed it to her, and Chris felt the blood drain from her own face as she read it:

"If you want to see your mother alive again, drop your current investigation at once."

"WHAT INVESTIGATION?" Chris asked a little wildly. "Have you been working on another case, something I didn't know about?"

"No." The color had returned to Max's face, and that hard light Chris thought of as his "dangerous" look glinted from his eyes. "But someone obviously believes I have been. The question is, who?"

He carefully folded the note in half and stuck it in the pocket of his jeans.

"I'll have to take this to Quinn. Stay here, in case whoever took her follows up with a phone call."

"All right," Chris said as she walked with him to the door. "If somebody does call, what should I say?"

"I doubt you'll have to say anything," Max answered grimly. "If they call, it'll be to make demands. Just make sure you write everything down." He seemed to hesitate, then put both arms around her for a fierce hug. "Damn, Chris, if anything happens to her..."

"Nothing will," Chris said with more conviction than she felt. "You and Quinn Vincent will have her back home in no time, Max. I know it." She gave him a hard squeeze of encouragement before she released him and stepped back. "Now go take him the note. I'll stay close to the phone, I promise."

After he left, Chris wandered restlessly around the small apartment, straightening pictures, fluffing pillows, wiping a sponge over the spotlessly clean kitchen counters and the table in the dinette. The phone on the wall was maddeningly silent. She lifted the receiver five times in ten minutes to make sure it wasn't out of order. Each time she heard the monotonous buzz of a dial tone.

For some reason Jess had carried the remote control tuner for the television into the kitchen and left it lying on the counter next to the sink, beside a box of pickling spices. Chris conscientiously replaced the box in the cabinet where it belonged and took the tuner back into the living room. She was placing it on an end table when the phone rang. The tuner fell from her hand, completely forgotten. She banged her shin on one of the dinette chairs racing to answer the phone.

"Is this Mrs. Decker? Mrs. Jessamyn Decker?"

Chris sagged against the wall. "No. Mrs. Decker isn't here. Can I take a message?"

It was the garage where Jess's car had been taken for repairs, calling to let her know she could pick it up any time.

"As I said, she isn't here at the moment," Chris repeated. She was impatient to get off the phone, in case Jess's kidnappers were trying to get through.

"Okay. But if she comes in later and wants to pick up her car, tell her we're open all night."

Chris thanked the man and promised to pass the message on to Mrs. Decker when she got home. She'd barely settled the receiver back in its cradle when someone knocked at the door. She started toward it automatically, then stopped. A chill swept up her spine. What if it was the people who'd taken Jess? What if they were the same people who'd tried to drag her into a dark blue car that afternoon?

She told herself she was being paranoid as she tip-toed the rest of the way to the door and squinted through the peephole. Still, the breath rushed out of her and her knees almost buckled in relief when she recognized Jess's neighbor, the old man who kept confusing horses and corpses. She opened the door to him reluctantly, determined not to let him draw her into a long-winded conversation.

"Hello there, little lady," he bellowed in greeting. "Thought that was you I seen come in with Max a while ago."

"Yes, Mr. Ferguson, but Max left again," Chris said in clear, distinct tones.

Bill Ferguson nodded. "Saw that, too. Barely set foot inside before he took off again. That's what made me decide to come over. I couldn't help but wonder if maybe there was some kind of family trouble. I mean, what with Jess goin' off with those fellas from the funeral home, and then Max tearin' off like a bat outta—"

"What!" Chris grabbed the old man's arm and dragged him bodily through the door. "What was that you said about Jess leaving with some people from a funeral home?''

He nodded again. ''Yep, she sure did. Has there been a death in the family?''

''No,'' Chris said tersely. ''How do you know the people Jess left with were from a funeral home? Are you sure they were?'' She couldn't help thinking that if his other faculties were as faulty as his hearing, he might have imagined the whole thing, or have Jess confused with someone else.

''Oh, I'm sure, all right,'' the old man assured her. ''A body lives to be my age, he gets to be familiar with all the morticians and their hired help. These fellas were from Holloway's.''

Chris literally begged Bill to stay right where he was while she called the police station. She wanted him to personally repeat to either Max or Quinn Vincent what he'd told her. When she got through, the officer manning the switchboard informed her that both Max and Quinn had just left. It didn't even occur to Chris that they could be reached via the radio in Quinn's car. She left a message for Max to meet her at Holloway's Eternal Rest, hung up the phone, then turned to Bill Ferguson and demanded to know if he had a car and a valid driver's license.

He did. Chris asked rather desperately if he would drive her to the garage to pick up Jess's car. Bill agreed willingly.

''I'd surely appreciate it if you'd tell me what's goin' on, though,'' he said as they pulled out of the parking lot. ''I ain't seen this much excitement around here since Daisy Winfield's drawers caught fire in the clothes dryer.''

Chris filled him in on the way to the garage. When they reached it, she climbed out of Bill's old Nash and hurried around to his open window, wanting to make sure he'd understood what she had asked him to do.

"Have you got everything straight, Bill?"

The old man nodded confidently. "Sure. Piece'a cake. I'll go back to Jess's place, call the police and tell 'em what I told you before... about seein' them two fellas from Holloway's take Jess away in a blue car. Then I'll just sit there and wait, in case somebody calls or Max comes back before he gets your message."

"Right. Okay, then, you'd better get going. And thanks again, Bill."

"Shoot, there ain't no need for thanks. Jess and Max are good neighbors, better than most. Glad to do anything I can to help 'em out."

After Chris had paid for the repairs to Jess's Civic with her Visa card, she took the car and headed for Holloway's Eternal Rest. She promised herself she wouldn't attempt any foolish heroics. She only intended to keep an eye on the place until Max or the police arrived.

She parked the Civic on a side street two blocks from the funeral home, just in case Holloway or any of his employees might recognize it. Then she crept up the alley at the back of the building until she found a hydrangea bush to hide behind and settled down to watch and wait. She figured that if they were holding Jess inside, and if they decided to move her, they would probably use the rear garage entrance.

She'd been in position for about five minutes when the twin beams of a car's headlights swept across the bush as the vehicle turned into the alley. Chris scrunched even lower, curling herself into as tiny a ball as she could manage, and stayed that way until the car drove past. There was a faint squeal as a set of exceptionally hard brakes was applied, and then a brief engine knock when the driver switched off the ignition. The next sound Chris heard was the slam of a door. She risked peeking out from behind the bush. Parked at the rear of the funeral home, directly in front of the garage door, was the dark blue car she and Max had seen at deCosta's.

Chris didn't allow herself time to reconsider the impulsive decision or think about the possible consequences if she was caught. The presence of the car convinced her that they—whoever they were—were holding Jess inside the funeral home. If she could find out exactly where, she'd be able to tell Max when he and Quinn Vincent arrived. She slipped from behind the hydrangea bush and swiftly but silently ran up the alley to the open garage door.

There didn't seem to be anyone in the garage. She crossed it quickly, stopping only when she reached the door leading into the funeral home. Taking a deep breath and mentally crossing all her fingers and toes, she started slowly easing the door open.

When a hand dropped out of nowhere and landed on her shoulder, she nearly jumped out of her skin. Five strong fingers curled in a firm grip as Chris's captor reached around her to flip on the overhead garage lights, at the same time turning her to face him.

"Well, well, look who's here." It was the man who'd driven the hearse out to the airport on Monday. He didn't seem at all annoyed to discover her sneaking in the back door of his employer's establishment. In fact, he was smiling.

"So you changed your mind about paying us a visit, did you?" the man said as he propelled her through the door. "The boss is going to be tickled pink about that. He feels real bad about this afternoon. When your friends with the guns came along, we had to leave in such a hurry he didn't even have time to say hello."

He took her down the hall to Holloway's office, where Jess was already being held. She was seated in an uncomfortable-looking chair with her wrists securely tied behind her, but thankfully she didn't appear to have been harmed. The man who'd discovered Chris placed her in an identical chair across the room and bound her wrists, as well, then excused himself to go find his employer.

As soon as the door closed behind him, Chris opened her mouth to ask Jess a few of the hundred or so questions she'd stored up since Bill Ferguson had appeared at Jess's door, but she didn't get the chance. There was a muffled exchange in the hall outside, and then the door was pushed open again—not all the way but enough for the women to hear clearly what was being said.

"All right, then. I'll go back to the house in case anyone gets impatient and calls about the next delivery date. The Decker woman should be safe here for the time being. We can discuss this regrettable situation and what to do about it later, after you've spoken with Freddie."

Holloway made a brusque response, but Chris was no longer listening. She was still reeling from the two separate revelations that had hit her one right after the other, each with the force of a knockout punch. Seconds after she'd identified the first man by his voice—which she now realized she'd heard several times in the past few days—he had made that casual but damning reference to "Freddie."

Of course! Julio deCosta was Holloway's partner! Why on earth hadn't she figured it out before? She was still calling herself a knucklehead when the office door swung the rest of the way open. Holloway entered the room alone, his eyes widening in surprise as he spied her. Apparently his employee hadn't yet given him the message that there were now two guests awaiting him in his office.

Ten minutes later Jess and Chris—both tied and gagged—were placed in the back of a hearse and curtly told to keep their heads down. Led by the dark blue Chevy, the hearse left the alley at the rear of the building and turned onto a side street at virtually the same instant Quinn Vincent's unmarked car and two blue-and-white cruisers screeched to a halt at the front of the funeral home.

MAX WAS ALREADY HALFWAY up the steps at the front of the building when the last of the four patrolmen scrambled out of his squad car. He charged through the door and across the foyer, drawing startled glances from several people who were apparently taking a break from their "visitations." When a neatly dressed blond man followed close on his heels, a couple of speculative murmurs were exchanged. And then four uniformed police officers burst through the door and hurried down the hall after the first two men, and the half-dozen people in the foyer forgot why they'd come to the funeral home in the first place.

CHRIS AND JESS HAD BEEN LEFT in an efficiency apartment above the garage of Frederick Marchand's house. Their hands were still tied behind them, but the gags had been removed from their mouths.

"Yell yourselves hoarse, if you want," the man Chris had labeled the hearse driver told them cheerfully as he'd unwound the muffling strips of cloth. "This place is completely soundproof. I'm afraid I have to leave you ladies for a little while, but I promise I'll be back later to check on you."

"Bastard," Chris spat when the door had closed behind him. Turning to Jess, she asked anxiously, "Are you all right? Those creeps didn't hurt you, did they?"

"Not at all. Except for that warning about keeping our heads down in the hearse, they've hardly even spoken to me. How tight are your ropes, dear? Do you think you could manage to work free of them?"

Chris twisted her crossed wrists experimentally. "Given enough time, I think so. I doubt the guy who tied them ever earned his merit badge in knots. How about you?"

"Oh, I'm almost free. I've been working on getting loose since they put us in the hearse. I'm so relieved that you understood my message. I was afraid it might have been a little too subtle, but I didn't dare try to come up with anything more conspicuous."

Chris stopped struggling with her ropes and stared at Jess in confusion. "Forgive me if I sound dense,

Jess, but I don't know what on earth you're talking about. What message?"

"Why the television tuner, of course, and the box of pickling spices. The tuner was supposed to make you think of Mr. deCosta, and the spices represented his friend Holloway, the undertaker. Don't tell me you didn't even see them? Then what were you doing at the funeral home?"

Chris closed her eyes with a groan. "Christine Hudson, you are incredibly stupid!" she said in disgust. "Yes, I saw the tuner and the spices, but I thought you'd left them out by accident. I came to the funeral home because Bill Ferguson told me he'd seen two men from Holloway's take you away in a blue car."

"Don't feel too bad, dear," Jess consoled her. "We'll just have to hope that Max understands the significance of those particular items when he sees them."

Chris felt sick. "He won't see them," she told Jess miserably. "I put the spices back in the cabinet and the tuner on an end table in the living room before I left."

There was an awful silence, during which Chris called herself every synonym for "idiot" that she knew.

"Oh, my. That is unfortunate. It looks as if we're on our own, then, doesn't it?"

As she spoke the last sentence, Jess gave her arms a vigorous shake and the ropes that had been binding her wrists fell away. She got up from the sofa where the hearse driver had placed her, flexed her fingers a few times and then crossed to Chris's chair and started tugging at her ropes.

"Don't worry, dear," she said calmly. "Message or no message, I'm certain Max will eventually work out who took us and where we are."

"How can you be so sure?" Chris asked skeptically. "For that matter, how did *you* figure out deCosta and Holloway were in cahoots?"

"Why, it was simple, really. The brake line of my car was cut *after* you and Max used it to go see deCosta. Either he or someone who was with him at his house obviously saw the two of you in it and assumed it belonged to one of you...probably Max. And I knew that Holloway had to be involved in whatever was going on, because of the address book." She briefly explained to an astonished Chris. "His reaction to hearing that I had it made me suspect that it was more than just an ordinary address book. I tried to catch Max at the police station to tell him about it. Unfortunately I missed him, and then before the two of you could make it back to my apartment a couple of Holloway's employees arrived. I recognized the car they were in as soon as they drove up."

"The dark blue four-door, you mean?" Chris asked weakly. "You knew it belonged to Holloway?"

"Oh, yes," Jess replied. "He often uses it to transport flowers out to the cemetary. That's why I impulsively decided to put the television tuner and the box of spices out on the counter before I opened the door. I also managed to hide the address book in the cookie jar. Are you feeling ill, dear? You look a little peaked."

Chris summoned a wan smile and assured Jess that she was fine. She didn't tell the other woman what she'd been thinking: that if she and Max had only confided in Jess about everything that had happened that afternoon, Jess might have identified the dark blue car for them hours ago...and deCosta and Holloway probably wouldn't be holding anybody prisoner above Frederick Marchand's garage right now.

CHAPTER SEVENTEEN

MAX BEGGED A CIGARETTE from one of the uniformed officers and lit up for the first time in six years. After a single deep drag, he grimaced and stubbed it out in the ashtray on Holloway's desk, just as Quinn Vincent entered the room.

"I thought you quit," Quinn remarked.

"I did. Still no sign that either of them has been here?"

Quinn shook his head. "Nothing, and we've been over every inch of the building twice. It's clean as a whistle."

One of the patrolmen entered the office to report that Mrs. Decker's car had been found parked a couple of blocks away. "It can't have been there long," he added. "The engine's still warm."

Max swore bitterly. The first officer left and a second arrived, carrying a list of vehicles registered under Holloway's name. Quinn glanced at the printout and then wordlessly handed it to Max. One of the cars listed was a 1985 blue Chevrolet four-door. Max swore again.

He thought that if Chris were there, he might well turn her over his knee and tan her stubborn little backside, like the arrogant chauvinist she'd accused him of being. It was just like her to go tearing off on her own, after she'd *promised* him she'd "stay close to the phone."

He and Quinn had gone straight to Jess's from the station. They arrived right behind Bill Ferguson, so they hadn't wasted any time getting to the funeral home. But quick as they'd been, evidently they'd still missed Holloway by mere minutes.

While Quinn phoned in an alert to locate the blue Chevy, Max sorted through the papers on Holloway's desk. Finding nothing useful there, he wandered over to the file cabinet. He frowned when he noticed that one of the drawers had been left standing wide open. Having nothing better to do, he started idly flipping through the manila folders inside.

The third file his fingers touched was labeled Markowic, Francis David.

His frown deepened as he withdrew the folder. According to the single sheet of paper inside, young Frank had died a little over five months ago, from injuries sustained in a motorcycle accident on a highway in southern California.

By the time Quinn got off the phone, he was halfway through a second file drawer. Several manila folders were stacked on top of the cabinet. As Quinn walked up behind him, he added another one to the growing pile.

"What you're doing is illegal," Quinn said dryly as he reached over Max's shoulder for one of the folders. He glanced at it briefly. "Estevez, Jorge. Anybody I know?"

"Estevez is Julio deCosta's real name," Max muttered as he continued to make his way through the E's. "Ernesto Estevez. According to that, Jorge was his uncle. He supposedly died of a stroke nine months ago...at his home in California."

"California?" Quinn reached around him to collect a handful of the folders. "If he lived in California, how come Holloway's got a file on him?"

"Good question," Max said as he closed the drawer. "Why would the body of a man whose family lives in California be shipped to Daytona Beach, Florida, for burial?" He tapped the top folder in Quinn's hand. "About half of these are for other members of the Estevez clan. There's also a hefty section of files labeled Markowic. Here." He pulled Frank's file from the bottom of the stack and opened it for Quinn to read. "According to this, the young man you questioned this evening was buried more than five months ago."

Quinn scanned the form inside, then closed the folder with a muttered oath. "How far back do these things go?"

"The oldest one I've found is from three years ago."

Quinn didn't waste time on idle speculation. He called one of the uniformed officers into the room and instructed the man to collect Frank Markowic from his uncle's motel and bring him to the funeral home.

"He can at least go through the Markowic files and tell us if the rest of them are as phony as his," Quinn said as he gathered all the folders Max had pulled and carried them to Holloway's desk.

The phone rang, and Quinn automatically answered it. Max slipped out while he was busy explaining that he wasn't an undertaker and had no idea what the cost of a cremation would be. His pickup was sitting in the police department lot, but fortunately he had a set of keys to Jess's Civic.

He didn't wait to hear Frank Markowic confirm that the rest of the files for his family were also fakes. They had to be. Whatever Holloway had been shipping into town concealed in coffins had come from California...home of the Golden Gate Bridge, the Los Angeles Rams and a certain balding television actor, who just happened to be visiting Daytona Beach.

He left the Civic at one of the many small stores along Atlantic that cater to the tourist trade. At this time of night the only people on the streets were students on their way from one party to another, which made it easy to slip onto Marchand's property unobserved. *Old habits die hard,* he thought wryly as he crouched beneath a window at the rear of the house. It had been more than six years since he'd had to exercise this kind of caution, but he was relieved to discover that all the old instincts were still in good working order.

The window above him was the same one Chris had seen someone watching them from that afternoon. Max had been drawn to it by the light visible through the drapes, and now he could hear voices from inside. Male voices, raised in argument.

"I can't believe you actually brought them here! Are you out of your mind? Decker's been here twice already, for God's sake. What if he comes back?"

Max tensed. Jess and Chris were here!

"Then you'll just have to deal with all three of them," an irritating nasal voice replied. "I had no choice but to bring them here. I could hardly keep both of them tied up in my office indefinitely, now could I?"

There was a moment of tense silence, and then the first man spoke again . . . directly above Max's head. Max instinctively sank into a squat as adrenaline spurted into his bloodstream.

"So you stuck them in the apartment over the garage? Way to go. You've led the cops right to us." Max belatedly recognized the voice as Julio deCosta's, sans phony accent. "It would be even riskier to move them again, but I still don't like it." DeCosta's voice rose in agitation as he suddenly turned from the window and walked back across the room.

"What in heaven's name possessed you to snatch both of them! I thought the idea was to keep Decker off our backs until the shipment arrived and we'd distributed it. By kidnapping both his mother and his lover or partner or whatever this Hudson woman is, you've virtually assured that he'll come after us, you imbecile."

Partner? Max couldn't help smiling a little at that. Now that he knew where Jess and Chris were being held, and that they were apparently unharmed, the tension that had gripped him for the past hour eased somewhat. He glanced at the garage and wondered how they were holding up. Knowing the two of them, they were probably at that moment working on a plan to escape. Pride swelled in his chest, and with it that other unsettling emotion he'd experienced repeatedly in the past few days.

"Stop fighting it," Chris had told him. "Just let it happen." Easy for her to say. Easy for her to *do*. But not so easy for a man who'd spent the better part of his life blocking his emotions, confining them behind walls of suspicion and mistrust.

The mortician spoke again, diverting Max's attention from his personal dilemma. "What was I supposed to do when that nosy Hudson bitch came snooping around again—pat her on the head and send her off to tell the police what she knows? And I suppose I should have left the book in Decker's mother's hands so he could put two and two together? I didn't count on her outfoxing us, but even if he has the book, he isn't likely to do anything that would jeopardize the women's safety."

Max scowled. *Book?* What book?

"The man's a former cop, Vernon," deCosta said icily. "He's not going to just stand calmly by and let us get away with kidnapping two people he cares about."

You got that right, Max thought grimly.

"I intended to wait, but I suppose I might as well tell you now," the actor continued. "After this shipment, I'm calling it quits. I've paid off all but ten thousand of my gambling debts, and I got word from my agent this morning that the network's agreed to meet my salary demands for next season. When Nick learns how much I'll be making, he'll be willing to wait a little longer for his money. So I'm pulling out. You and Freddie will have to find yourselves another partner. That is, if you're still in business."

"Exactly what is that supposed to mean?" Holloway demanded. "We've barely tapped the market in this part of the country. Granted, we may have to stop the shipments for a while after this trouble with Decker, but by this time next year we could double our sales, maybe even triple them."

DeCosta's tone was sardonic as he replied. "By this time next year, you might not have a product to sell. If the new encoding device goes into widespread use, you could be out of business in six months."

Max frowned. *Encoding device?* This was beginning to sound like one of deCosta's TV shows. What kind of "product" were they talking about, for crying out loud?

Holloway made a disparaging noise. "That doesn't concern either Freddie or myself. They're always coming up with some new antipiracy device, but there are ways around all of them. And since we're springing surprises on one another, this seems a good time to tell you that Freddie's decided to give me control of the entire west coast operation. I've already arranged for one of my cousins to take over the funeral home. As soon as this delivery's completed, I'll be relocating to California."

"But what about Decker?" deCosta asked anxiously. "And the women?"

Holloway's reply was cool and unconcerned. "They're your problem, Julio. Do whatever you like about them."

A third man entered the room briefly to say that he was going to check on the ladies and ask for instructions.

"It should be safe to untie them, Greg," Holloway told him. "They're not going anywhere. By this time tomorrow they'll be of no further use to us, anyway."

Max had been trying to decide whether to follow Greg or hang around to see if he could learn anything more about the mysterious shipment they were expecting. But after those last ominous remarks by Holloway, he lost all interest in finding out what kind of merchandise Holloway and his partners had been smuggling into Florida.

He knew that at this point he should call Quinn and let him take over. That would be the responsible, sensible thing to do. On the other hand, the unseen Greg was going up to check on Jess and Chris. This might be his only chance to see for himself that they were all right. Not allowing himself time to reconsider, he darted across the space between the house and garage and ducked under the wooden staircase leading up to the apartment. As he crouched in the shadows, he experienced a disturbing sense of *déjà vu*.

Six years ago he had impulsively decided to act on his own rather than wait for assistance, with disastrous results. The similarity between that situation and this one was unnerving. And, he suddenly remembered, this time he didn't even have a gun. It was still locked inside the glove compartment of his truck, which was sitting in the police department parking lot. He swore under his breath and edged deeper into the concealing shadows. Like it or not, he'd made his decision.

"GET READY. I hear him on the stairs."

As she hissed the warning, Chris stepped away from the door to collect her weapon. She and Jess took up their positions and then stood poised and silent as they waited for the door to open. When the hearse driver stepped through it, he was going to receive a nasty surprise. Chris was wielding a short, sturdy leg she'd unscrewed from one of the end tables, while Jess had armed herself with a ten-inch frying pan she'd found in a kitchen cabinet.

Max unlocked the door with the key Greg had been holding when he'd mounted the stairs. Giving the knob a firm twist, he started to push it open and step inside. Then he reconsidered. Taking a cautious step backward on the small landing, he pursed his lips as he contemplated the door and the suspiciously silent apartment beyond it.

"Anybody home?" he said dryly.

The women stared at each other for a moment in mute astonishment before Chris yanked the door open and they both flew through it. Their assault drove Max back against the flimsy wooden railing surrounding the landing, making him fear for a second that all three of them were going to end up all over Freddie Marchand's gravel driveway.

"Max! Oh, Max, I've never been so glad to see anybody in my life!" Chris declared as she hung around his neck and scattered fervent little kisses over his face. As he tried to drag her away from the railing without completely dislodging her hold on him, he felt a second pair of arms give his waist a quick hug.

"I knew you'd figure out where they'd taken us, but I must say I didn't expect you to do it so quickly."

The pride in Jess's voice gave him almost as much foolish pleasure as the way Chris kept kissing him as she clung to his neck. Good grief, you'd think he was the cavalry riding to the rescue, or the Marines or something.

"Are you both all right?" he asked gruffly.

They assured him that they were, and he gave them each a brief one-armed hug before turning them toward the stairs. When Chris let go of him to start down them, he noticed the club clutched in her right hand. She grinned at the expression that crossed his face.

"We were lying in wait for the hearse driver," she explained. "When he came through the door, we were going to clobber him and make our escape."

"I figured you might have something like that in mind," Max drawled. "Assuming the guy I intercepted was 'the hearse driver,' he ought to be grateful I got to him first."

Halfway down the stairs they heard the wail of approaching sirens. Apparently so had deCosta and Holloway. The two men ran around the near corner of the house and spotted them before they could reach the concealing darkness at the bottom of the staircase. Max saw Holloway's arm fly up, one long, bony finger stabbing in their direction.

"Run!" he ordered curtly. Reaching past Chris, he gave his mother's shoulder an urgent nudge to get her moving. "Both of you. Get out to the street and wait for Quinn."

Jess followed the instructions without question. Thankfully, for once so did Chris. As soon as they were off and running, Max turned his attention to the two men. DeCosta had evidently decided to leave while he still could. He headed straight for the garage and the De Lorean inside it. The clatter of the metal door rising along its track distracted Max for a moment as he vaulted the last two steps. When he glanced around to find out what had become of Holloway, he saw that the mortician was reaching inside his suit coat as he raced after Chris.

Something inside Max cracked wide open. He ceased to be aware of deCosta, his mother or the pain that had seared his knee joint when his feet hit the ground. As he sprinted after the undertaker, a scene from six years before was flashed through his mind . . . in glorious Technicolor.

Chris heard the crunch of running feet on gravel and glanced over her shoulder, expecting to see Max right behind her. Her eyes widened in alarm when she found Holloway breathing down her neck instead. His thin lips compressed in determination as he withdrew a gun from under his coat with one hand and grabbed for her arm with the other. His fingers grazed her skin as she swerved to the left, and a combination of fear and revulsion slithered through her stomach.

The shrill, undulating scream of sirens grew louder, nearer. Up ahead, Chris saw a flash of white as Jess emerged from the drive onto the comparative safety of the brightly lit street. But the relief that surged through her was abruptly replaced by fear when Holloway managed to grasp a handful of her blouse.

"Oh, no you don't, you nosy little bitch," he snarled as he tried to drag her to a halt. "You're coming with me. You're my insurance policy."

"Like hell!" Chris panted grimly. Two buttons at the front of the borrowed blouse popped off as she strained to break free of him, and she felt the right shoulder seam rip open. Undaunted, she gritted her teeth and lunged forward. She didn't care if the whole damn blouse came off in his hand. She raised both arms to balance herself for another lunge, fully prepared to have Jess's blouse torn from her body, and suddenly realized that she was still clutching the table leg in her right hand.

She spun around, swinging the makeshift club in an arcing backhand stroke, savagely hoping it would connect with the undertaker's head. It connected with something. There was a satisfying crack, and the force of the blow jarred her arm all the way to the shoulder socket. Holloway howled in pain, but his fingers remained clamped on her blouse. Chris sucked in an enormous breath and prepared to swing the table leg again. There was a low growling noise behind her, followed by a solid-sounding thud. She suddenly found herself teetering as Holloway's restraining hand was removed, and with it, a large portion of the back of Jess's blouse.

Max's knee gave way the instant before he launched himself at the mortician in a flying tackle. His leg twisted under him painfully, pitching him slightly to the right. He still managed to bring the man down, though, and then immediately put all his weight behind a pile-driving blow to Holloway's jaw to make sure he stayed down.

"Son of a bitch," he wheezed as he pushed himself away from the undertaker and fell onto his back. He knew better than to try to get up just yet. In fact, he wasn't sure he'd ever be able to.

"Max!"

The anxiety in Chris's voice penetrated the waves of agony emanating from his knee. He turned his head toward her as she dropped beside him on the grass at the edge of the driveway.

"Max, are you all right?"

He was in too much pain to put up a stoic front. "No."

Her hands darted out to flutter over his body. The De Lorean roared past them, its left front tire missing Holloway's prone body by inches. Chris didn't even spare the car a glance.

"Oh, God, he didn't shoot you, did he? I didn't hear a gunshot."

Her voice quavered as she bent over him, her fingers splayed across his chest. Max gave her a feeble smile.

"He couldn't have shot me if he'd wanted to. He dropped the gun when you whacked him with that club. I wouldn't be surprised if you broke his arm."

"I hope I did!"

The ferocity in her voice brought his smile back for a moment. He lifted one of her hands from his chest and carried it to his mouth to kiss the palm. "You're something else," he murmured against her skin.

"So are you," Chris told him huskily. "Now tell me where you're hurt. What can I do?"

Max shook his head. "Nothing. It's just my damn leg. I twisted my knee when I tackled him."

"Oh, darling..."

The soft, infinitely gentle sound was as much a caress as the brush of her fingers against his cheek. Max lifted his gaze to her face, and the sight of her leaning over him, love and concern shining openly from her clear blue eyes, caused the muscles in his throat to convulse painfully. His arms trembled as he reached for her.

"Come here," he said thickly.

He held her as if he never intended to let her go, his hands restless on her back as they alternately stroked and clasped her to him.

"I saw him going after you, reaching for his gun, and..." He pressed her fiercely to his chest and buried his face in her hair. "God! It was happening all over again, and I couldn't do anything to stop it."

Chris felt as if a giant fist were squeezing her heart. She pulled back to take his face in her hands, forcing him to look at her. Tears glistened in her eyes, but her voice was steady and sure.

"But you did, Max," she told him firmly. "You did stop him, darling." Her lips curved in a tremulous smile. "He probably won't be able to eat solid food for a month."

The last word was muffled by Max's mouth as he pulled her down. He kissed her as if he'd never get his fill of her, trying to communicate all that he felt but didn't know how to put into words. When Quinn

Vincent's car braked to a stop five feet away and he and Jess climbed out of it, neither of them noticed.

IT WAS ALMOST DAWN before they returned to Jess's apartment. Chris drove Max's truck from the police station, claiming he was in no shape to drive it himself. Max didn't argue.

Julio deCosta had been apprehended less than five miles from Frederick Marchand's house. Both he and a slightly battered Holloway were now residing under lock and key. It had been deCosta who'd provided Quinn with the details of their partnership, on the advice of his attorney.

The merchandise he and his partners had been shipping from California to Florida at regular intervals for the past three years turned out to have been pirated videocassettes. Marchand made the illegal copies, then sent them to Holloway for distribution to a network of black-market dealers. Holloway had kept a record of his clients in the little black book that was now safely in the hands of the police. DeCosta had served as the delivery boy on the east coast, while at the same time using his connections in California to help Marchand acquire the original tapes for copying.

During the course of deCosta's confession Steven Kline and Frank Markowic were exonerated of any involvement in the videocassette scheme. It had simply been a case of bad timing that the two young men arrived in town the same week Holloway was expecting the next shipment of videocassettes.

A middle-of-the-night call from a grim Quinn Vincent to Elliott had produced yet another confession. Elliott admitted that he'd smelled something fishy from the beginning, when a youthful-sounding female phoned him claiming to be "Mrs. Gollum"—according to Frank, the caller had been Steven Kline's girlfriend. But, Elliott claimed defensively, he'd had no proof that the woman wasn't who she said she was, and she *had* agreed to the unusually high fee he'd quoted. She even promised to get a certified check in the mail to him that day.

"Greedy skinflint," Chris said when Quinn repeated the conversation to her, Max and Jess. "By the time he pays me back for the trip Holloway's hearse made to the airport and having Jess's car repaired, he could well end up losing money on this job. Serve the old miser right if he does."

Max draped an arm around Chris's shoulders, leaning on her heavily as they rose to leave Quinn Vincent's office. When they reached the door, she paused to glance back at Vincent with a questioning frown.

"I just remembered...did that credit card thief you were looking for ever turn up?"

Quinn stuck his hands in his pockets and studied the toes of his shoes for a second or two. Clearing his throat softly, he lifted his head with a sheepish smile.

"Yeah. He was arrested yesterday, in Denver."

Chris stared at him without comment until she saw a faint blush spread across his handsome face. Then she and a limping Max left.

When Chris had parked the truck, she turned to Max. "I think I should stay downstairs with Jess for a while."

He swallowed his disappointment and nodded. "She probably won't want to be alone, after what she's been through."

Not trusting himself to stay inside the confined space with her, he quickly opened his door and stepped down from the cab. Then, not trusting himself to speak, he lifted one hand in a poignant farewell and limped off toward the stairs leading to his own apartment.

With an ache in her throat, Chris watched him go. Proud, stubborn man. Didn't he know how badly she wanted to come with him, how much she needed him? The torn edges of Jess's blouse fluttered against her back as she trudged across the pavement. When she entered the apartment, Jess looked up from the sofa with a disapproving frown.

"What are you doing here?"

Chris floundered for a moment. "I thought... Don't you want me here?"

"Well, of course I do," Jess replied as she rose to her feet. An incredibly gentle smile touched her mouth. "You'll always be welcome in my home, dear. But right now my son needs you more than I do." She removed something from her purse and placed it in Chris's hand. Chris glanced down and saw that it was a key. "Go to him," Jess urged softly.

Chris didn't have to be persuaded. She went just as she was, in Jess's tattered blouse and grass-stained slacks. She found him in the shower, leaning back against the tiled wall while the steaming spray pounded his chest. She quickly undressed. In the instant after she opened the door, before he realized she was there, she saw the torment on his face.

"Hi," she said cheerfully as she stepped into the stall with him. "Want me to wash your back?"

Max quickly arranged his features in a smooth, bland mask that he was convinced would break into a million pieces at any second. "Actually, I'd rather you washed my..." He'd been wrong. It was his voice that broke. He stopped, horrified. Chris's face suddenly blurred, and he realized it was because he was crying.

"Max!" She stepped closer, her arms winding around him like vines. "Oh, darling, it's all right. It's all right."

He bent his head, hiding his face against her neck. "I'm not cracking up, honest," he said in a weak attempt at humor. "Everything just...I think I must be having some kind of delayed reaction."

Chris stroked his back with loving compassion. "To what happened tonight, or what happened back in New York six years ago?"

His arms contracted in a fierce embrace and he shuddered beneath her hands. "Both," he admitted hoarsely.

They clung to each other blindly until Max regained enough control to release her and turn off the shower. They dried one another in an impatient rush, leaving lots of damp spots, before they moved to his bed. Their lovemaking was silent save for the soft little pleasure sounds neither could suppress, and when it was over Chris knew beyond a shadow of a doubt that Max loved her with his whole heart and soul.

The question was, did he know it? And if he did, could he admit it, to himself first and then to her? She lay awake long after he'd fallen asleep. His head rested just beneath her breasts and his arms were locked around her like the bars of a cage, as if even in sleep he was afraid she might leave him. As she held him, stroking his hair with an unconsciously comforting touch, the first hint of daylight seeped into the room. A serene little smile played around her lips as her eyes drifted closed. She knew exactly what she had to do.

Max stirred sluggishly, one hand groping over the sheet in search of Chris's warmth. When he realized she wasn't there, his eyes snapped open. Panic rose in his throat for an instant until he forced it down. He threw off the sheet covering him and rolled to his feet in one smooth, economical movement, grabbing clothes at random on his way to the bathroom. Dammit, she'd better be downstairs with Jess, he thought irritably as he splashed cold water in his face.

Then, as he lifted his head and met his own apprehensive eyes in the mirror, *Please God, let her be downstairs with Jess*.

"She's gone," his mother told him as soon as he stepped through the door. "She left for the airport about half an hour ago."

Max stared at her in numb, disbelieving shock. He tried to brace himself as he waited for the pain to start.

"She left a message for you," Jess added calmly. "She said you know what she wants, and where to find her when you have it to give." She picked up a tan overnight case sitting at the end of the sofa and thrust it at him. Max accepted it wordlessly. "Her plane leaves at 4:05, so don't waste a lot of time packing." When he just continued to stand there, looking stunned, Jess huffed at him in exasperation.

"For heaven's sake, Max, get a move on! I'd like a grandchild or two while I'm still young enough to enjoy them."

His mouth tilted in a lopsided smile as he gave her a rib-cracking hug with his free arm. "You're something else," he murmured roughly.

"I love you too, dear," Jess replied. Her eyes looked suspiciously moist as she patted his shoulder. "Now hurry, or you'll miss the plane."

He took the stairs to his apartment two at a time. When he was halfway up them, Jess stepped outside to yell, "I meant it about those grandchildren, Max."

"You'll get 'em—don't worry. At least three."

"And see if you can talk her into living in Florida," Jess added as he wrestled with the lock on his door. She smiled as his impatient swear words carried to her, and for once didn't reprimand him for using them. "I'm getting too old for those northern winters."

"So am I," Max answered with a grin as he shoved the door open and hurried inside.

Chris fastened her seat belt and tried not to cry as she settled into the narrow seat. He wasn't coming. Her brilliant plan had been a flop. She'd been wrong; he still wasn't ready to admit that he loved her, much less make any kind of commitment to her.

She sighed and turned toward the window, wishing the plane would just take off and get her the hell away from Max Decker and the entire state of Florida. There was a flurry of activity at the front of the cabin as a tardy passenger came aboard and the flight attendant checked his boarding pass to direct him to his seat. Chris glanced up with a frown. She hoped he wasn't going to be sitting in the seat next to hers. She didn't feel like company at the moment. Hastily snatching a magazine out of the pocket in front of her, she opened it on her lap and pretended to read an article about Windsurfing.

Out of the corner of her eye she saw an immaculate dark blue suit draw level with her and then stop. Terrific; he *was* going to be sitting beside her. Bending her head, she feigned absorption in the article as the man stowed his luggage in the overhead compartment. She caught a faint whiff of Old Spice and nearly groaned out loud. She didn't look up as he eased himself into his seat and fastened the belt over his lean hips. Maybe if she didn't acknowledge his presence, he wouldn't try to start a conversation with her.

"I ought to wring your gorgeous little neck," a gruff voice growled at her shoulder.

Chris's head jerked up, her eyes like saucers. The magazine slid out of her hands and off her lap. Max leaned over to pick it up and replace it in the pocket.

"Max! You're wearing a suit!" The way she said it, he might not have been wearing anything at all.

He frowned as he fiddled with the knot of the maroon tie he had paired with a classic blue-and-white pinstripe shirt.

"You're positively gorgeous," Chris breathed. She was amazed to see a flush rise from the collar of his shirt.

Max shrugged self-consciously. "I didn't want to look like some kind of overage beach bum when I meet your parents."

Chris was almost afraid to trust her hearing. "You want to meet my parents?" Her voice was little more than a whisper.

"The sooner the better," he said. "I don't know how long I'll be able to tolerate this damn suit."

Chris took a couple of deep, calming breaths as she reached over to loosen his tie and unfasten the button under it. Still, her fingers trembled slightly. "You might feel uncomfortable, but you look terrific... sort of Paul Newmanish." She sat back with a smile. "Funny, I never suspected you even owned a suit."

Max grinned sheepishly. "I didn't. I just bought it at the mall across from the airport. Thank goodness it didn't have to be altered. I was afraid I was going to miss the plane, as it was."

Chris drew another deep breath and took her courage firmly in both hands. "Why, Max? Why are you here, on an airplane headed for Evansville, Indiana, wearing a suit and tie and making plans to meet my parents?"

A full minute passed in utter silence as he gazed deep into her eyes. He saw hopeful expectancy there, and love. All the love a man could ever wish for; much more than he would ever deserve. When he spoke, his voice was hoarse with emotion. "Why do you think?"

Color bloomed high on Chris's cheeks and resentment flickered in her eyes. That definitely had not been the response she was hoping for. It took every ounce of willpower Max possessed to keep the joyous smile inside him from spreading to his face.

"Max!"

"Serves you right," he said wickedly as he lifted her clenched hand from her lap and gently uncurled her fingers. "For running out on me."

Chris's hand jerked in his. "I didn't run out on you!" She sounded hurt that he'd accuse her of such a thing. "I just wanted to make you realize...I wanted you to admit..." She trailed off helplessly, unable to explain without saying the words that were supposed to come from *him*.

Max raised her hand to his mouth, gazing at her steadily as he placed a tender kiss on each knuckle. The look in his eyes caused her breath to catch audibly.

"To admit what?" he whispered. "That I love you? You know I do, Christine. I'd have told you this morning, if you'd stayed around long enough to give me the chance. Last night..." He hesitated, groping for the right words. "The last wall finally came down, and everything that had been locked up inside me for years just sort of...overwhelmed me, I guess." His lips curved in a rueful smile. "Am I making any sense, or do I sound like a raving lunatic?"

Chris gave him a luminous smile. "You're making beautiful sense. Especially the part that went 'I love you.' If I asked you nicely, would you say that part just one more time?"

The smile inside him finally broke to the surface as he shoved the armrest separating them up out of the way and wrapped both arms around her.

"I love you, Christine Hudson," he breathed against her lips. His mouth caressed hers softly, tenderly, and he repeated it twice more to be sure she got the message. He pulled back a little, grinning at her dazed expression. "Happy now?"

Chris was too short of breath to speak, so she nodded an emphatic affirmative.

"Cat got your tongue, Christine?"

She nodded again, a smile tugging at the corners of her mouth.

Max hesitated for all of two seconds. What the hell. As long as she was being so agreeable, he might as well go for it. "Jess wants us to live in Florida. Is that all right with you?" The third nod was a little slower in coming. He held his breath until it did. Then his courage abruptly deserted him. His gaze dropped to her mouth as he muttered the next half under his breath.

"She, uh, also said something about wanting some grandchildren."

The ecstatic smile that slowly took possession of Chris's mouth was the most beautiful thing he'd ever seen. "Legitimate ones, I hope," she said huskily.

When Max lifted his eyes to hers again, the relief and joy in them almost made her cry. "I should hope so," he said in mock horror. "She'd kill us both if they weren't."

"Then I guess we'll have to get married," Chris said with a resigned sigh.

Max settled back in his seat, but kept one arm around her shoulders. "I guess so." He couldn't have wiped the silly grin off his face if he'd tried, and he wasn't trying.

Chris snuggled as close as she could without unfastening her seat belt. "We'll need a bigger apartment. And eventually a station wagon, to haul the kids' stuff around in."

"If you say so."

It took a moment for Chris to realize that the funny feeling in the pit of her stomach was caused by the plane's ascent and not the fact that Max wanted her to marry him and have his babies.

"What will I do in Florida until Jess's grandchildren start to come along?" she said dreamily. "Sunbathe? Collect seashells? Learn to fish?" *Make love with you day and night, night and day?*

"I've been thinking about that." The serious tone of Max's voice made her lift her head from his shoulder. His mouth was curved in the sexy half smile she was so crazy about. "We just might be able to turn you into a halfway decent private investigator."

Chris shot bolt upright, her face alight with excitement. "Max, do you mean it? Would you really let me work with you?"

His smile became a wry grin. "It's the only way I can think of to keep tabs on you and at the same time hopefully keep you out of trouble. But you'd be working *for* me, not with me," he added firmly. "Get that straight, Christine."

"Of course, Max," Chris said demurely. "You'll be the boss." She threw her arms around his neck with a gurgle of laughter. "But I get to handle all the missing coffin cases, okay? And Jess can be my assistant."

Max reared back in alarm. "Whoa. Hold it right there. I never said anything about including—"

"Have I told you today how much I love you?" she asked gently as she leaned into his chest.

"Now listen, Christine—"

"Later, Max," she whispered against his lips. "I'll listen later, I promise. Oh, look, we're above the clouds. The last time I was this close to heaven was when you—"

Max muttered something to the effect that, with his luck all their children would be girls, just before his mouth came down on hers. He was wrong. Two of the three were boys.

Harlequin Superromance

COMING NEXT MONTH

#206 SOUTHERN NIGHTS • Barbara Kaye
The past is waiting when Shannon Parelli, newly widowed, returns to the family farm in North Carolina. Blake Carmichael, who'd silently worshiped her as an adolescent, is now a prosperous contractor, determined to fulfill his dream of homesteading her parents' old place—with Shannon by his side.

#207 DREAMS GATHER • Kathryn Collins
When gallery owner Amanda Sherwood signs Grant Wellington for an exclusive showing, she quickly learns that he isn't just another temperamental artist. The terms he sets for their contract prove that he is a man's man who always gets what he wants. And what he wants is Amanda . . . with a hunger he's never known.

#208 FOR RICHER OR POORER • Ruth Alana Smith
Despite appearances, Britt Hutton is *not* a Boston socialite and Clay Cole is *not* a wealthy Texas oilman. They're both fortune hunters, determined to triumph over life's hardships. And, moving in the same elite circles, it is inevitable they will discover the truth: the powerful attraction they feel is no illusion. . . .

#209 LOTUS MOON • Janice Kaiser
While searching the back streets of Bangkok for the daughter he may have fathered during the Vietnam War, Buck Michaels and social worker Amanda Parr find themselves locked in a passion as sultry as the Oriental nights. Everything is perfect, until Buck's quest becomes an obsession. . . .

WHAT READERS SAY ABOUT HARLEQUIN INTRIGUE . . .

Fantastic! I am looking forward to reading other Intrigue books.

*P.W.O., Anderson, SC

This is the first Harlequin Intrigue I have read . . . I'm hooked.

*C.M., Toledo, OH

I really like the suspense . . . the twists and turns of the plot.

*L.E.L., Minneapolis, MN

I'm really enjoying your Harlequin Intrigue line . . . mystery and suspense mixed with a good love story.

*B.M., Denton, TX

***Names available on request.**